HERE THERE BE MONSTERS

A Bianca Jones Collection

John L. French

PADWOLF
PUBLISHING

A waiter came over with a drink. "Compliments of the gentleman at the bar."

She looked up. Satan raised his glass in greeting.

Bianca made eye contact, daring to stare the Devil down. "Take it away," she said.

Looking around the room, listening to the silence, Bianca wondered if there were any so foolish as to believe that their souls were not at stake.

"And what are you going to do about it?" The voice of her conscience asked.

"What can I do?" she answered herself. "It's up to them. We each chose our own path. It's called free will."

"Letting people condemn themselves is not in your job description, especially not these days."

Thoughts of good men doing nothing while evil triumphed came to her. "Damn it," she said out loud. As she stood she realized that this was perhaps not the best time to use that particular phrase. Screw it, she thought and walked over to face the Devil.

Satan smiled. "Miss Jones, come to offer your body in exchange for eternal happiness? Or at least a better body? Or maybe you'd like to be taller, or should I say 'less short?'"

Up until now it had been a matter of doing her duty, of protecting the people gathered here from themselves. But Evil Incarnate or not, now it was personal. She decided to find out if the Devil had an ass she could kick.

PADWOLF PUBLISHING BOOKS BY JOHN L. FRENCH

Here There Be Monsters, a Bianca Jones collection
Monsters Among Us, a Bianca Jones collection
The Devil of Harbor City
Past Sins
Rites Of Passage: a DMA casefile of Agent Karver and Bianca Jones
(with Patrick Thomas)
The Grey Monk: Souls on Fire
The Nightmare Strikes
Bad Cop, No Donut (editor)
Mermaids 13 (editor)
Camelot 13 (editor with Patrick Thomas)
Bullets & Brimstone: a Mystic Investigators™ book (with Patrick
Thomas) featuring Bianca Jones
From The Shadows: a Mystic Investigators™ book (with Patrick
Thomas) featuring the Nightmare

OTHER BOOKS BY JOHN L. FRENCH

The Last Redhead
Paradise Denied
The Assassins' Ball (with Patrick Thomas)
To Hell in a Fast Car (editor)
With Great Power (editor with Greg Schauer)

For the joy she has brought into my life,
this book is dedicated to my daughter
Karen French Rudolph

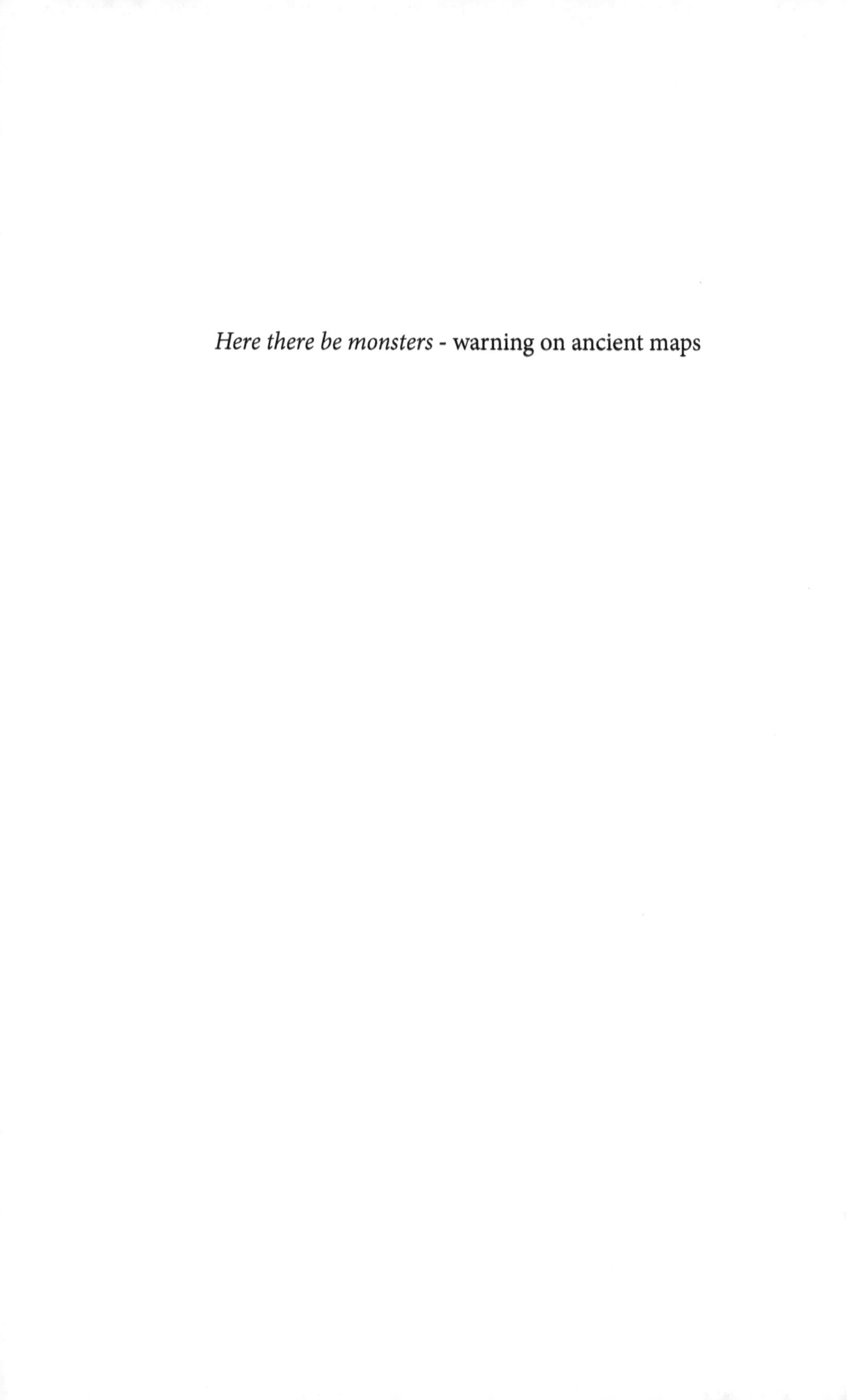

Here there be monsters - warning on ancient maps

Table of Contents

OUT OF THE BLACKNESS

It's night; she's alone. For some reason, something in the air maybe, she's nervous. She shouldn't be. She's walked these streets alone at night before. This is a safe neighborhood, one of the safest in the city. And why not? The community association's called the mayor enough to get added police patrols. Plus there's the private security the association hired. And the Neighborhood Watch.

She laughs off her fears. I've been watching too much TV, she thinks. Still, only a few blocks from home, she quickens her steps to get there that much faster.

Something ahead, going into the alley. She didn't see it clearly. A rat? Probably, every neighborhood had them. Again she sees it. Bigger than a rat. She slows her walk, ready to jump out of the way if an angry dog came after her. Should she cross the street? No, someone might see and what would they think?

Reaching into her purse, her hand wraps around the pepper spray. "Triple strength," the ad had read, she assures herself. "Pit Bull ready" it had said.

She steps off the curb, looks down the alley. Nothing. She relaxes. Her hand comes out of the purse. She looks again. A slight shimmer. What? She blinks it away. Another blink. There was something, someone in the alley. And then he, she, it was gone.

It's the worry, she decides, tension from work. She passed the alley, steps up on the opposite sidewalk. As she does something grabs her ankle, latches on, pulls hard. As she's dragged into the darkness she thinks to scream. She turns, and the scream dies in her throat as for an instant she clearly sees what has taken her. And then there is nothing but the blackness.

***

I've got to get on dayshift, Bianca Jones thought as she pulled into the ER parking lot at 3a.m. The police spaces all taken, Bianca waited for an ambulance to pull out and slipped into the vacant spot. Getting out of her car, she saw the security guard coming over to her.

"Hey, you can't ..." then he saw who she was. "Sorry," he said quickly and ducked back inside.

And a good thing too, Bianca thought. It wasn't that she minded playing by the rules, but not when it overly inconvenienced her. With all the visitor and cop slots taken, she'd be damned if she'd park down the ramp and on the street.

She'd had problems with security here once before, only once, right after she'd transferred to the Sex Offense unit. Like tonight, the only spaces open were reserved for the ambos. So she took one. Then the rent-a-cop came out and yelled at her, ranted really, demanding that she move her car, her vee-hick-cull, he called it, or else. What "the else" was he never made clear. Bianca tried to explain that she was a detective there on a rape case. He didn't care -- it was illegal for her to park there and she had to move.

"You're right," she said suddenly, "I apologize." That shut the officious jerk up. "Cars should not be illegally parked. I'll move my vee-hick-cull right away." Had the guard known who she was, or what the calm tone of her voice usually meant, he not only would have insisted she leave the car, but might have washed and waxed it for her while she was inside. Instead, he said snippily "Good, see that you do, and don't do it again."

Bianca moved her car, finding a legal spot a block away. Then she got her old ticket book out of the glove compartment and on the way back to the hospital cited every car she found parked in violation of the law. Most of these cars belonged to hospital personnel.

"Sorry I'm late," she told the SAFE nurse once she finally got inside that night, then she told her why. The word quickly spread to let Bianca Jones park wherever she damned well pleased.

As a member of the BPD's Sex Crimes Unit, Bianca had free access to the ER. Punching in her code, she walked over to the charge desk.

"Can I help you, sweetie?"

Oh great, another new one, Bianca thought as the nursing assistant at the desk looked down on her -- literally. Five foot even (five-three if you asked Bianca) and slightly built, Bianca was often mistaken for being younger, much younger, than she was. She'd had that trouble all her life -- unable to get into R-rated movies, getting carded in bars, and, the worst of all, being handed a child's menu at every restaurant all through her teens.

"Are you lost, dearie?" the assistant asked again. Obviously thinking Bianca was some teenager who had wandered through the wrong door.

"Being small has its advantages," her mother used to say. "Not as many as I'd like," had always been Bianca's silent reply.

"Can I get the guard to help you find the way out?"

Bianca decided that she'd made the woman wait long enough. Stepping back, she let her jacket open just enough to give the assistant a glimpse of the 9mm pistol under her arm. The brief look of fear on the woman's face was payback enough for the "sweetie" and "dearie." Then Bianca flipped out her badge. "Police, where can I find the SAFE nurse?"

Killer teen turned cop? Bianca watched as fear gave way to confusion on the assistant's face. "A safe nurse? Why? Is there a problem? I thought we were all safe in here."

"SAFE," Bianca said slowly. "Sexual-Assault-Forensic-Evidence. I'm here to take a rape report."

The assistant looked at her charts. "They would be back in critical care. Should I get someone to show …"

Bianca cut her off. "I know the way -- hon." She walked to the back of the ER leaving the assistant wondering just what the city was coming to, hiring girls that age as police and giving them guns.

When Bianca got to Critical Care, she found the SAFE nurse waiting for her. "How you doing, Bee?"

Bianca didn't normally respond to nicknames, but somehow it was okay coming from this woman. "Just fine, Maggie, just fine." Margaret Tate had been the nightshift SAFE nurse for three years now, had in fact, started the program at City of Hope Hospital. The SAFE program trained nurses in the collection of forensic evidence from sexual assault victims. Hairs and fibers, cavity swabbings from the victim, photos of bruises, lacerations and other injuries, the SAFE nurse collected them all and turned them over to the investigating detective.

"We got a bad one this time, Bee," Margaret said. "She's back in exam one." The nurse led Bianca to a rear examination room. Opening the curtain, she gave the detective her first view of the victim.

The woman on the table was unconscious, with strange bruising around her neck, arms, wrists and thighs. A small white towel covered her genitals, otherwise she was nude.

"She come in like this?" Bianca asked.

"Her clothing was in shreds, medics who brought her in bagged them for you."

Margaret pointed to a red bag in the corner. Bianca shook her head.

"We've got to get them to start using paper bags. That plastic's no good for bloody evidence." The detective got out her notebook. "So what's her condition?"

"Comatose, higher brain functions minimal. She's not going to be waking up anytime soon. Someone found her in an alley down on Federal Hill. Called an ambo. They took one look at her and called you guys. Then they brought her here."

"Yeah, there's uniforms and the crime lab down on the scene now looking for evidence. What did the exam show?"

"She wasn't raped, not in the usual sense. Whatever was used on her wasn't attached to any guy I know, or want to know. Too long and too wide, based on the amount of damage done. Whatever it was, it was covered with some kind of strange lube. A sample'll be in the rape kit."

Bianca looked the victim over, studying her features, memorizing the damage done to her. She'd get the photos Margaret took later, but she wouldn't need them. She'd remember what was done to this woman long after she caught the bastard who did it and made him pay.

"What do you think caused these marks?" she asked Margaret, pointing to the circular bruises on the woman's neck and limbs.

"Don't know. They look like suction marks, the kind you get if you hold a suction cup against your skin too long, but they're so many of them."

"You got photos, right?" Bianca asked, knowing the answer. In reply she got an "of course" look from the nurse. "Maybe the freak uses cut-up bath mats to bind his victims."

"Victims?" Margaret said with some alarm. "There's been more than one?"

"Not yet," Bianca said, again looking at the woman lying on the table. What kind of Hell did you go through, she silently asked her. Bound, beaten, assaulted -- pushed past the point of endurance into the darkness of a coma. At least Bianca hoped it was darkness and that the woman wasn't trapped inside her own mind, constantly reliving the torture of her violation. "Not yet," she repeated, "but there will be. Whoever did this was one sick son of a bitch. They'll be more like her."

It's only going to get worse, Bianca thought as she drove home much later that night. Night? Try morning. Sunrise would be in a few hours. She might get to sleep sometime. Shower and breakfast, read the paper, try not to think about how bad things are.

The hospital was the bright spot of her night. There'd been nothing at the scene. She hoped the woman's purse would be found so her relatives could be notified and she would at least have the dignity of her name.

Sleep; don't think of sleep, she told herself. You can sleep when you get home. From the scene she went back to the office, submitted the evidence, wrote her report. Then there was her boss.

"Lieutenant, got a minute?" Lieutenant Herbert Moran walked over, stood next to her desk, his six-eight towering over her as she sat. Bianca hated it when he did that, especially when, like now, he stood so close that she couldn't get up without uncomfortable physical contact. So she had to sit there and let him look down on her.

"What is it, Jones?"

"I think we got a serial rapist starting up."

"How so?"

She handed him her report, them described how the victim was abused, Moran reading the report as she detailed the odd binding marks and the artificial means of penetration.

"And how many does this make?" he asked, his tone indicating that she should make her point and stop wasting his time.

Bianca sighed. "How many what?" Bianca knew what was coming. Moran was newly promoted, sent to the Sex Offense Unit because it was the only spot open. He was also an idiot who'd spent most of his career inside -- Planning & Research, Personnel, the Academy -- his rank due solely to his ability to impress an interview board and do well on written tests. Any street smarts he might have had were long gone.

"How many victims?"

"This is the first."

"One does not make a pattern, Jones. It doesn't even make a line." Moran paused, waiting for the laugh.

Ignoring him, Bianca said, "So let's stop it before it does."

"Jones, for all we know this is rough sex that got out of hand. She passes out and her partner panics. Thinking she's dead, he dumps the body. Let's not get everybody all worked up over what might be some love play that went too far. Work it as you would any other case."

Taking her silence for assent, Moran started to walk away. Bianca let him take ten steps before asking, "So we just wait for him to do this to another woman, Lieutenant?"

Moran turned. "And just what do you have, Jones?" he asked, eyes flashing anger for a moment. "Nothing from the scene, no DNA, no witnesses. Just hickeys and some funky lube. You get something to work with and then we'll talk."

Pulling into the lot of her apartment complex Bianca thought back to that conversation. That could have gone better, she decided. But I'm home now. I'll think about work later. Now -- home, breakfast and bed.

Bianca's next shift was uneventful. No calls came in. She spent the night doing follow-ups to previous cases. About two in the morning she called the hospital.

"How's the patient?" she asked Margaret Tate.

"Not good. Still comatose, and now her pressure's up and there's swelling in her abdomen. Nothing on X-Ray but the CT scan shows some kind of tissue mass."

"Something to do with the attack?"

"Hard to say how, unless she had some weird allergic reaction to whatever was used on her. We moved her to regular ICU. They'll probably do an exploratory in the morning." Margaret paused, then asked, "What about on your end, anything?"

"A little more than nothing. Clothing, slides and samples went up to Lab. No ID yet. Ms. Doe's never been arrested and there's no missing persons report that fits her. Her purse hasn't turned up either."

"Souvenir?"

"Maybe, remember, this is Baltimore. It's just as likely the same person who found her and called it in snatched up her purse."

"What about your boss? He agree that this is the start of something?"

Bianca gave a disgusted laugh. "Lt. Moron? He's about as useful as a limp dick. He thinks she went down because of kinky sex gone bad."

"Can kinky sex go bad?"

"Not the way I do it. Anyway, he'll sing a different tune when the next one comes in."

"You know something, Bee?"

"What?"

"If it's a choice between you being right and him being right, I hope it's him."

"Yeah," Bianca admitted, "so do I."

She hung up the phone. Sitting back and looking out over the city from her seventh floor window, she repeated softly, "So do I."

It was a false hope, she knew. Baltimore's newest freak was out there -- reliving last night's assault, planning a new one or doing the deed this very minute. And right now there was nothing Bianca could do about it.

***

It all quickly goes to Hell.

With the image of the mass causing her swelling continually shifting, the surgeon doing the exploratory on Jane Doe is unable to get any kind of reading on the scope he's inserted inside her. In the end, unable to discern its nature, he decides it has to be removed. As the first cut is made in her abdomen, Jane Doe is ripped open by a force from inside. What looks like a tentacle wraps itself around the doctor's hand and pulls itself from her womb. The nurse, frozen in shock, can only watch as something emerges from the bleeding body of the woman on the table, something that crawls up the doctor's arm and fastens itself to him, drawing the life from his body, something that turns on her as the doctor falls.

Slime-covered limbs come forward, breaking her stupor. She screams as a blast of white foam hits both her and the creature. As it falls to the floor the nurse looks up to see the anesthesiologist standing near her, a spent fire extinguisher in his hands.

The nurse's scream attracts the attention of those outside. The doors of the OR fly open and people pour in.

"Get it," the anesthesiologist calls, pointing to the floor.

"Get what?" asks the security guard who was the first to rush in.

"That."

"That" is now a lifeless form on the OR floor. Whatever it was, it had not been able to survive a premature birth, its exertions immediately afterwards and

the chemical spray from the extinguisher.

"It ... attacked the doctor," the nurse tells the unbelieving crowd of people.

The OR is locked down, hospital officials called. Someone suggests calling the police and is quickly silenced. The tentacled mass is taken away for a necropsy and the cover-up begins.

Jane Doe's death is later attributed to a severe infection, the doctor's to a heart attack. The nurse's comments are dismissed as hysteria. Substantial pay raises convince her and anesthesiologist to remain silent. The lump of tissue from the patient is officially classified as "a pre-cancerous tumor" and taken down to the pathology lab for further study.

***

Bianca's sleep was interrupted by her telephone.

"Yeah," she mumbled into the receiver, not quite awake.

"Detective Jones," a voice replied, "this is Joe Russo in the Lab. Can you come in this afternoon?"

"Why?" And you better have a good reason for waking me up, she silently added, or I'll break a test tube off in your ... but Russo was talking again.

" ... DNA in the lubricant you submitted. Matches with others in the database."

Hot damn! The momentary elation she felt was enough to wake her up entirely. After telling the criminalist that she'd be there by one, she realized that unless the DNA was associated with a known sex offender, the match did nothing to bring her closer to her suspect. At least, she thought, it'll give me enough to convince even Moran that there's a serial out there.

"What you got for me," Bianca asked Russo after arriving at the Lab.

"A mess, that's why I asked you to come down. Coffee?" At her nod, Russo took a beaker off a hot plate under the chemical hood and poured her a cup. The inky liquid was thick and bitter, but at least it was hot and had enough caffeine in it to keep her going thorough her sleep-shortened day.

"We got three hits, all murder cases from up north -- one from Norwalk, that's in Connecticut, one from Portsmouth, Rhode Island and the other from some place in Massachusetts called Arkham. Actually, they're in reverse order. The Arkham one being first and Norwalk last."

"I'll call and ask for copies of the reports."

"Already done," Russo said, pleased with himself. "Norwalk and Portsmouth PDs are going to fax what they've got. They'd both appreciate copies of your report."

"What about the Arkham PD?"

Russo shrugged. "Funny thing. When I told," Russo checked his notes, "a

Detective Armitage about the match, he laughed, wished me luck and hung up. But he did finally send something, not much, but something."

"Any chance it was a suspect's name?"

Russo shook his head. "Not likely. The DNA came from what you called lubricant. It matches similar stuff found on the murder victims and well …" Russo sighed, as if not believing what he was about to say, "… it isn't human."

It took a minute for Bianca to realize just what Russo had told her. Just when you think you've heard everything, she thought. To Russo she said, "You're telling me that our Jane Doe was raped by some kind of animal?" The criminalist nodded. "What kind of animal?"

Russo shrugged his arms in the air. "Don't know. It's not a primate, not even mammalian. I've sent a sample down to College Park. Maybe their Zoology people can ID it."

"My God, he raped her with a snake," Bianca thought aloud.

"No scales. Snakes aren't slimy. Besides, unless you froze it, how could you get something like a snake up into … you know." Russo turned red.

"I've a few boyfriends who tried," Bianca said, embarrassing the chemist even more. She picked up his report. "Thanks, Russo, I'm sure this will help."

I'm not sure how, she thought as she walked from the Lab to her office. But at least I've got more to go on than I did.

Back at her desk, Bianca looked over the reports from the other agencies. There was a fax from Arkham, a 24-hour sheet describing the finding of female remains scattered over a wide area in a field just inside the town limits. Under "recommend follow-ups" were the phrases "check with London" and "call China Alley." She supposed China Alley was the Arkham equivalent of Baltimore's Block; a place where legalized vice was concentrated and barely controlled. The London reference she didn't get at all. Surely the Ripper's not still around, she thought.

The report from the Portsmouth PD provided more details. Their murder victim had been found in slightly better shape, but only slightly. Arms ripped off, her pelvis broken and her legs at unnatural angles to her body. A note was made of the strange suction type marks found on her savaged limbs.

While the victim from Norwalk had suffered some trauma, she had been found intact, cause of death strangulation, no doubt from the ligature wrapped around her neck that had left the same suction marks.

Something, she wasn't quite sure what, bothered her about these reports, hers and the three from out of town. She read them again, and again, and a third time. She was halfway through a fourth reading when she figured out what it was. Her perp was working in reverse. Most deviant killers build up to their crimes -- they start out small, peeping into windows, abusing small animals. Some then graduate to B&E, sneaking into houses at night to rape or just fondle their victims. The fondlers will sometime progress to rape, and the rapists to murder. This guy, started off committing a horrific mutilation murder and is working down to simple rape, if there is such a thing.

Bianca was pondering the why of this when she heard Lt. Moran come in. Major Chester Williams, head of the Detective Division, was with him. She smiled at the sight of the two of them together. She got up and quickly made photocopies of all her reports. Then she walked over to the brass.

"Good evening, Major," she said, politely, "Sorry to interrupt. I just want to update Lt. Moran on a case."

"Go ahead, Detective."

"Lieutenant, remember the case from the other night, a jane doe found in an alley, tied and raped with an unknown object?"

"What about it?" Moran looked uncomfortable. He clearly didn't like discussing this in front of his boss.

Bianca smiled again, in what appeared to be a last ditch plea before his superior officer. "I was wondering, sir, if you'd reconsider treating the case as an isolated incident."

Had Moran been paying attention, had he more experience in the Sex Offense Unit and with Bianca Jones, the "sir" would have tipped him off. Bianca never called a ranking officer "sir," preferring to use the rank itself. But Moran didn't know that, and so he said, "I told you the other night, there is no basis for thinking this case something other than a one time attack." The condescending way he said this, made the next all the more sweet.

Bianca handed him the copied reports. "What's this?" he asked.

"Three dead in New England, our jane doe is number four, at least." Turning to Williams she said, "We got a freak here, Major, and he's loose in the city."

She spent the next hour reviewing the case with Williams, Moran ignored and forgotten in his own office. In the end she got the promise of extra resources and detectives to help her work the case. As she left the office, she heard Williams say, "You know, Herb, it wouldn't hurt to listen to your people more. They're the experienced investigators."

Payback's a bitch, Herb, Bianca thought, and so am I.

Bianca's glee at putting Moran in the jackpot was short-lived. No sooner had she sat down at her desk then the phone rang. It was Margaret calling from the hospital.

***

Alice Simkins hovers between here and there, her consciousness on the edge of darkness and light. Slowly, memory returns.

Working late at the convenience store, walking home, this she remembers.

Home -- she thinks of home -- she didn't get there. She was grabbed, grabbed by the leg, pulled into the darkness. A smell comes back, the smell of the State Fair and 4H animals. She's forced down, arms -- too many arms for one person -- rip her clothing, spread her legs. She closes her eyes.

No! She doesn't want this, tries to reject the images, but the memory floods her.

She cannot struggle -- her arms, neck, legs held fast during her violation. It's over quickly.

Bad, but you lived through it, Alice's mind tells her. Now come back, back to the light. Then a final image, a last memory. The sight of her attacker, all limbs and legs, hideous and unclean. And inside me.

It is too much. Consciousness flees, memory fades, and Alice Simkins sinks down into the blackness

***

"Bee, we got another one."

Alice Simkins's condition was much the same as Jane Doe's -- unconscious, violated, clothes torn off, suction marks on her neck and limbs. Her purse was found this time, lending credence to the belief that someone had snatched Jane Doe's from where it lay near her battered body.

"Same kind of violation?" Bianca asked Margaret.

"The same, whatever it was."

Bianca then told her about the Lab reports -- the unknown DNA, the murders in New England, what she did to Moran.

"Well," the nurse said, "here's the rest of the bad news -- Jane Doe is dead."

"Damn it! What happened?"

Margaret told Bianca what she'd heard -- nothing official, but hospital gossip had a way of coming close to the truth.

A moment of clarity, pieces coming together. Bianca didn't quite know what was going on, couldn't explain it to herself, but knew what she had to do.

"Maggie, Alice is going to go the same way as Jane. Once the swelling starts, have a D&C done on her. Scrape her good, get everything, and send it to our Lab."

"Bee, I just can't …"

"Then she'll die, just like the first one. Do anything, sleep with an intern if you have to, better yet, lie to one, but don't let Alice come to term."

"Bee, you're talking crazy, did you just say …"

"Come to term, yeah. Maybe I am crazy, but it makes sense to me. Now, can you get me to your morgue? I need a DNA sample from the mass that came out of Jane."

"I could talk to our pathologist tomorrow, see what he says."

Bianca shook her head. "It has to be tonight. Jane Doe died, that makes it a murder. Tomorrow her case, and Alice's too, will be taken from me and given to those cowboys in Homicide. While they're rounding up the usual perverts and sickos, more women will die and then this monster will leave town. Tonight's all I got."

Margaret led Bianca to the hospital morgue. She distracted the attendant by asking about the personal effects of some non-existent patient. This caused him to check the record in his office while Bianca snuck into the freezer and sliced off a generous piece of the thing that had emerged from Jane Doe.

"Are you sure she died?" Bianca heard the attendant ask Margaret as she crept past the office door.

"That's what Admissions & Discharge told me," she heard Margaret reply. "They have 'reason for discharge' as deceased." *You're a good liar, Maggie.*

"Then it's Admissions problems. Take it up with them. Trust me, I'm sure your girl's not here. I know everything that goes on in my morgue."

"Did you get it?" Margaret asked once she left the attendant.

"In a specimen cup in my purse. Tomorrow it goes right to the Lab. They won't get the word I'm off the case for at least a day or two. By then I'll have the results."

They were back with Alice Simkins. "Remember what I said about the swelling, Maggie. Whatever's growing in her is not entirely human. Kill it as soon as you can."

Margaret Tate trusted her friend. "Bee, if the swelling starts, I'll do what I can. Some of these first-year residents believe anything a nurse tells them. I'll find one to do it and make him think it was his idea."

It went as Bianca predicted. When she reported the next day, Moran happily pulled her from the case and put her back in rotation. But not before she'd given the samples to Russo.

"Rush it," she asked.

A few days went by. No results from the Lab, no progress on the case. At least as far as she knew. Homicide wasn't great at sharing results. There were, however, no more victims. None found anyway, Bianca thought. *Maybe the monster is hiding them, maybe he's moved on.* If so, then the case was dead. With no solid leads, and without more victims to spur them further, the detectives on the case will soon be pressed into service on other, more current murders. Jane Doe and Alice Simkins will become old business, and soon find their way to a file in the cold case squad.

The next day, Russo sent the results. The DNA Bianca had recovered was a 100% match with the other samples. So was the sample that Nurse Tate had sent over from City of Hope. *Good going, Maggie!* In a way she felt relieved. She'd had this half-assed theory of something --some *thing* -- inducing conception, then extremely rapid development of the fetus. Maggie was right, it sounded crazy, but at the time it fit, and Bianca was too good a detective to throw out an idea that fit the facts, even if it did sound like something out of a mad scientist movie.

But where did that leave her? Certainly not with half human/half whatever little monsters running around. Just some nut job with some sort of beast trained to assault women. And whatever he used to make it horny got into its jism and caused an allergic reaction. So where did the DNA come from? Bianca didn't have the answer for that one. She tried telling herself that it wasn't her case anymore, that you work your own and didn't worry about somebody else's problems. That the detectives in Homicide would break this one, and the solution would be a simple one, with a perfectly rational explanation.

She didn't believe it.

What she did believe, with no evidence whatsoever, was that she was the only one who could do something to stop this monster. She just wished she knew what it was.

"Start over," she told herself, and pulled out the duplicate case files she'd copied before turning the originals over to Homicide. She read them all, nothing, and nothing on the second reading. She'd decided to read them one more time ....

"Jones, line one."

"Jones here."

"Detective Jones." It was an old voice, thin and dry as dust.

"Yes, can I help you?"

"I may have some information in a case you're working on."

"Which one?"

"The assaults on women in Federal Hill."

Bianca took a deep breath. Don't blow it, girl. This guy could be an informant or just some nut case, or he could be the perp. But how did he know she was working on it? That wasn't public knowledge. She tried to sound calm when she answered.

"What about them?"

"I dislike talking over the telephone. Could you come to my shop tomorrow?"

"Possibly, Mr. ..."

"Morgan, of Morgan's Rare Books and Collectibles. I'm in Fells Point, Historic Fells Point, as our mayor insists we call it."

Bianca was quite familiar with the area. Her first post had been in nearby Canton. Fells Point was in southeast Baltimore, right on the water. A collection of shops, restaurants and homes, it was a tourist area still untouched by the chain stores. It also boasted the highest density of bars and taverns per block in the entire metropolitan area. She knew the area well, but hadn't heard of Morgan's bookshop.

"I'm not familiar with your store, Mr. Morgan. Just where is it?"

There was a raspy sound that may have been a laugh, or maybe just a chuckle. "It's an alley shop, Detective Jones, just off Fleet Street. I don't get much walk-in business, but those who need to manage to find it."

"If you could tell me something about what this is about …"

"As I said, Ms. Jones, it is not something to talk about over the telephone, especially since the police operator warned me that my conversation may be taped. But I'll say this -- Arkham, Portsmouth, Norwalk. Anytime tomorrow after one, Ms. Jones. I'll be waiting." He hung up.

Now what was all that about? Bianca wondered. Who was this Morgan and, more importantly, what did he know?

Morgan's Rare Books proved to be closer to Aliceanna Street than Fleet. As Morgan told her, it was a small shop fronting on what had once been an alley. Yielding to the need for more specialty shops, the backs of many stores had been converted to storefronts. Bianca found the bookstore on the newly named Lisbon Street.

"Come in, Ms. Jones," came a voice from the back as Bianca entered the store, the bell above the door announcing her presence. A gnomish looking man came into view, his appearance matching the voice. "Come in," he said again, moving past her to lock the door and turn the "Open" sign around to "Closed."

He is old, Bianca thought as Morgan led her to the back of the store. Just how …

"Eighty-nine next month," Morgan said over his shoulder as if reading her thoughts. "And except for a few rough spots along the way, enjoyed every minute of it. So far, that is."

There was a table in the back. "Please sit, I'll get us some tea, unless you'd like something else."

"Tea would be fine," Bianca started to say, but Morgan was already gone.

As Morgan fussed with teapots and cups, Bianca looked around. As befitted any decent bookshop, the walls were lined with bookcases with volumes overflowing onto chairs and tables. She supposed that some of these books were Morgan's private stock, not generally available to the walk-in trade.

Many of the books were in foreign languages. On the table in front of her something called *Les Cultes des Ghoules* sat on top of a book entitled *Las Reglas De Ruina*. Propped up against these was *The Undead* by John Seward, M.D. Looking over at the shelves across from her she saw Holmes's *The Whole Art of Detection* and *Practical Handbook of Bee Culture* bracketing the slim form of *The Dynamics of an Asteroid.*

"Find anything you like," Morgan asked as he came from the kitchen carrying a tray.

"Just looking around, I'm not really here to buy."

"Of course not, you're here to catch a monster."

Bianca stopped stirring her tea. "Mr. Morgan ..."

"Morgan, please, just Morgan. It was Captain Morgan to the Army many years ago, then Dr. Morgan to a few universities a bit later, but now it's just Morgan."

"Is that a first or last name?"

The old man shrugged. "Your choice. It's what I've gone by most of my life. Safer that way. But we were talking about monsters."

"What do you know about them?"

"Monsters in general, or the one you're hunting?"

This cute little man was starting to get on Bianca's nerves. He clearly knew something, and was having too much fun making her work for it. Bianca briefly thought about picking him up and shaking the knowledge out of him, but she thought he might crumble into dust if she did.

"The one I'm hunting," she said. "You can start with how you know I'm hunting it."

"Fordleigh alerted me after the first victim died. He told me about the creature that poor woman gave birth to, as well as your collecting samples from it."

"And Fordleigh is ..."

"The night time morgue attendant. He did tell Nurse Tate that he knew everything that happened down there. And from his description of her body, it fits with what happened further north."

"You know about that?"

"Miss Jones, there are those of us who take an interest in the strange and unexplainable. Some, like myself, can only observe and advise. Others play a more active role and from time to time step in when circumstances go beyond what the normal authorities can do. In this case, we were alerted to the first death in Arkham by the local police. They've had similar problems in the past and by now know what to do and who to call."

"China Alley and London."

Morgan smiled. "Yes, although in this case both are busy elsewhere. The resident of China Alley is currently on the West Coast, and Mr. London, I believe, is in Europe. We are, for the present, on our own."

"Just what are you talking about, Mr. ... er, Morgan?"

"About things beyond normal comprehension, Miss Jones. The DNA, it wasn't human, was it? Nor have you matched it to any known animal. You won't, and currently there is no way to cause the acceleration in fetal development that you have witnessed."

"It wasn't a fetus," Bianca corrected. "No DNA from the mother."

"Exactly," Morgan said, as if he already knew. "And again, no way to explain it, not by what you know."

"Cloning?" Bianca offered lamely, searching for something.

"Yes, but a clone of what? Nothing in nature." Morgan turned toward the books Bianca had been looking at earlier. "What was it Mr. Holmes always said? When you've eliminated the impossible ..."

Bianca finished the quote. "Whatever's left, however improbable, must be the answer."

"So if there's no answer in nature, what have we left, Ms. Jones?"

Sitting here, sipping tea in the back of a bookshop that seemed too large for the space it occupied, what Morgan said made sense. After she left here, when she got back to her office and looked again at the cold hard facts, it might be different. But for now ...

"You're saying this thing is supernatural?"

"Let's say, preternatural -- before nature, before the Chaos of Creation was formed into Order. There was life even then, before the First Day ended. Not life as we understand it, or could understand it, but life. This life was not seen as good, and thus was banished to its own time and place. There are moments, however, when a rift between that place and ours opens."

This is bull, Bianca thought, and even if it were true, what did it have to do with today? Still she listened politely. Back in patrol she'd learn that even the craziest story -- cosmic rays, sacred bleach bottles and God watching through electric sockets -- was true to someone, and sometimes led to a more general truth.

"For some reason," Morgan was going on, "these rifts usually occur in New England, generally centered around Arkham. Would-be magicians seeking power, religious fanatics looking to end this sinful world, the curious playing with the occult -- they tap into power, open a door, and something leaks through."

"So what you're saying is that someone summoned a demon from another world who is now impregnating Earth women."

Morgan slowly shook his head. "Miss Jones, please, accept for one minute that what I'm saying is the truth, and not the makings of a cheap movie. Think like the detective you are. Clearly the women are not being impregnated. The DNA of the offspring proves that. What else could be the reason for their violation? What leads to a child without the genetic contribution of the birth mother?"

Bianca's eyes widened as she realized where Morgan had led her. "Son of a bitch, they're surrogates. This thing isn't raping them to spread his seed, he … she's laying eggs and using them as incubators."

"Exactly. When the first woman was discovered, investigators found a cult devoted to a goddess called Shub-Niggurath. Mostly female, this cult had learned of Shub-Niggurath from an old book of occult lore. Believing her to be a variation of the Phoenician goddess Ashtoreth or the Assyrian Ishtar, they began worshipping her as an alternative to the male gods that dominate most modern religions."

"And this Shub …, whatever, is one of these chaos beings you mentioned."

"Yes, among her many names is the All-Mother. The victim in Arkham was a member of her cult. Apparently this group summoned her and an aspect of her being came and stayed."

To herself Bianca said, "I don't believe I'm listening to this crap." To Morgan she said, "This is all very interesting, but it doesn't help me …"

"Miss Jones, let me finish, if for no other reason than to humor an old man. When you leave here, you're certainly free to ignore or forget everything I've said. Okay?"

At Bianca's nod Morgan continued. "It is believed that ever since their banishment, these creatures, these elder gods if you'll permit, have been trying to return to our time and place. And so far, every time they've tried, they've been beaten back. This, I believe is a new tactic. Rather than invade from the outside, Shub-Niggurath hopes to raise an army from within by planting pieces of herself, her 'Dark Young' as it were, here in our world."

It was beginning to make sense. Not the monster stuff, but the cult. These weirdoes had some mutant animal and were using it to bring about the second coming or some stuff. As Bianca thought to ask Morgan if that was possible he grabbed a book from the table and opened it. Displaying a woodcut, he said, "This engraving was found in the temple called Tsathoggua. It displays Shub-Niggurath in all her glory."

Bianca looked, then instantly turned away. Whatever that thing was, it was … disturbing. There was no creature on earth that came close, an octopus or squid, maybe, if either had horribly mutated then mated with a goat. But those tentacles. Bianca looked again. The marks on the victim could have been caused by tentacles.

"I see enlightenment, Miss Jones."

"Morgan, let's just say I'm glad you called. I think I have it figured now. But Shubby here gets to stay in the monster closet. I'm sure if she were walking the streets of Baltimore someone would have noticed by now."

Morgan took a coin from his pocket, nothing exotic, just a quarter. He held it straight up so that Washington was facing her. "Imagine this in two dimensions, Miss Jones. All you would see was a round disk." He turned it sideways. "And now all it is is a thick line. The Old Ones can exist both in their plane and ours. What we see and how we see it depends on which side they present to us."

"The blind men and the elephant."

"Exactly. Now, is there anything else?"

There wasn't, and after thanking him for his time, Bianca left.

***

She knew her from the neighborhood, just to nod "hi" to. They'd never spoken, only seen each other jogging, walking their dogs, sweeping the sidewalks. It was like that now in the city, be friendly but not too close.

She's sitting on her front step, looking toward the southwestern sky. Some big game at Camden Yards, supposed to be fireworks later. From here she should see some of the high ones.

Her neighbor comes by, her little pug on a long leash, taking him to the park for his nightly business. She nods, then goes back to studying the stars.

A muffled cry, just one, up from where the woman and dog had walked. She looks to see the dog running back toward her, its leash trailing behind.

Every instinct of city life tells her not to get involved. Still, she gets off her stoop and runs toward the alley, looking for the woman. She sees legs being dragged around a corner. Hoping to get a look at the attacker, a description she can give to the cops, she runs after them.

She comes to where alley meets alley, turns the corner. She had time for her own quick scream before she too is taken and dragged into the blackness.

***

That night, Bianca got called to the hospital. "What we got?" she asked Margaret.

"A girl claiming to be raped."

"Claiming?"

"She called 911 from his place, said he raped her. Patrol brought her here. Him they took to Central Booking."

"And there's doubt?"

"More than that. No bruising, no tearing. During the exam she admitted that it was consensual."

Bianca could see where this was going. "And afterwards?"

"He broke up, said it'd been nice but he'd found someone else. Offered her cab fare home."

"And that's when she called the cops?"

"From the bathroom. Locked herself in until they showed up. I guess we write this one off."

Bianca looked at the nurse. "Like Hell. That son of a bitch should have dumped her before her got his freebie. Let him rot in CB."

"But what about her statement?"

Bianca smiled. "Privileged communication, Maggie. Legally, I never heard a word of it."

"You're a nasty piece of work sometimes, Bee. So what happened with your informant?"

Bianca told Maggie about the bookstore and her conversation with Morgan.

"So you got up early and on your own time for a ghost story?"

"It wasn't all a waste of time." Bianca laid out her cult theory.

"So where did they get this strange beastie?" Margaret asked.

"Genetic engineering."

The nurse gave her an "are you kidding" look.

"Can we rule it out? Not so long ago there was another cult claiming to have cloned a human. And that claim hasn't been disproven. Who's to say some other group hasn't been playing Frankenstein?"

Margaret nodded. "Possible. You going to tell Homicide?"

"And let them take all the credit?"

The one thing bothering me, Bianca thought when back in her office, is that there should have been another victim by now. The cult had been chased out of New England by Morgan's Fearless Monster Hunters. But no one here in Charm City was a threat to them, not yet. There should have been another vic. While at the hospital she'd had Maggie check the other ER's in the area. Nothing even similar turned up. With no other leads, she again turned to the case folder.

Complete destruction in Arkham, mutilation in Portsmouth, strangulation in Norwalk. Each time they got better. Jane Doe almost made it, Alice Simkins did, but both would have died when the infant monster burst through their abdomens.

Bianca suddenly realized why other victims had not been found. Almost frantic, she called Missing Persons.

The report she got back was disturbing. Two women in the Federal Hill area were missing, had been for several days now. So far, no sign of either of them had been turned up.

They were taken, Bianca knew, taken by The Daughters of Shub-Niggurath, taken to be used as breeders for whatever monster they'd cooked up.

Despite her words at the hospital, Bianca knew she couldn't do it herself. Alone, she didn't have the resources to search the Hill for the missing women.

Reluctantly, she went to Homicide.

"Interesting," was all Detective Earl Beasley said after she'd laid out her theory. She'd avoided any mention of elder gods from other dimension and instead talked up the cult theory, using Ishtar as the goddess being worshipped. When she'd finished she could tell by the look on Beasley's face that she'd wasted her time.

"It's like this, Jones," Beasley said, "we haven't forgotten about these murders, but given that the killer came down the coast and no more bodies have been found, we're kinda thinking that he's moved on. The FBI profiler thinks so too. And kidnapping's not in this freak's M.O. Those two missing gals are probably up in Atlantic City losing at the slots. Give 'em a few more days they'll be back."

Bianca wanted to lash out, call Beasley all kinds of names, to question his intelligence, parentage and sexual habits. Instead, she bottled her rage, controlled it. Adding to her rep as a witch on wheels wouldn't change Beasley's mind. He was the primary on the case, and what he said went. And no matter if he was later proven wrong, the FBI had signed off on his theory. Any comeback would be dumped on them.

"Well," she said as pleasantly as possible, "just thought I'd pass on what my informant told me."

"Thanks, I appreciate it," Beasley said, with about as much sincerity. "Should anything break in the case, I'll look into the cult idea."

He wouldn't. But she'd tried, damn it, she'd tried. Now she'd have to go it alone.

"Damn it!"

A detective looked up as Bianca entered the Sex Offense Unit. "Something wrong?" he asked.

Bianca hadn't realized she'd sworn out loud. I've got to get out of here, she thought. To the detective she said, "Did you know that they're moving all the bathrooms to the Homicide Unit?"

"No, why's that?"

"Because that's where all the assholes are." With that she went into Moran's office, slapped a leave slip for a week's vacation on his desk and left without saying another word.

On the way out she stopped at the lab and found Russo.

"The blue light you guys use to detect semen on crime scenes, does it work on that stuff from the DNA lube?"

"We got two calls about you."

"From who?"

"One from Moran, the other from Beasley in Homicide. Both of them wanted us to let them know if you came down here asking about the Federal

Hill murders."

"And?"

"If you ever do I'll call and tell them. And for your general information, the blue light will work on certain samples of non-human DNA, should you ever run in to some on a future case."

"Can I borrow one?"

"You're not planning to do something stupid, are you, Bianca?" He handed her a black plastic case and waited to see if she objected to his using her first name.

Not objecting at all, Bianca smiled instead, "Probably, Joe. Why, want to help?"

"What do you need?"

"First off, how do you use this thing?"

Russo opened the case. "You got a standard rechargeable flashlight. Put this blue lens over it, then put on the orange goggles. Shine it on the sample, or where a sample might be. If something glows in the dark, you got a positive."

He closed the case and handed it to her. "Any thing else I can do for you?"

Bianca hesitated. This was her fight, her career she was risking. And Russo was a civilian, a noncombatant. Still she wasn't fool enough to turn down help when offered. "Ever use a gun?"

Russo shook his head. "But what's the problem. Point and shoot, just like a camera, right?"

He'd shoot himself or me, she decided. Better go it alone. "Thanks anyway, Joe. If all goes well, I'll owe you big time. Dinner on me, or something." She surprised herself as much as Russo with the offer. Oh, what the Hell, she thought, he is kinda cute.

"Sure, anytime, Bianca."

She left the Lab and a beaming Russo. Don't get your hopes up, kid, she thought back at him. Chances are things are not gonna go that well.

That night, Bianca started where the first victim was found, the still unidentified Jane Doe. There wasn't anything left of the scene -- she hadn't expected there to be, it had been too long. But she wanted to get a sense of the area, of the hunting ground. She walked further down the alley, found it connected with another one. That's the way it was in Baltimore, a city of row homes, all with alleys in the back, each one linking up with another just like the streets in front. If you had to, you could cover quite a distance without going on to a major street.

Reading her map by the light of her flash, Bianca saw that the alley where Alice Simkins was found was only a few blocks away. Between here and there was the general area where the two missing women were last seen. She got the blue lens out of her knapsack, slipped on her orange goggles and started the slow process of scanning the alleys of Federal Hill.

From time to time she found the luminescence Russo had told her to look for. Each time, however, the cause turned out to something mundane --freshly used condoms, puddles from dogs and people relieving themselves. She searched for three hours and found nothing.

The next night she went back, this time starting where Simkins was found and walking a different path.

I've got to be out of my mind, she thought. Spending my own leave looking for cult weirdoes and DNA monsters. With this blue ray in my hand and the orange specs, I'm the only thing around here that looks like she's from the Twilight Zone. Bianca wondered how many calls the Southern District had gotten and dismissed reporting an alien.

She looked at her watch. Another hour and I'm gone, she thought. I'll go home, shower and sleep. When I wake up it's down the ocean for the rest of my leave. Old Shubby can make all the little monsters she wants.

When that hour went by, Bianca was still searching. More condoms, more urine, more of the sense that she was wasting her time -- her time and not the Department's. I'll just finish sweeping this alley, she promised herself.

Then -- movement ahead. Nothing much, just a glimmer of something in the next alley over. She stood still and waited. Something appeared then was gone, some sort of animal. It suddenly occurred to Bianca that if the cult and their pet beast were still around, they could still be on the hunt. And here she was making herself the biggest target in the neighborhood.

Fine, that way works too, she thought as she unzipped her jacket and made sure her Glock was close to hand. She reached back into her knapsack, feeling for the reassurance of the sawed-off Mossberg she'd put in the umbrella sheath. Her hand gripped the cut down stock. Ready for the quick draw. She moved forward.

Whatever it was didn't reappear. Sometimes a dog is just a dog. She hit the alley pavement with her blue light, was rewarded with a glow like a slug trail, only much wider. She followed it to the yard of a vacant house, the windows broken out, the 4x8 covering the back door ripped off.

Her first thought was calling for back up. Going alone into an unknown situation was the first thing the Police Academy taught her not to do. And if the place was empty? How to explain an unauthorized investigation, an illegal shotgun and the crime lab equipment Russo shouldn't have lent her?

Her next thought was to back off. Find a phone, call it in as an anonymous tip. Yeah and wait how long? Call it in as a Signal-13, officer needs help. Right, and send patrol into the unknown situation you didn't want to handle.

She even thought about calling Morgan, telling him to get his monster hunters down here. But how long would that take? What the Hell? How much trouble can a pack of loonies and their pet be?

She did wait until dawn, when the light of a new day would shine through the broken windows and give her light to work by. Checking her Glock, she took the shotgun out of her knapsack. Leaving the bag in the back yard, she went into the house.

The first floor was clear. Nothing but the trash left behind by the people who'd moved out. Basement or second floor? Her decision was made when she heard noises coming from above. Slowly she climbed the stairs.

Bianca was no stranger to death. Suicide, homicide, accident -- she'd seen it before in all its many forms. So the eviscerated bodies of the two missing women on the floor of the front bedroom did not disturb her that much. What did were the creatures feeding on what remained of the bodies.

They were repulsive. Short hairy legs ending in hooves. Round torsos out of which sprang tentacles which were in the process of digging into the open abdomens and shoveling their internal organs into the open gashes that served as mouths.

They hadn't been feasting long. The victims were still mostly intact. No doubt the creatures had just ripped open their surrogate mothers' wombs to emerge into new life.

Bianca's entrance had interrupted the feeding. As one, the two beasts stopped, turned and advanced on her.

Not stopping to think about the horror in front of her, Bianca brought up the shotgun and fired on the new-born monsters. Once, twice, again and again, the noise deafening, the flechette loads from the shotshells ripping the creatures to shreds. She only stopped when she ran out of ammo.

The shooting over, the threat abated, Bianca surveyed the scene. She saw how it would look to the Internal Investigations shooting team. Two dead women, her with the only weapon. *I am in major crap,* she thought. Before she could dwell on her problem any further, something tugged at her ankle.

Bianca broke away, turned to face whatever was behind her.

The babies had been bad. Their mother was worse. A myriad of limbs and tentacles were all she saw as she was grabbed by the legs and pulled down. The thing snatched at her clothes, tearing them off. Bianca got her first full look at what had to be one of Morgan's Dark Young as it fully phased into this plane of existence, as it prepared to do to her what it had done to the others, to replace the offspring the detective had blasted out of existence.

She'd dropped the useless shotgun. Hand freed, Bianca grabbed for her Glock. Fighting to stay conscious, fighting the dark that tried to take over her mind, she let her police training take over. She fired again and again, aiming for the center of the wriggling mass, hoping that somewhere there in there were vital organs and that somehow her copper-jacketed slugs would do the lethal job they were designed for. She kept firing until the blackness came.

***

"So you're suspended?" Morgan asked over a cup of tea a few days later.

Bianca gave him a weak smile. "Until they can figure out just what to do with me, and what happened in that vacant house."

"What's the official word?"

"Let's see -- two dead women, three creatures beyond anything known to physical science, but whose DNA all match that found on the murder victims. The Department's calling it a cult slaying and hoping it will all go away."

"And what about you?"

"Conducting an unauthorized investigation, illegal weapons and ammo, disobeying orders, contributing to the corruption of a crime lab tech -- I'm in more trouble than anyone in the history of the BPD. The only way I might not get fired is that I know too much of what everyone hopes isn't the truth."

"And what is the truth, Miss Jones?"

Bianca looked around at the books on the shelves, tables and chairs, then at the old man. "It's all true, isn't it? What's in these books? There was no cult; there was something out there that tried to get in, to come out of the blackness into our world."

"And there are more of them out there," the old man said. "And they have to be stopped each and every time."

Bianca nodded. "That's the horror of it. There's a saying in the Department, 'Do a job once and it's yours.' I guess even if I get fired, I've still got a job to do."

A WORLD INSIDE

Terrance Ziegler faced the assembled group. The four were, like him, seekers of knowledge and power. They had met at an occult gathering some months previous, but the dark priest who led it had proven too much the charlatan, too interested in how many men he could influence and how many women he could bed.

"There must be an offering," he told them. "Without one, none of us will ascend."

"Does it have to be one of us?" Peter Shelton squeezed his sister's hand, more afraid for her than for himself.

"A willing sacrifice would make the summoning more powerful, but no, it can be anyone."

"You got a place picked out?" asked Mark Gaines. It had been his idea to break away from their old coven, but leadership of the group had quickly fallen to Ziegler.

"Janine found us one." Ziegler looked toward Janine Conners. The small full-figured blonde had joined the old gathering mostly for laughs, but had quickly become a serious student of the dark arts.

"There's this place in Pennsylvania, off I-83. The owner just died. It'll be perfect." Then she told them about the Soto House.

"That will do."

"It will more than do," agreed Gale Shelton. "And we won't have to use the grimoires we took from LeVaey, not that any of his books were the real thing."

"Maybe we should invite our old master along," suggested Gaines. "He'd make the perfect sacrifice."

Ziegler shook his head. "Let's just pick something up on the way."

***

"It's called the *Ravings of el-Hazred*," Morgan explained to Bianca Jones. "If the stories are true, it may be one of the most dangerous books in the world."

A week ago, Bianca Jones had been a detective in the Baltimore Police Sex Offense Unit. That was before one of her investigations had led to her almost being killed by a creature from another dimension out to remake the world in its own image. In defeating the monster and sending it back to the Blackness that had spawned it Bianca managed to disobey several direct orders and break quite a few rules. Now on suspension and waiting out an investigation by Internal Affairs that could end her career, she filled her time by working at Morgan's Rare Books and Collectibles in the Fells Point area of Baltimore's waterfront.

Morgan was more than a book dealer. The wizened old man was one of a small group of people who had devoted their lives to a struggle against the dark forces that threatened humanity, a struggle into which Bianca had been drawn. If he said a book was dangerous, it was likely so.

"Dangerous how?" she asked him.

"Have you ever heard of *The Necromonicon*?"

"A creation of H. P. Lovecraft, wasn't it? He wrote about it in some of his stories."

"Lovecraft wrote about it, but it wasn't his creation. It is a work of forbidden lore, a grimoire if you will, said to have been written in the 8th century, although parts of it are no doubt much older. Its author is supposed to be one Abd el-Hazred. *The Necromonicon* is thought by many to be his only work."

"But it's not?"

Morgan shook his head. "Supposedly, there is one other. A small volume, hand-written. No copies were ever made. It is thought by some to have been the true reason for the First Crusade, and that the Knights Templar had it in their possession until their demise in the 14th century. Another story is that it was part of Hitler's occult collection and was burned by him before he took his own life."

"But it still exists, doesn't it?" Bianca asked, knowing the answer.

"Yes. The book is, or rather, was in the possession of Adam Soto, a colleague of mine from Pennsylvania. Just today I was informed of his death."

"How did he die?"

Morgan smiled. "Nothing mysterious, just the ailments of old age finally catching up with him."

"And what's in this book that makes it so dangerous?"

"As I said, *The Necromonicon* contains much that is forbidden. One who reads it with less than a pure heart and mind may be doomed. He will surely go mad. Imagine then the fate of its author."

Morgan paused, allowing Bianca to consider the possibilities. "el-Hazred died in madness. Just how and when, well, there are several stories, each more horrible than the next. But it is believed that before he died, he recorded in this book those rituals and incantations too horrible even for *The Necromonicon*."

"Did Adam Soto have any family?"

"Sadly, Miss Jones, no."

"And I presume he lived alone."

"Correct. Of course you see the problem."

"This dangerous book is now sitting unprotected in an empty house."

Morgan nodded. "It must be retrieved and destroyed as soon as possible."

"I'll leave first thing in the morning."

The bookseller held up a cautionary finger. "Given that others may have heard of Adam's death, it might be best if you left now."

***

Jennifer Ames was just out of high school. She knew the dangers of hitchhiking, but that didn't stop her. She was eighteen and at that age, mortality was for other people. Nothing bad was going to happen to her; she'd been thumbing since eighth grade. She knew the rules. Never hitch at night and never take rides from guys driving alone or in pairs. Truckers were okay, so were old guys in big sedans, no pick-ups or vans. And always keep your hand on the knife in your purse, just in case.

She'd just been left off in Pennsylvania at Interstate 83 at old Exit 4 by a middle-aged couple on their way back from an afternoon Orioles game. She stopped at a diner for a quick bite and then started walking west on Forrest Avenue, thumb out, of course, hoping to make Stewartstown by nightfall. There she'd sleep over at a friend's house.

She was hesitant when the van pulled over a little ahead of her. The driver was male, as was the passenger riding shotgun. But the van's side door slid open and a short blonde came out, followed by a slightly taller brunette.

"Where you heading?" the brunette asked.

"You going as far as Stewartstown?"

The blonde nodded her head. "Sure, climb aboard."

Jennifer got in the van with the two women. There was another guy in the back. Introductions went around and everything seemed cool. She relaxed and sat back to enjoy the ride. She even took her hand out of her purse.

***

"This is not a good idea," Bianca told herself as she head north on Interstate 83. "Breaking into a dead man's house to look for a forbidden book is not a smart thing to do."

Following Morgan's directions, once she was across the state line Bianca took Exit 4 and turned east towards Hopewell. Passing Orwig Drive she soon found the road that led to Soto House.

The dirt road gave way to macadam, and the house slowly revealed itself as Bianca drove up the paved surface. "House" was not the right word for the building she found. It was three stories high and at least as long as two football fields. It wasn't a house, it was a mansion.

An empty mansion, she remembered. An empty mansion whose owner, whose dead owner, was a collector of the occult. Bianca suddenly remembered every horror movie she had ever watched and again thought that this was not a good idea.

"But horror movies aren't real," she reminded herself, "and you've fought and beaten actual monsters. So why worry about a vacant house?" So, forgetting about all those horror movies she'd seen, Bianca got out of her car.

Reaching into her pocket, Bianca took out the key Morgan had given her. "It's not burglary if you have the key," Morgan had told her. As a member of the Baltimore Police Department, Bianca knew better. But that didn't mean she wouldn't try that explanation on the York County PD if they suddenly showed up.

"You won't have to worry about that," was Morgan answer to Bianca's concern. "Soto House is somewhat isolated and not visible from the main road."

Bianca looked around and saw that Morgan was right. In the failing light there was nothing to be seen but trees. But just to be safe, she decided, I'll park around back.

***

Things were working out better than Ziegler could have planned. Not only did they have an offering tied to the large oak table in the library, but he and his followers had also found Adam Soto's trove of occult books. They had been hidden behind a bookcase that swung out to reveal a second set of shelves.

"Tie her tight," Ziegler ordered as he watched the Sheltons bind their victim to the make-shift altar. "We'll begin when she wakes up." Finding a chair, he turned his attention to the books.

Gaines came up to him. "Which one are we going to use?"

"I was thinking something from *The Book of Eibon*."

"If that's the McBride translation it's not reliable. Is the Junzt text there?"

"Yes, but it's in German."

Janie Conners came up to them holding a small book. "Try this one," she said, her voice somewhat distant.

Ziegler took it from her, examined it. "It's not something I've seen before. No title on the front but I've seen this symbol before."

"One of LeVaey's grimoires?" suggested Gaines.

"Hardly," Ziegler said as he opened the book. "Damn, this is no good. It's in Arabic, I think." He started to close the cover when a chill ran trough him and understanding flooded his mind.

"Terry, you okay?"

Ignoring the question, Ziegler stood and closed the book. "We are ready," he said in a tone as quiet and controlled as Conners's. "Gather round the offering."

***

Jennifer woke to a headache and tried to remember what had happened. She had been in a van. A man grabbed her; a woman stuck her with something. Slowly she realized that she'd been drugged. She tried to move and discovered that she was tied to a table. Five people were looking down at her. One of them, a woman, held a knife over her chest as a man reading from a small book chanted in a language grating to her ears.

Screaming, Jennifer strained against the ropes, struggling to free herself from her bonds. It was no use, she was tied too tightly. As she screamed again, knowing there was no one to answer, the cadence of the chant grew louder and she watched the knife slowly descend.

***

When Bianca pulled around to the back of the house she found a van parked there. Looking up, she saw light coming from that part of the house where Morgan had told her the library was. Through the window she saw silhouetted figures moving around.

Maybe they were there on legitimate business, but Bianca's cop sense told her that this wasn't so. As Morgan had warned, it was likely that they were every bit as interested in the el-Hazred as the bookseller was, although possibly with less than his noble intentions.

Weapon drawn, she went in through the open back door. Finding no one on the first floor, Bianca carefully climbed the stairs to the second. A rough yet hypnotic chant coming down the hallway drew her towards the library. Unnoticed, she entered to see a partly-clad young woman tied to a large table in the center of the room, surrounded by several people. One of them was about to stab her in the chest.

Damn, she thought, now I'll never get my job back. She took aim and squeezed the trigger of her Glock. An explosion filled the room and the woman with the knife flew backward.

Hearing the gunshot the four still on their feet turned and looked towards Bianca. One of them rushed her and she took him down with a head shot. As Mark Gaines fell the three survivors raised their hands and slowly backed away from the little woman with the big gun.

"Are you okay?" she called to the woman on the table.

She took a minute to answer. "I am now. How did you …?"

"Later." Keeping her eyes on the three cultists Bianca retrieved the knife Janie Conners had dropped. She cut the rope binding the girl's right hand.

"Can you manage the rest?" Assured that she could, she handed her the knife then turned to her prisoners.

"You're too late," said the one holding a small, bloodstained book. There was a smile on his face as he laid it on the table. "However it was done, blood was spilled, the ritual complete. The way is opened and He will come."

The temperature in the room dropped ten, then twenty degrees. "Get over here," Bianca shouted. Jennifer scrambled off the table just as the air above the book began to shimmer.

"What's he talking about?" she asked her savior.

"You don't want to stay around and find out. Get out of here. Run away from here as fast as you can and keep running until you find some help."

"What about you?"

"I'll be right behind you," Bianca lied. She was going to stay, to do what she could to take down whatever crawled out of the vortex forming in the room. She had to. With no time to warn Morgan about the Hell that was going to be unleashed, she somehow had to stop it before it gained full strength.

Who calls?

The words screeched through Bianca's mind, announcing whatever had been summoned. Fighting off a psychic migraine, Bianca struggled to see what had arrived.

At first, it had no shape then the air twisted and turned in eddies over el-Hazred's book. Tentacle-like limbs formed, flailing about. The couple in the corner was too close to them. One struck the woman, smashing her skull and sending her lifeless body against the wall.

"No!" His head throbbing, Peter Shelton rushed the monster he had helped create. He didn't care that he hadn't a chance against it. Gale was lying dead at his feet. He'd make it pay for his sister's death.

The creature was now a mass of eyestalks and tentacles with an amorphous body that seemed to have little solidity to it. Solid enough to kill, Bianca decided and took what she hoped was deadly aim. Before she could fire, the man who had cried out charged the thing, only to be impaled on a thrusting tentacle.

Who calls? The thing asked again as it flicked Peter Shelton's body off its limb. And this time, as the monster's sending seared the inside of her head, Bianca caught the trace of something else -- anger, fear and a pain far deeper than what she had felt. It was enough to make her hold up her shot.

"Shoot it, shoot it!" came a desperate voice from behind her. The girl hadn't left. Instead she clung to the detective's back in panic.

Bianca could understand this. There were things mankind was not meant to see and this was one of them. She herself might right now be screaming down the stairs and running for her life had she not confronted something similar several days ago. Confronted and beaten, she thought, reminding herself that these things could be defeated.

"Not yet," she told the frightened girl.

The thing was not attacking. It was just sitting there, waving its limbs and eyestalks, awaiting an answer to its question.

Who calls?

And this time the blood-splattered man on the other side of the room claimed, "I did. From the ravings of el-Hazred I summoned you. From the nether plain I have brought you and now I command you to do my bidding."

And what is your bidding?

With this reply, Bianca understood. The fear, the anger, the pain that the creature projected was what it itself was feeling. What she herself might have felt under similar circumstances. She readied her pistol.

"Having summoned you from the darkness, in the names of the Old Ones, I command you to …"

Bianca fired, cutting off Terrance Ziegler's command and silencing him forever.

When Ziegler fell, the eyestalks that had been focused on him turned toward Bianca.

"Okay," Bianca said to herself, "I think I have its attention. Now I only hope I'm right." To the creature she said, "I spilled the blood that called you here. I command you."

Yes.

Although lessened, the pain, the anger from the creature's thoughts was still present. Bianca ignored it. "From where do you come?"

This. A tentacle indicated the book. *We come from this.*

"We? How many are you?"

Legions.

"And you are all bound to the book?"

We are the book.

"Then return to it. You are not wanted or needed here." She indicated the bodies of the Sheltons. "And take those with you."

A jumble of thoughts -- disdain for one who would refuse its power, suspicion and confusion as to her motives, relief that it could return home -- was projected into Bianca's mind as the creature unformed and currents of air drifted down into the bloody tome on the table.

***

"What happened then," Morgan asked. Bianca was back in the safety of his bookshop. She and the bookseller were in the back room drinking tea, *The*

Ravings of el-Hazred lying on the table between them.

"I called the Pennsylvania State Police on my cell phone. When they arrived I told them that I had witnessed Ms. Ames being abducted, had followed the abductors' van to Soto's House and had to use deadly force to prevent her from being sacrificed in an occult ritual."

"And the two you -- sent away?"

"No choice, Morgan. There was no way to explain their injuries."

"And what about Ms. Ames? I don't suppose her version of events agreed with yours."

Bianca shook her head. "She told the police some wild story about us fighting a monster that had killed two people that weren't there anymore. But what do you expect? She had been drugged and was in a panic."

Morgan smiled. "Yes, I can see why they wouldn't believe her. Such things aren't possible, are they?"

"What was that thing?" Bianca asked.

"Hard to say. It clearly wasn't one of the Old Ones or any of the Other Gods. They can be summoned but not commanded. Some lesser demon perhaps? The important thing, Miss Jones, is that you are safe. Now all that is left is to destroy the book, thus ending its threat forever."

"No."

Morgan looked at Bianca then down at the book between them "You mean to say that the threat won't be ended, Miss Jones?"

"I mean to say, Morgan, that I'm not going to let you destroy that book. However it's associated with Abd el-Hazred, whether it was somehow created from his madness or if that's just a story that sounded better than the truth, it's not just a book. It's a physical manifestation of an entire world, defined by the words inside it. Destroy it and you might just set its inhabitants loose. Or else you'll kill everything that lives there. I can't let you do either."

The bookseller was quiet for a moment. "Very well, Miss Jones. The book will stay with me, locked in my safe. At least until the safest course can be determined to our mutual satisfaction. Agreed?"

"Agreed."

"It is late, and this old man needs his rest. But one last question. Why did you not just shoot the monster?"

Bianca thought about this. Thought about a possibly intelligent creature forced into servitude. Then she thought about the man who had dragged it from its world, the man who would use the creature for his own ends. She calmly said, "I did."

EVERY VICTIM

"So what do you think, Reynolds? Gang sign?"

Looking up from the body on the sidewalk, the older cop looked at his partner, shaking his head. "Three red streaks on the cheek? Not any gang in this district, Jay. They just shoot 'em down. Later they tag a wall or three."

He stepped aside to let the crime scene tech take close-up photos of the marks.

"Hey, Crime Lab, any word on when Homicide's getting here?"

Joe Russo shrugged. "Who knows? As crazy as this city's been in the last few months, this guy may have to wait until one of you get promoted before a detective's assigned."

"Then he's gonna wait forever."

"This guy's got forever," Joe told the veteran officer as he finished taking his pictures. "Me, I got two more scenes waiting for me." Just then his radio crackled. "Forever isn't what it used to be. A detective's on the way."

The three men waited only a few minutes before a standard Baltimore Police unmarked sedan pulled behind the Crime Lab's jeep.

When Joe saw who was getting out of it he swore to himself quietly. He was always glad to see Bianca Jones, but not on a crime scene. That usually meant only one thing.

"What the … they hiring kids now?"

The rookie cop had a right to his question. Small and slender, the person walking toward the scene looked like she might be in her late teens, very early twenties at best. The other two knew better.

"Explain it to him," Joe told Reynolds. "I'll fill in Jones."

As the older cop took his partner aside, the Crime Lab Tech greeted Bianca. "Please tell me this guy isn't going to jump up and bite me on the throat."

Bianca smiled and shook her head. "That was our last case, remember. And from what I've heard, the M.E.'s still looking for him."

"So if there's nothing … special about this case, why are you here? I thought you and Homicide didn't get along."

"You don't see me with a partner, do you, Joe? The flu's still running through CID. With the murder rate up and half the detective squad down, Special Investigations is pitching in. We're all working together until things get better."

Over Joe's "That'll be the day," Bianca added, "What've you got?"

"Dead guy on the street."

"That I can see. How'd he get dead?"

"Typical Baltimore murder. Drive-by, no casings, no bullets, no witnesses."

Bianca looked around her. "Maybe typical for some parts of the city, Joe, but not here, not in Lauraville. Upper middle class with their kids mostly in private schools. To these people a drive-by is when someone slows down at your yard sale but doesn't stop. Officers …"

Reynolds had just finished telling his partner about Bianca's sensitivity to her height, or rather, lack of it. "Don't let her size fool you, Jay. I've seen her take down guys as big as me."

"Bigger, actually," Bianca interrupted. Having drawn their attention, she went on.

"Officers, this is your post. Do either of you recognize him?" They both shook their heads. "Any ID?"

"We were waiting for the M.E. There was that warning about handling dead bodies."

Bianca nodded. She remembered the warning and the reason for it. Officers going through the pockets of dead people tended to contaminate any evidence on the body. "So we wait. Meanwhile, any known problems in the neighbor that that might make this man dead?"

Jay spoke up, "None that we know of, Detective, maybe a gang drop off, you know, from the marks on his face."

"I saw them." Bianca walked over to the victim and bent down for a better look. Lighting the victim's face with her flash she studied the marks closely. Satisfied, she stood up.

"Lipstick, Radiant Red, I think. It's a popular shade right now."

"Lipstick?" the young cop asked, "You're sure?"

"Contrary to popular belief, Officer, I have been known to wear it." Then, less harshly she added, "When you get him ID'd, call my office. Joe knows the number. And tell the M.E. I'll meet with him in the morning."

It was a woman. Of that Bianca was sure. A man intent on marking his crime would have used a pen, a marker or the victim's blood if nothing else was available. Which explained the lipstick -- the woman no doubt used what she had on hand, or in her purse. The same purse where she no doubt had carried the gun. Dumb place for a gun, Bianca thought, thinking back to stories of fictional women detectives she'd read. The only place worse was on the inside of the thigh. Made you walk funny. Bianca smiled as she thought about the few times she had done it, none of them line of duty. Men and their fantasies.

Shaking off stray thoughts Bianca turned to thinking about the marks themselves. Why make them at all, and why three? A private farewell, a warning to the survivors, some attempt to confuse the police. She hoped it wasn't the last. If the killer thought that far ahead then it might well be a very clever man.

The one possibility that worried her was that there were three marks.

Three suggested that there had been two others, each with a smear or two of red on his cheek.

Bianca pulled up the NCIC on her computer and started a search for similar markings on homicide victims. She didn't have much hope of getting a hit. She'd been in police work far too long. Such marks, if noted at all, would be tested with the results being "blood" or "not blood." Those that came back "not blood" would most likely be filed and forgotten.

Thoughts of lipstick reminded Bianca to freshen her own. Unlocking her lower desk drawer, Bianca got her own shade of red out of her purse. Not "Radiant Red" but close. A thought occurred to her as she was putting it on, one which led to several other thoughts. But first, there was the autopsy.

***

"Hello, Little Sister."

Aside from their last names, Bianca and Dominic Jones had nothing in common. He was tall and dark and from the Caribbean Islands. Bianca's people came from the cold, wet British Isles and it was once suggested, although out of her hearing, that she was descended from the "wee folk."

That had not stopped the pair from forming a bond. Conversation over many a dead body that Dominic was cutting up had lead to friendship and to the two "adopting" each other as brother and sister.

"Hello yourself, Big Brother. Lose any bodies lately?"

"Now, Bianca, you know we've only lost two, and we did get one back. Are you here for Mr. Durham?"

"If that's the name of the guy with lipstick on his cheek."

"That's him, Adam Durham, if his wallet is to be believed."

"What can you tell me about him?"

"He's dead, but you knew that. His last meal was burger and fries. He had zero alcohol and no drugs in his system. Death was due to natural causes."

This last was said with as straight a face as Dominic could manage.

"Natural causes, Big Brother?"

"Of course. You get shot three times in the chest …" He paused to let her finish the old joke.

"… it's only natural that you die. So nothing unusual?"

"Nothing, unless you count the fact that his pubic region is completely bare."

To Bianca's raised eyebrows and her reply of "Really?" Dominic whipped the covering sheet off the deceased like a magician revealing a trick.

"Well?"

"Nothing I haven't seen before, Dominic, although this one's not quite as lively."

"Well, if it's lively you want …"

"May I remind you, brother, that you are married man?"

"You don't have to. My wife makes sure I remember."

Durham's denuded pubic area was another part of a puzzle growing in Bianca's mind. It was time to gather more pieces. "Dominic, can you do a search for other bodies found with marks on their faces and/or no short and curlies. Oh, and would you please send a sample of the lipstick over to our Crime Lab?"

"Sure thing, Bianca. Anything else."

"That will do it, unless you want to check this guy for traces of wax. He may not have wanted to shave."

"Ouch."

***

It was few days after her trip to the Medical Examiner's and Bianca was in one of her least favorite places in Headquarters, the DNA Lab. One of the few BPD units with a seemingly unlimited budget for equipment and personnel, the Lab was staffed almost exclusively by fresh out of college bright young things, mostly women, all of whom thought they were oh so cool because they were doing CSI work just like on TV. Of course, none of them had any idea of what things were really like out on the street, their experience in that matter being limited to a two night ride-along with the Crime Scene Unit.

The morning had not started well. Bianca had not slept much. She had been up late on a triple shooting at a carry-out that had started over an argument about someone's burger having too much ketchup. It was a dunker; with each suspect admitting taking part in the shooting but insisting he had only been defending himself against the other two. Bianca charged them all with aggravated assault, copied the case file to the State's Attorney's Office and again checked the calendar to see how many days she had left on her detail to Violent Crimes.

After signing in and being directed to the Criminalist assigned to her case, Bianca had stood for a few minutes before the young woman noticed her.

"Oh, I'm sorry," the young woman, Tammy Dolan, according to her ID card, said with a smile too wide for so early in the day, "I didn't see you standing there."

Since Bianca needed something from this person, she ignored the giggles from the two women the next workbench over and decided that that had not been a joke about her height,

She's young, Bianca thought, she's new. And she probably hasn't heard too much about me yet or she would know not to make fun of a short person with a gun. She'll learn, and then she'll worry.

With the calmness of someone who knew she had the authority and the ability to make Tammy's career in forensics short and sweet or long and miserable, Bianca gave the chemist the case and property numbers of her evidence and asked,

"What were the results?"

Tammy looked over her case work then cheerfully replied, "It's negative for blood."

"It's lipstick, it should be. What else did you find?"

"Nothing, once it tested negative I didn't go any further."

Try to stay calm, Bianca told herself. To Tammy she said, "Ms. Dolan, what part of "check for DNA" did you not understand?"

"I'm sorry, it's our procedure. And if it's lipstick it wouldn't have DNA, would it, Bianca?"

Years of being a cop had given Bianca the ability to command attention and respect with her voice alone. As Tammy turned to her friends for their approval of her logic, Bianca used it on her.

"It's 'Detective Jones' to you, Ms. Dolan."

Tammy's head whipped around, her full attention on Bianca as she realized that there was a line, that she had crossed it and that everyone was watching this woman yell at her and no doubt enjoying it.

"First of all, Ms. Dolan, your procedure is secondary to my requirements. Next, I expect a *scientist* such as yourself to consider every possibility in the pursuit of evidence. That's what you're being paid to do. And finally, how do you think DNA might get on lipstick?"

Bianca grabbed a tissue from a box on the counter. Wiping her lips with it, she showed reddish marks to Tammy. "No contact without transfer. Remember that from class?"

"What's the problem out here?"

Ernie Prevost, the DNA supervisor, had heard the commotion and come out to investigate.

"Everything's fine, Ernie."

Ernie couldn't see Bianca, but he recognized her voice and from it, the mood she was in. Deciding that he had reports to review, he eased back into his office, leaving Tammy to what he was sure would be a "learning experience."

"This is what you are going to do, Ms. Dolan. You will examine the sample for DNA. If you find any, and you better hope you do, you will extract it and enter the profile into the CODIS database. You will then do the same for the blood sample from Adam Durham and for every other sample – blood, lipstick, marker ink, whatever – I send you, giving these samples your highest priority, even if it means you have to stay late and miss reruns of 'Fashion Idol.' Is that clear?"

"Yes."

Faced with the glare Bianca used to stare down armed drug dealers, Tammy amended her reply.

"Yes, Detective Jones."

"Good. I expect daily reports and you are to call me anytime if and when you hit on a name."

Bianca left the lab following Tammy's second "Yes, Detective." She was in a much better mood than when she had come in.

****

The first report from Tammy Dolan came in the next morning. Skin cells not belonging to Durham were found on the lipstick from his body. They were on the "Rush" list along with Durham's DNA profile. Results were expected within a few days.

Bianca thought back to when, as a new detective, she worked in the Sex Offense Unit. Back then DNA results could take weeks, sometimes months, to come back. And there wasn't a database to help solve the case either.

But profiles and computers were only tools; there was still detective work to do. If Bianca was right, the DNA on Durham would not yield any immediate results. It was what was in him that might give it all meaning.

The profiles in, Bianca was waiting for the CODIS results when her "big brother" faxed a report from the Medical Examiner's. Records showed that a body from Anne Arundel County had had two red streaks across his forehead and one from Baltimore County had had a single similar mark. Like Durham, both had been murdered. The AA County victim shot while the other had multiple knife wounds, only one of which was fatal.

Her theory closer to being confirmed, Bianca nodded then read on. Thank God for procedure, she thought as the report went on to state that as matter of routine samples were taken from each "red smear" and submitted along with other evidence from the bodies.

Two more DNA profiles. Two more samples to test for skin cells. Not to mention a chemical comparison of all three lipsticks. Bianca checked the time – three thirty in the afternoon, close to quitting time for a criminalist who started at eight a.m. Bianca briefly thought about ruining whatever plans Tammy Dolan had for that evening. No, she decided, the young lady had been doing good work with well-written reports and frequent updates. Let her go home early. Tomorrow was soon enough.

***

A body found in the woods in two separate trash bags and a home invasion that left three dead meant that it was several days before Bianca could get back to the Durham case. By then most of the analyses and profiles had been completed or were running. None of the three lipstick samples matched any of the others. Bianca hadn't expected them to; what woman wore only one shade of lipstick? Okay, there were some Goths she knew, but even they had different flavors of black.

The good news regarding the lipsticks was that, other than the victims', the same DNA profile was obtained from each. The bad news was that it wasn't in any of the offender databases. Durham's DNA, however, hit on three rape/abductions in the Baltimore area. Not on semen or blood, but skin cells from under the victims' nails.

Bianca quickly turned to the reports from victim's I and II. As she'd expected, they too were in the databases, hitting on the same cases as had Durham plus adding two more assaults to the list.

A team. Predators hunting in a pack, grabbing young girls off the street and brutalizing them. And one of their victims had found them, hunted them down, and marked them the way they had marked her.

Bianca knew what the next steps should be. Pull the rape reports, get the names. Run the victims' profiles, make the match and then the arrest. Close out three murders. It was what police did, what procedure demanded. Every crime must be paid for, every victim deserved justice.

Except – these three weren't victims, not as Bianca understood the word. They were monsters, monsters who had given up their place in decent society the minute they decided that raping women was a fun night out. From her years working Sex Offense and Special Investigations Bianca had faced her share of monsters and knew there was only one sure way of dealing with them.

All crimes must be paid for, all victims deserve justice. To Bianca the deaths of Durham and the others had been paid for in advance, and she knew of at least three victims who now had a form of justice.

With this thought, Bianca was tempted to drop the Durham case into the open/inactive file and go on with one of the other murder investigations for which she was responsible. When her detail was over, someone else might pick it up, might make the same connections, and might decide to follow procedure.

Or maybe not.

No, that may have worked thirty years ago, when all reports were on paper and no one was connected. Now everything was linked and if her colleagues in the counties didn't already have the information, they would soon. Better to finish this herself, in her own way, rather than let someone else write the ending.

Bianca pulled the files, began tracing the assault victims. One was in jail awaiting trial on traffic related drug and alcohol charges. Bianca made a note to alert the public defender as to the possible underlying cause of the woman's substance abuse problem. Two other victims had moved out of state. Several phone calls and online searches confirmed that neither had come east in several months.

That left two, Anita Jakes and Diana Mayo. Running two profiles would not take that long. By tomorrow or the next day it would be all over. But Bianca was reluctant to take that last step. With the result she'd have to act. Bianca liked to have options.

Again she read the reports and this time noticed that of the two profiles generated from the evidence in the Jakes case, only one had been matched, to the AA County body. The other was still an unknown and likely to stay that way. The profile was incomplete, enough to eliminate the dead men, but not enough for an ID. That meant that there was a fourth man, one who was still alive.

Every victim deserved justice. Every crime must be paid for. There was someone out there who hadn't paid his bill and only one way to find him.

On a hunch and a whim Bianca called Anita Jakes.

"Ms. Jakes, this is Detective Jones of the Baltimore Police Department. What shade lipstick do you wear?"

***

Anita Jakes had a small room in a Fullerton townhouse. It was her aunt's home and she'd been staying there since the attack.

"I used to live alone," she explained to Bianca, "but ever since …"

"I understand. Do you want to tell me about it?"

"That's why you're here, isn't it?"

The young woman was remarkably calm. Her reply to Bianca's lipstick question had been, "I've been expecting this call." She then gave Bianca her address.

"Yes, that's why I'm here, Anita. Start from the beginning, if you can."

Bianca sat quietly and listened to Anita Jakes's story.

***

I should have waited for the bus. But it was cold, and raining. And I should have run away when that van pulled up. But the driver looked so nice and friendly. I took the ride.

As soon as I got in I knew I'd made the biggest mistake of my life. I heard the van's doors locked and the driver's face went from nice and friendly to cold and mean. And he wasn't alone.

Somebody grabbed me and pulled me back on to a smelly mattress. They ripped off my clothes and, and forced themselves inside me.

It lasted for hours, or seemed to. And when they finished using me one way they turned me over and used me in another.

When they were done they dumped me somewhere like so much used garbage. The police told me that I'd been found by someone whose dog had gotten loose. I don't remember. I was in the van then I was in the hospital.

They tell me I should have died. For the next few months I wished I had. But, I got better, not well, but better.

I talked to a detective. He was kind, patient and kind. But I couldn't remember anything. I'd only seen the driver's face but he looked kind of average and my description didn't help at all. There was something else, numbers and letters that kept running through my mind. But they didn't seem important and I didn't say anything.

The county victim's services got me some good counseling. I moved to my aunt's house and when I was able to leave it on my own I got a job at women's shoe store at an open air mall on Belair Road. It had bright lights and lots of security. I felt safe there, especially with my aunt dropping me off and picking me up each day.

I was while I was waiting for my aunt that I saw it, a dark van, just like the one from that night. My therapist told me that would happen, that I'd see things that reminded me of that night. I did like she told me, started my breathing exercises and told myself there were lots of vans like that around.

Then it pulled into a spot close to me and I saw it. I saw the license plate and those numbers and letters came back all of a sudden. I must have seen the tag before getting into the van that night. Then the driver came out and walked past me into the auto parts store. And it was *the* driver.

I froze, then I grabbed my cell phone. I remember thinking about calling the police then thought what could they do? What would they do? I'd already told them I didn't remember that much. And I hadn't told them about the tag. Could they arrest him? And if they did, what then? I was getting better. I was afraid going through it all again for a trail would make things worse. By then my aunt showed up and I dropped the cell back in my purse.

I took three showers that evening. But as I sat alone in my room I suddenly realized that I wasn't afraid anymore, or rather, I was less afraid. I'd had dreams where the men came back and raped me again, that they knew who I was. But The Driver had walked right past me. He hadn't known me.

How could he not know me, I asked myself. How could he have changed my entire life and not known me? I was confused, then angry when I realized it wasn't my face he had been interested in.

Then I realized something else. He hadn't known me but I knew him. That gave me ... something over him, not much, but something. I went to bed with that mind and by morning I knew what to do. My therapist had told me that I had to take back control of my life and I had an idea of how to do exactly that.

***

Bianca knew that she should halt Anita's narrative there and do things by the book. But then Jakes might not continue. With what she had, Bianca didn't need the confession, but she did need to hear the rest of the story.

***

I got a knife, it's was my uncle's. When he was alive he hunted all the time, he always had lots of guns and knives around. I took one of his guns as well but I needed the knife first. Then I waited. I told my aunt that I was working extra hours, but all I was doing was waiting for that van to pull up again. It took two weeks.

If he recognized me when I told him my car had broken down and asked if he could give me a ride home he didn't show it. He just grinned like he did the last time and told me he sure would. It took all I could do to get in but I did. It smelled the same and the same old dirty mattress was in the back. Of course he didn't drive me home. He drove me somewhere and told me that no one rode for free and I should get in the back and pay him. I did like he said. He didn't see the knife until it was in him. I didn't think it would be but it was easy, and it felt good me sticking something in him. I stuck him twice and told him I would stop if he told me who else had raped me. He pretended not to know what I was talking about so I stuck him again, close to what he'd used on me. I told him I'd cut it off if he didn't tell. Then he gave me names and addresses.

I stabbed him once more and left him there, the way he left me. I walked home, well, walked to where I could catch a bus.

***

Anita's confession trailed off, as if she expected Bianca to say something.

"What about the mark on his face?"

"I did that at the last minute. They had all marked me, coming on me and peeing on me. So I marked them."

"So you did kill two more, or was it three?"

"Two," Anita confirmed. "When I started to drive again, I stalked them and shot and marked them."

"Why not use the knife?"

"I only used that to get what I needed to know. The gun was quicker and safer."

"What about the fourth man, Anita?" Bianca leaned in to woman. "The fourth man who raped you. Did you kill him?" Anita shook her head. "Who is he?"

Again Anita shook her head. "I don't think I want to tell you. Am I under arrest?"

That, Bianca admitted to herself, was a good question. By every rule in the book, Bianca knew that she should cuff this woman and take her downtown. But there still a crime to be paid for, and only Anita Jakes knew where to send the bill.

She'd give up the name eventually, after she was charged with murder and after her lawyer saw the case against her. The name would become a bargaining chip, something to use to get her sentence reduced.

But there was no hard evidence, only Anita. And what weight would the testimony of a three time killer, a self-confessed vigilante carry with a jury?

Every victim deserved justice. Every crime had to be paid for. Bianca could see only way to accomplish this.

"Not yet, Anita," she said, surprising the young woman. "You see, I didn't read you your rights. So I can't use what you told me against you. But in a day or two I'll have other evidence, evidence that will prove your guilt. Then I'll come and arrest you. So if here's anything you have to do, do it soon. Tomorrow at the latest, tonight if you can."

Bianca let that sink in then added, "Do you understand?"

Anita nodded. "I do. And thank you."

Bianca left the young woman alone and both made plans to do what they had to do.

***

The house was in Brooklyn, on 6th Street off Patapsco Avenue. Anita had only been there once or twice, each time watching Leon Kingston come home from work and go out again two hours later. She'd followed him the last time to a bar on Potee Street. Daring to go inside, she saw him working the bar, pouring beers and serving customers. He left and went home shortly after closing.

Hoping that he was working that night, Anita waited in her car for Kingston to come home. And if by three he hadn't appeared, she was prepared to wait until he did. Why not? She had nothing else to do, nothing for the rest of her life. The woman detective was kind enough to give her the time to finish her job and Anita was going to do just that. Wait on Kingston, kill him and mark him, and then it would be over. She'd go home and wait for the police. She'd tell her story again and again, and finally let a jury decide how guilty she was for killing men who did not deserve to live.

A car pulled up and parked in front of the house Anita was watching. A man got out. Gun in hand, Anita left her car and walked toward him. When she was close enough so that she could not miss, she called his name and prepared to raise her weapon.

"Is that the man, Anita?"

Startled by the voice behind her, Anita let her gun hand drop. That detective, that nice detective who had given this time, this moment, had followed her and now was going to stop her. No!

"If you raise that gun I will kill you. If you don't get back in your car I will kill you. If you leave I will hunt you down and kill you. Now go sit and wait." Detective Jones's command was not to be denied. Anita did what she was told.

Hearing his name, Leon Kingston had turned in time to see two women, one with a gun. They argued, then the one with a gun got back in her car. The other one, the smaller of the two, then came toward him.

A badge was flashed, Kingston heard, "Detective Jones, Baltimore Police. And what's your name, sir?"

Damn, he thought, they're making them younger every year. And because he was what he was, Kingston briefly thought about making this one himself. But the more cautious part of his brain had already processed the word "Police" and he heard himself replying, "I'm not sure if I want to give you that information, officer."

"Fair enough," came the unexpected reply. The woman's coat opened and the hand that had shown the badge now rested on what seemed to be a very large gun for such a little person. "But let me give you some information. The woman in that car over there seems to think you and your running buddies gang-raped her. So do I."

Kingston was about object, to protest his innocence, but the cop before him talked over whatever he was going to say.

"If I had any proof you'd be under arrest right now. So would she. You for rape and her for murdering your rapist friends."

So that's what had happened to Adam and the others, Kingston realized, why they hadn't called to set up the next hunt. Why his own phone calls had gone unanswered. Someone had killed them and that someone was in the car across the street.

"But as I said," the detective went on, "I don't have any proof, not against you. And I won't have any against her for a day or two."

"So?" Kingston tried hard to sound unconcerned.

"So I just wanted to warn you that I believe the young lady I think you raped has a gun and probably intends to shoot you just as soon as I leave. So be careful and have a nice day, or as much of one as you can."

Bianca started to leave. On hearing Kingston's frantic "Wait!" she turned back to him.

"Why?"

"Because if you leave she'll kill me."

"Good."

"But you're a cop," Kingston protested.

"That I am," Bianca agreed. "And as a cop I'll make an arrest, just as soon as a crime's been committed, or confessed to."

As Kingston nodded in understanding it occurred to him that it might all be a bluff, a con to get the evidence this cop said was missing. Then a car door closed and he saw the other woman standing beside it, staring at him, her right hand behind her. And in the glow from the street lamp he recognized her, recognized her from the dreams he had of his hunts, those wonderful dreams. And he knew that this was no bluff, and that he was probably less than five minutes away from dreaming no more.

Kingston did the only thing he could do.

"Me and the others, we …"

"Wait," Bianca interrupted. She turned and called Anita over, adding, "Leave it."

Metal hit pavement as Anita walked to them.

"Now then, before we start." Bianca took out her Miranda card, read it, and made things official. "You were saying?"

Eyes to the ground, not looking at either woman, Leon Kingston briefly told what he and his friends had done to Anita Jakes. It was not as detailed a statement as he would later give, but it was enough for Bianca to take out her cuffs. With Kingston's hands behind him, the detective took out a second pair.

"Your turn, Anita."

"You used me," Anita accused as she submitted to arrest. "Why?"

"Because," Bianca explained, "there were other victims who deserved justice, and one more bill to pay."

***

"And what happens when Kingston recants his confession?"

Bianca had met Joe for lunch, to let him know how the case went down.

"He won't, Joe. He won't because as I was putting him in the patrol wagon I whispered to him that if he's back on the street in less than ten years that I would personally finish the job Anita Jakes started."

"Was that before or after you made four slashes on his cheek with your lipstick?"

"Just before, and it was Anita's lipstick. It seemed only right."

DARK PLACES

There are dark places in the city -- clubs and bars that cater to wants and needs that most would call perversions. Forgoing clever signs and bright neon, they are known only to those with reason to seek them out. Some have names, others merely reputations.

A few are meeting places. You come in with your wife, husband, boyfriend or girlfriend and leave with someone else's. Others provide private rooms that will accommodate anywhere from two people to a small crowd. And there are those where you perform your deeds in full view and to the cheers or catcalls of those assembled.

No one is left out, whatever the taste or deviance. Male or female, human or animal, healthy or diseased, whole or maimed, the very young or extremely old -- whatever your preference, Baltimore has a place for you.

There are darker places than these, establishments where vices other than drink, drugs, and sex are practiced. Places where people meet in secret to worship old gods and conjure new ones. They discuss forbidden books and talk of sacrifice both animal and human. Some are poseurs, people jaded by normal sins and looking to commit new ones. Others are seekers, looking for new paths in the wrong places. Still others are in deadly earnest, willing to devote their lives in this world and souls in the next to the pursuit of power over their fellows. And there are the few who have the power and the knowledge to use it, and are just waiting for the right time, the proper motivation, and the most lucrative reward.

Damon LeVaey was rumored to be one of the few. He was considered by some to be Baltimore's supreme black magus, a man of power to be feared and not one to cross. It was said he had once called up Hell's Wrath on five members of his coven who had betrayed him. They had broken the circle, stolen his grimoires and tried to perform their own ritual of empowerment, only to meet a horrible fate at the talons of demons summoned by LeVaey. LeVaey did nothing to deny this story and did what he could to spread it.

Bianca Jones was a detective with the Baltimore Police Department assigned to Special Investigations. Her specific duty was to investigate all things occult and supernatural. She knew the truth about the coven members, having killed three of them herself and watched the other two die.

LeVaey's name came up in her follow-up investigation and she sought to learn more about him. Some of those she interviewed denounced him as a charlatan and others uttered his name in awed tones. But most of the people Bianca approached refused to have anything to do with the police.

Which is why she was where she was that night. Looking to find more about LeVaey than just story and rumor, she went to the dark places to listen and learn, hoping for a word here, an address there, a whisper about a meeting. So far she had learned nothing.

The club she was in was another dead end. Despite her informant's assurances, none of its fifteen to twenty patrons were anything more than wannabe witches and never-were sorcerers. Whatever it had been in the past, it was now simply a hangout for young people with a penchant for dark clothing and a passion for scary movies and horror fiction.

Dressed as she was, Bianca fit in with the crowd. With her small size and slender build it was easy for her to pass as someone younger. Padding gave her curves she didn't have and platform shoes added inches to her five-foot height. She topped her outfit with a long blonde wig dyed shoe-polish black to match her clothing. She was the perfect picture of a neo-Goth and so was able to mingle without being noticed.

This is a waste of time, Bianca thought, nursing her drink at a forward table, trying her best to look bored and disinterested but in reality listening in on as many conversations as she could. Another half hour, she promised herself, and then I'll go home and take off this ridiculous outfit.

She hated having to wear the disguise, but she couldn't take the chance that someone she had interviewed would come into one of the clubs and recognize her as a cop. Wearing tight jeans and a low-cut top that revealed more cleavage than she naturally had, she wondered what her co-workers would think if they saw her dressed as she was. No, she didn't have to wonder, she knew what they'd think, especially a certain crime lab technician.

A conversation at the bar drew her attention.

"No, it's true. A friend who goes to York says he read about it in some local paper. They were eaten alive by wild dogs."

"The way I heard it, it wasn't dogs. I got a cousin who's dating a Pennsylvania State cop. He said it was some kinda occult ritual that went bad. They all killed each other."

They were talking about the dead coven members. Maybe this wasn't a waste of time at all.

"Nah," said a third one, "Way I heard it, it was a sex thing -- four guys and two girls and someone didn't want to share. Knives came out and then a gun. After that it was all over except for cleaning up all the blood."

"Think maybe the house is haunted?" The lone girl at the bar seemed excited by this possibility. "That'd be something, to spend a night in a haunted house where people have died."

The three guys at the bar looked at each other then at the girl, all of them weighing their chances, deciding if a trip to Pennsylvania and a little B&E would be worth what she would do once they got there. If she would do it, and if they could find the house. By the nodding of their heads, they had all decided that if she would do it, any old house would be the right house.

Then someone mentioned a new horror movie, a remake of a classic that wasn't as good as the original, but which featured more horrific special effects and much more nudity. The conversation turned to the immense physical attributes of the lead actress. Bianca prepared to leave.

"Man, what I wouldn't give to do that chick," said one of the guys at the bar, not realizing that he'd just blown any chance he might have had with the "chick" sitting next to him.

"What would you give?"

The speaker was not at the bar. He was instead a few feet in front of it, standing in the center of the room and commanding its attention. If asked, no one present would have been able to swear that they had seen him come in.

Like everyone else in the place, his clothing was black. But his was a black that went beyond the mere absence of color. Instead, the fabric of his shirt and pants spoke of the void, as if there was nothing truly there and that nothing was part of who he was. Physically, he was the most beautiful person Bianca had ever seen. Everything about him was perfect. His hair was the right shade of blonde and styled just right. He was tall enough, but not too tall, and had the kind of body that women dream of and every man wishes he had. Bianca could not help but picture him naked and think of things they might do together.

Then he turned her way and she looked into his eyes. They were ice blue and failed to mirror the perfect smile he had on his face. There was no warmth in those eyes, only a cruel humor and a disdain for those they gazed upon.

Instantly Bianca knew him for who he was. She'd fought evil long enough to recognize its pure form. She had come looking for a practitioner of dark magic and instead had found his master.

He stood in the center of the room long enough for all to notice him and guess his name. With a nod and a smile towards Bianca, he approached those at the bar. He addressed the one who had previously spoken.

"So what would you give? Because she can be had. Has been, several times in fact. It was part of our deal." He laughed at the looks on their faces. "Why so surprised? Surely you didn't think she made it on her talent?"

"I did," said one of the four at the bar, "and don't call me 'Shirley.'"

The Devil smiled. "A brave soul to jest with me. Tell me, Simon, what would you have from me? Fame, fortune, a new car every year? This lady here, forever young and your slave for life? Or that one over there?"

He pointed to Bianca and she tensed, ready for a fight. Why, she wondered, was he focusing on her?

The man at the bar turned away. "Perhaps not, not that one. I'm not found of the company she keeps." He turned, addressing the crowd. They listened, knowing that whatever promise he made would be kept and whatever price he asked would have to be paid.

"What would you give for your heart's desire? Your souls, small though they be? I think not. Whatever their worth, they are not mine to buy nor yours to sell. You must give them away, as some here already have. What then? A year of service? Ten years off your life, five off the life of a loved one? Maybe a child's beloved pet? Or a simple favor, one to be named later and payable on demand?"

He waited, letting them think. The bar quieted as each patron contemplated his secret wants and desires, thought about what could be made better or different in their lives, maybe even wondered how someone else's could be improved. And they counted the cost. What service would be asked, what sacrifice demanded?

Without meaning to, Bianca found herself focusing on her life, what she wanted, what she lacked, what she would change if she could. A lover? Children? A normal life where she did not have to sit in bars and stare at the face of Damnation itself?

As if in appreciation of the irony she felt cold eyes fall upon her and she knew that all she had to do was consent and it would be hers. It was tempting, but even if given with no further obligation, the price was too high. She was a straight cop, always had been, and had never accepted favors from the other side. She wasn't about to start now

A waiter came over with a drink. "Compliments of the gentleman at the bar."

She looked up. Satan raised his glass in greeting.

Bianca made eye contact, daring to stare the Devil down. "Take it away," she said.

Looking around the room, listening to the silence, Bianca wondered if there were any so foolish as to believe that their souls were not at stake.

"And what are you going to do about it?" The voice of her conscience asked.

"What can I do?" she answered herself. "It's up to them. We each chose our own path. It's called free will."

"Letting people condemn themselves is not in your job description, especially not these days."

Thoughts of good men doing nothing while evil triumphed came to her. "Damn it," she said out loud. As she stood she realized that this was perhaps not the best time to use that particular phrase. Screw it, she thought and walked over to face the Devil.

Satan smiled. "Miss Jones, come to offer your body in exchange for eternal happiness? Or at least a better body? Or maybe you'd like to be taller, or should I say 'less short?'"

Up until now it had been a matter of doing her duty, of protecting the people gathered here from themselves. But Evil Incarnate or not, now it was personal. She decided to find out if the Devil had an ass she could kick.

Bianca raised her leg, kicking out in a practiced move that connected with the Devil's knee. Having taken human form, he was subject to human frailties and he went down. Bianca caught him as he fell, raising her own knee and ramming it between his legs. The air went out of him and he went down.

However evil this creature was, Bianca felt momentary shame at her pleasure over dropping him. She stepped back to allow him to stand, which he did with as much dignity as any man who had just been felled by a woman half his size.

"I'd say 'Get thee behind me,' but I wouldn't trust you there. So, Prince of Darkness, Father of Lies, I cast you out from this place. Leave now, or I'll drop your ass again."

The Devil took his time replying. He studied Bianca, conscious of the audience watching them. Despite his humiliation, he was still a master showman and so had to play to the crowd.

"From time to time I am drawn to a place, forced to leave the Pit to wallow among you humans. Now I know what brought me here."

Bianca felt him probing, testing her, taking her measure and looking into the depths of her soul for her strengths and failings. She let him look, hiding only a small part of herself.

"It has been interesting, Bianca Jones," the Devil said loud enough for all to hear, "and not a total loss. I look forward to our next meeting -- Detective."

And he was gone, leaving Bianca alone in a dark place, exposed as a cop.

The mood of the crowd turned quickly. A quiet evening had suddenly become the chance of a lifetime and this woman, this cop, had ruined it for them. That she may have just saved their souls didn't matter. They didn't care about that. It was time for a new game with her as the target.

Bianca didn't care either. She'd just beaten the Devil. This crowd didn't frighten her. She calmly walked over to her table, opened her over-sized purse and took out a very large gun. Holding it casually, her challenge was clear. Who wants to meet Satan on his own turf?

Time to leave. Despite what had happened, the night was a bust. No sign or word of LeVaey and now that her cover was blown she'd have to find a new way to trace him.

At least I got to knee the Devil in his jewels, Bianca consoled herself, so it wasn't a total loss.

Which is what he had said. He had accomplished something, but what? Protecting his minion? No, there were other ways to find LeVaey, that was only a matter of time. Then what? Bianca thought of the temptation of a normal life and the silent offer and rejection. And she knew that she had not acted quickly enough, someone here had fallen.

"Who was it?"

They knew what she meant but no one answered. Instead they glared at her, silently casting her from their midst.

"Fine then, whoever it was can go to Hell." She gave the crowd her cop look, the one taught in the Academy, the one that can control with just a glance. As she caught the eye of each person in the room, only one turned away in guilt. She noted him, left and waited outside.

He walked home. Bianca followed after changing her platforms for more sensible shoes. He walked slowly, head down, as if he didn't want to arrive at wherever he was going. Three blocks away, when it was just those two on an empty stretch of Charles Street she caught up with him.

"What did you ask for?"

He turned at the sound of her voice, recognized her right away. From the look on his face Bianca could tell he was getting ready to book out of there.

"You run and you'll go to jail tired." She had nothing to hold him on but it was enough to freeze him in his tracks.

"What deal did you make?"

"It ... it was only a thought, about my mother. She lives with ... I live with her. She doesn't approve ..."

Spiky hair, torn black clothing, lips, cheek and who knows what else pierced. Maybe okay for a sixteen-old in a rebellion phase, but not a twenty-something slacker. Mother must be so proud.

"It was just a thought, but for a moment I wished her dead, really thought I'd be better without her. And then a voice, *his* voice, said that soon I'd be free of her. To go home and all would be over."

"What did he want? What did you offer?"

The young man shook his head. "Nothing."

Bianca understood. The guilt alone would keep this one in an earthly hell until despair drove him to the real one.

"Name and address." He was Roger Zales and gave an address three blocks away on Read Street. Close enough. Maybe there was still time to cheat the Devil.

She called it in. Investigate trouble, possible prowler. This neighborhood, this time at night at least two units would respond. She hoped it would be enough. They walked the three blocks as fast as they could.

Flashing blue lights greeted their arrival. She badged an officer standing at the door. "Jones, Special Investigations" and as his eyes roamed over her body added, "working undercover, just off duty." He nodded and she became just another cop.

"What have we got?'

"9-1-1 call about a prowler. Caught someone trying a second floor window, found some lady nearly scared to death."

"Her name Zales?"

"Yeah, I think so, why?"

"This is her son, let him go up."

Bianca watched Zales disappear into the building. She didn't follow. She'd done what she could; the rest was up to him. Maybe he'd forgive himself, maybe not.

She thought about getting a patrol unit to drive her back to her car, then decided the walk would give her time to think. She was halfway back to the club when the shadows spoke to her.

"You cost me a soul, Miss Jones."

"One who regretted what he did. He was never truly yours."

No answer from the darkness. A few blocks later the shadows spoke again.

"He wasn't the only one, you know."

She knew. How many had been lost because she hadn't acted sooner? One, two, a dozen? But she had saved one and maybe stopped others. She'd take comfort in that, she had to.

For the rest of her walk, the shadows remained silent. Still, it wasn't over. It never would be. As long as lust and desire lived in human hearts and minds there would always be dark places where souls were at risk.

INNOCENT MONSTERS

A Bianca Jones/ Lai Wan story
by John L. French and C. J. Henderson

Bloodbath. It was the main word going through Joe Russo's mind as he walked through the scene. He had known it was going to be bad when he arrived. Too many police cars for a simple murder, yet all the police were outside and all of them were facing away from the house.

"What do we have?" he asked the primary officer.

The uniformed man would not meet Russo's eyes, keeping his own toward the ground as if searching for something. "A mess," he said finally, lifting his head slightly. When he did Russo noted the man's face was sickly white, the same deathly pallor he could see on a number of the others.

Those who've been inside, he thought.

"How many dead?" Russo braced himself for a high number, but still was not prepared for the answer he received.

"Don't know, we'll have to wait until they're pieced together."

What Russo did next was cruel but he had to do it to someone. "Take me through it," he told the officer, knowing he was asking the man to step back into some sort of Hell. The cop looked as if about to refuse, but then the job and pride took over.

"Yeah, sure," he said, his face growing a touch paler. Walking to the house, Russo stopped at his crime lab van. Getting shoe covers from his safety bag, he offered a pair to the officer. The uniform shook his head.

"Too late for that." Looking down, Russo saw what the officer had been staring at when he first approached him. He nodded in response, and the pair walked around to the back in silence. The rear basement door was open; the officer stepped aside to let Russo go in first.

At first all the crime scene technician saw was red. The walls were a Rorschach, so many crimson spatters that the mind tried to make sense of them by finding patterns that could not be there. Russo had seen blood before--even that much of it. He had also seen bodies, and once he pulled his attention away from the walls he found two at his feet.

"I think they were the lucky ones." The words sounded as if out of a horror film ad campaign.

"How could that be," wondered Russo, looking down at the battered bodies. The heads were oddly crushed, the limbs twisted at unnatural angles. They looked like the toys of a spoiled child--broken and tossed aside.

"It gets worse as you go in."

The voice behind him was right. Looking past the two closest, Joe saw bodies and pieces of bodies the length of the basement. A few had their chests caved in, others their limbs pulled off. Two had been decapitated and one thrown so hard into the basement's concrete wall that what was left of its head was merely pulp, gray ooze festooned with bone chips.

As a crime scene tech, Joe had seen death before, death in all its variety, things the public never saw even on their television's endless catalogue of crime shows. But, he thought coldly, never this many, never this bad.

Russo fought down the unfamiliar sensation of nausea even as pinpricks of adrenaline tickled his arm. He wanted to flee, to run back to his van and drive away, but that was not in his job description. Then again, the back of his mind whispered, neither was this kind of mindless savagery. Slowly, he moved forward and began to catalog the dead.

"There's more upstairs," said the officer from the doorway. Russo had expected as much. He had seen the stairs, noted its twin sets of bloody shoeprints--one of running shoes, the other work boots. Red smears coated the stairway walls. There was no way he could sidestep the prints.

"Front door open?" Still standing in the basement doorway, the officer nodded.

"How many more upstairs?"

"Three or four."

"Like this?"

"One looks like he was shot. The rest, well, ripped apart or smashed."

"Let's take a look."

The upper floors were as bad as the basement. He'd had to step over one body at the front door--the gunshot victim, maybe the first one taken down before the true carnage was unleashed. Two more dead in the living room, one dead on the stairs to the second floor. Most of him anyway, one leg was on the floor by the front door.

Stepping over the leg and gunshot victim, Russo walked back outside. He would need help with this scene, but not immediately. First, he would photograph everything, starting with the upper floors then working his way down. Anything else could wait until the Medical Examiner removed the bodies.

Concentrating on the job, the technician mentally listed what needed to be done. As usual, he had moved the horror off to one side of his mind to be able to do his job. He knew with a cold assurance, however, that it would come back, would in fact never leave him, coming to him in those cold, lonely moments when he wondered just how one human being could do such things to another.

Back at his van, Russo was loading his camera when he again asked "How?" This time the question was less philosophical and more practical. How had all he had seen been accomplished? Except for the gunshot wounds there were no signs of any weapons play. The detached limbs had seen no blade. They had been torn free, not severed. Was any human that strong?

A chill not caused by the night air suddenly ran through the tech. Thoughts of undead monsters and unseen creatures came to him and he knew that whoever was responsible did not have to be human. It had happened before. Not wanting to, but having no other options, he took out his cell phone.

***

Bianca Jones knew that there was only one reason that Joe Russo would call her in the middle of the night. He was one of the few people in the Baltimore Police Department who knew that while she was nominally a member of the Special Investigations Unit, her real job was to investigate any case with a connection to the occult or supernatural.

It was not an assignment she had chosen for herself. Instead, a series of cases had drawn her deep into a shadow world of which most people have no concept. When offered the opportunity to continue to battle against the darkness she felt she had no choice but to accept.

That did not mean she liked it, however. It was not that she was afraid to die. She had accepted that risk when she pinned on her badge. Rather, with each case she handled she knew that with any misstep she could unleash plagues greater than those faced by ancient Egypt upon the world. She knew with unshakable certainty that vampires and zombies were real. That monstrous creatures locked away on the other side of unseen barriers waited their chance to devour the world. As she pulled on to the scene Bianca wondered what it would be this time--and if she would be equal to the task. Russo met her outside the house.

"It's the worst thing I've ever seen," he told her before she could say anything. As he led her inside, he added;

"So go through it and let me know what you think." They walked through the basement in silence. After looking at the bodies on the first floor Bianca whispered;

"This is worse than Federal Hill. No human did this."

"You know what I'm thinking." She did. She was thinking the same thing. She made to step outside, but Russo told her, "I already checked, Bianca. No moon tonight."

"Maybe that part's wrong, Joe. Just the same, I'm loading the silver bullets when I get back to the office."

"Like I'd argue." Bianca smiled at her friend's slight jest. The two were about to go into the house just as a voice called out;

"You, Crime Lab." Russo and Bianca looked back to see a uniformed major approaching, closely followed by two men in plainclothes.

"This doesn't look good. Do you know those guys, Bianca?"

"No, but I don't think they're BPD. Let's go inside." Once in the living room, Bianca said;

"Quick, give me your film." He handed her one roll just as the trio came in.

"Mind the body," Russo warned, watching carefully as the strangers stepped over the shooting victim. "Can I help you?" Major or not, this was his crime scene and he did not need or even particularly like anyone disturbing it.

"These ... gentlemen are from Homeland Security," the major explained. "They have a federal court order authorizing them to take control of this scene. You are to turn over to them any film and other evidence you may have in your possession."

The crime scene tech took a minute to consider the major's information. He, Bianca, and the major knew there was nothing right about it. The feds knew it as well, but their look said they did not care. Finally, as firmly as he could, Russo answered;

"No. The film is in my possession and I'll submit it per the General Orders. You two want it, you can go through channels." It was a useless gesture, but one he had no choice but to make. Just as the major had no choice.

"Russo, as Duty Officer I'm ordering you to turn over your film, prints, blood samples, and anything else you've collected tonight."

"On your order, Major." Russo reached into his pocket and handed over two exposed rolls. "There's another in the camera." He indicated his case in the corner of the room. One of the feds went over and unloaded his Nikon. Then he searched the case and, to be sure, took all of the unexposed film as well. Finding the tech's clipboard near the case, he asked;

"This the scene diagram?" Russo nodded. "Nice," came the reply as the fed crumpled it and thrust it into a pocket.

"That it," asked the government man still with the major.

"Photos and sketch. I hadn't started to sample yet."

"We should search him," suggested the man who had taken the film. The other fed thought this was a good idea and moved toward Russo.

"Don't."

Everyone looked toward Bianca. She had moved to a position in the room where she could easily cover the two feds without anyone else getting in the way. Her gun was out but she had yet to point it at anyone. Her body language announced quite clearly, however, that that could be easily changed.

"You can take the film. You can take the sketch. You can take the whole damn scene. Less work for us and we get to go home early. But you so much as touch Technician Russo and I'll arrest you for assault. And if you resist, well, there'll just be a few more blood samples to recover."

"Major?"

"That is Detective Jones, gentlemen, and she is not under my command. And I support her sentiment about your manhandling members of the department, if not her means of expressing it. Russo, Jones, secure from the scene."

Back at the crime lab van, Russo and Bianca took off their shoe covers. "Don't throw them away, Joe."

"Why not?" then it occurred to him.

"And while we're still here," Bianca added, "let's go find as many officers as we can who went inside the house."

✶✶✶

"It's not a werewolf, if that's what you're thinking."

Bianca was at Morgan's Rare Books and Collectibles, an alley shop on Lisbon Street in Baltimore's historic Fells Point area. Its owner looked old enough to have been on hand when William Fell bought the land in the 1700's and for all she knew he might have been. The little man was more than just a bookseller. In her first case involving what he called the preternatural it was Morgan who had revealed to her the things that existed in the realms hidden from this world. Since them he had served as mentor and guide in her battle against the darkness.

Bianca and Morgan were looking at prints made from the film the detective had kept from the feds. She and Russo had also downloaded any pictures that other officers at the scene had taken with their cell phone cameras. There were enough images to give Morgan an idea of the carnage on the scene.

Morgan held up a hand to keep Bianca from interrupting. "Before you object and point out the ripped off limbs and caved in chests, let me point out that when were-creatures shift to their animal selves the transformation is complete. There is no man/wolf, man/tiger or any other hybrid form. It is all one or the other, human or beast. I take it there were no reports of any wild animals roaming the city?" Bianca shook her head. "And look at the wounds. Had animals been involved there would be teeth and claw marks. No, your killer is human, or at least human-shaped."

"Not a werewolf then. I don't know whether to be relieved or disappointed. Any ideas what it could be?"

"It could be one of a hundred creatures, Miss Jones, but given the setting, none are likely. You say the murders happened in an area known for drug use."

"It was a crack house. That's why most of the victims were in the basement. They were using."

Morgan again looked through the photos. "No signs of occult summoning. And I can't imagine any of the victims being enough of a threat to warrant a sending. Miss Jones, for once I am at a loss. Have you anything else?"

"Joe's back at the lab running blood tests."

"I thought those agents intervened before he could collect any samples."

"They did."

"Then how ..."

"At least four officers walked through that scene. So did Joe and I. And with all that blood ..."

"One could not avoid stepping in it." A hint of a smile curled one corner of Morgan's mouth. "You two took samples from the officers' footwear."

"And the shoe covers Joe and I were wearing. There's one other thing. I doubled back after everyone left and watched from an alley. When they carried out the bodies they put one in a van by itself and the others in a panel truck. Then they sent in a cleaning team. No investigation, no crime scene processing. That means they already know what happened."

"Then perhaps it would be best to let the federal government handle it?"

"Like hell! Whatever went down happened in my city and I'm going to find out what, then stop it from happening again. That's my job." Bianca's cell phone chirped and she excused herself to take the call.

"That was Joe. So much for it not happening again. He just got a text from a friend in Brooklyn, the real one, not the one in South Baltimore. The friend works in the NYPD crime lab and just got thrown off a crime scene by the feds. At least a dozen dead, all ripped apart. This is bigger than just Baltimore, Morgan."

"Indeed, and potentially bigger than us. I for one have never been too proud to call for help." He wrote a down a name and phone number. "This woman might be willing to assist us. Indeed, she might be the only one who can."

***

Four hours up and four back. This trip better be worth it, Bianca thought as she drove the long loop from Martin Luther King Blvd to I-95. New York's a long way to go for nothing.

Her journey would not actually be for nothing. The official reason for her trip was to talk with the officers who had been on the scene of the Brooklyn massacre, to find out if their observations matched hers. But, her real purpose in traveling to New York City was to find a woman named Lai Wan, the one person Morgan felt would be able to shed any light on the situation. If she was willing to shed any light on the situation.

"She can be quite difficult," Morgan said. "She may not want to involve herself."

"And if she doesn't ..."

"Then you will have to convince her. If appeals to civic duty fail, try offering money. I'm told she is somewhat mercenary." Any authorization to hire outside help would have taken days to approve and her boss, Major Lewis, turned down Bianca's request to tap into the informant fund.

"Baltimore has its own psychics for hire, Detective. Anyway, isn't that why we're paying you?"

Psychic for hire was not quite how Morgan had described Lai Wan. He called her a "psychometrist," explaining she was someone who through touching an object could get a sense of people and events associated with it.

"Hand her, oh say, this book for instance," he explained, "and she'll be able to tell you the names of everyone who has ever read it. She'll know what store it was first sold in, where it was printed and from what forest the trees that were used to make the paper came."

As a police detective, Bianca could see where that could be a useful talent. Pick up a gun and learn who fired it. Touch a bloodstain and know who shed it. Shake hands with a suspect and find out right away all you needed to close the case.

"And if someone had ever slapped anyone in the back of the head with it ..."

"Oh, things like that," Morgan had answered, "those she answers easiest of all."

It couldn't be that simple, could it? It never was. There was always a price to pay and as she drove north Bianca wondered what her gift had cost Lai Wan.

She was just past Wilmington when she figured it out. Touch a gun and learn not just who fired it but its entire history -- where it was made, how it had been used, how many times it had wounded or killed. Would you also feel the rage and anger, or worse, the indifference to life of everyone who pulled its trigger? Would you relive every life it took and experience the deaths? Were you to touch a bloodstain, would you suffer as did the victim? And if you shook hands with a suspect, would you for a time become him and know what it was like to be a rapist or a killer?

Suddenly Bianca had the distinct impression that this gift of Lai Wan's might be more of a curse, that the woman constantly lived on the edge of sensory overload. No wonder she was known to be, as Morgan put it, "quite difficult." And she was about to ask this woman to take one step more, to go past this world and into another.

Can I really do that, she asked herself. I've seen horrors that still chase me through my dreams. This woman would feel them, become them. I'll be asking her to enter a nightmare while fully awake.

Halfway up the New Jersey Turnpike, only a few miles from where she would need to exit for New York, Bianca pulled into a rest stop. Perfunctorily, she had her gas tank filled, used the restroom, bought a dreadful cup of coffee. Her main reason for doing so, though, had been to think about heading back home. She was willing to risk her life, her sanity and her soul, but not those of anyone else. Not if it was not necessary. It just was not right.

Then she thought of the massacres in Baltimore and Brooklyn and of the other deaths that were sure to come. Throwing away her coffee, Bianca got back into her car and pulled back onto the turnpike, heading for Exit 14. Right or wrong, it was her duty to ask this Lai Wan for help.

The woman could always say no.

***

Lai Wan showered, dressed in what she considered her "work clothes"-- multiple layers of grey and black--then made a small pot of water for tea. She had received a call from the Baltimore Police asking her help in a case. A female detective was coming to talk with her, but about what the psychometrist was not certain. The woman was not too clear over the phone, indicating only that it was a grave matter was best discussed in person.

Very well, Lai Wan thought, I shall go over whatever "grave" nonsense she brings and then send her department an outrageous bill for my services. That should encourage them to handle any future "grave matters" themselves.

"Stranger ..." The mere mention of his name brought a large black dog to Lai Wan's side. He joined her on the sofa, his head comfortable in her lap. As the psychometrist gently petted him a warming sense of peace wrapped itself about her, the dog's happiness and contentment with his life washing over her every time she stroked his fur. As she had told a friend, Stranger was the closest thing she had to therapy--a safe haven to which she could retreat whenever the ever-encroaching sensations of the world threatened to overtake her. As always, enjoying this calm before a potential storm, she wondered why it had taken her so long to adopt such a companion.

The eventual knock on the door disturbed her rest. It did not surprise her; nothing did that.

"That would be our policewoman," Lai Wan told the dog. "Stay," she said as she got up. Stranger noted the grin on his mistress's face, and was put at ease. His dog mind had been certain she knew he had no intention of leaving the couch's piles of pillows.

The young woman at her door was of a slender build and just over five feet in height. It was the woman she had spoken to, had sensed over the phone- -same hard eyes masking such horrid depths of sadness. Simply speaking to the officer had told the psychometrist volumes. As close as they now were, however, Lai Wan actually had to put effort into deflecting the waves of feeling radiating from the woman. Resentment at being judged by her size, anger at her own resignation that it was and always would be so, frustration over being a woman in a man's universe, terror of loneliness, fear of companionship--Lai Wan shut her eyes, slamming the stormtide of emotion broiling around the woman on her doorstep.

"I'm Detective Bianca Jones, BPD," the woman announced, flashing her badge. "May I come in?"

"Of course." Lai Wan stepped aside, allowing access to her home. In passing, Bianca came close to accidentally brushing against the psychometrist. So much did Lai Wan wish to avoid direct contact with the troubled officer than she actually threw herself back slightly, bouncing her head off the wall. It was a slight thing, something most would not have noticed.

Lai Wan knew the officer was not most, however. Closing the door, she stood passively in the hallway, saying nothing else. She offered neither seat nor refreshment. The policewoman was not making a social call, and Lai Wan felt no compunction to turn it into one.

"I need your help," the detective finally said. The silence broken, she told Lai Wan of the massacres in Baltimore and Brooklyn. She also told her of the feds taking over both scenes, not for the purpose of investigation, but for that of covering something up.

"There's some thing loose out there, slaughtering people. And it has to be stopped."

"No doubt it does," Lai Wan answered. Long seconds ticked by, time Bianca experienced with more than a little discomfort. The psychometrist waited until she sensed the officer was about to speak, then said;

"Oh, I see, you were waiting for me to say more. Shall I wish you luck in your endeavors to stop this thing which is loose, slaughtering people?" Bianca was somewhat taken aback. What was this woman's problem? Again, Lai Wan allowed the precise amount of seconds to pass, then said;

"Wait, I understand, you expect me to aid you in your quest to stop this creature. Out of some sort of civic pride, as if I were some character from a television show ... yes?"

"Not really," answered Bianca. "I mean, I would like to get your professional opinion, and yes, I did think you might want to get involved, considering ..."

"Considering what?" Lai Wan snapped the words the way a woodsman cracked kindling. "You thought I might want to get involved. Why? Why would I? And for that matter, why have you? Federal agents are working the case. Why not let them handle it?"

"Because they got to the scene too fast, before anyone could call them in. That means they knew what was going to happen and did nothing to stop it; not in Baltimore and not in Brooklyn. Whatever their game, they can't be trusted."

"Of course they cannot be trusted; they are the government. But again, government agent, why is it my concern? Why should I risk the displeasure of federal authorities much less take the chance of being dismembered by a monster?"

Bianca felt her temper rising. She had expected some resistance, Morgan had warned her, but this woman ... it seemed as if she did not want to help anyone in the least. Had she not just been told there was a monster loose, one that had to be stopped? Did she not care that over twenty people had been murdered--slaughtered--and that the feds were covering it all up? What would it take to make her see ...

Of course, thought Bianca, and she held out her hand, palm up, offering;
"You want to know why? Take it."

Rarely had anyone offered themselves so freely and openly to Lai Wan. Not wanting to offend, already knowing what she would find, Lai Wan accepted the detective's outstretched hand and casually invaded her soul.

She saw it all in a blur--*childhood racing by. Teen years, a special hell for someone who stopped growing at five foot, no further development, no height, no curves--where was the figure everyone thought she would have? Like a little girl--poor Bianca. Constantly being overlooked, undervalued, ignored, forgotten--*

Education, completed--shoved aside, made useless by an anger that throws her where she can demand to be noticed. Joins the police to make a difference--double meaning--to serve and compensate; recruit excels, patrol officer then detective, assigned to sex crimes, learns what evil lurks in the human soul. More.

Monsters. Federal Hill. A creature from the shadows planting its seed in women, tearing them apart to make more of its own in this world. Monsters. A summoning in Pennsylvania brings forth yet another. More die, most by her hand. Monsters. The undead in Druid Hill Park. Blood and redemption. Monsters. Facing the ultimate Evil and stealing a soul from it.

Lai Wan sighed, then broke contact. As Bianca waited to see something like understanding in the psychometrist's eyes, she was surprised when the woman only told her;

"You are a fool." The detective, still shaky and slightly pale from the sharing, looked surprised. The look would soon harden as Lai Wan continued.

"Worse yet," the psychometrist charged, "you are a dangerous fool. You charge into situations for which you are not prepared, trusting that you will find a way to prevail--somehow--as if there was a God to be on your side. One day you will learn that if there is a God that he is on no one's side but his own. And on that day, when you finally discover not every problem can be solved with a gun, I hope your failure does not damn us all."

Bianca was still weak. Without asking she shuffled to a chair and collapsed into it. "You're right," she admitted, "I'm probably not the best person to go after the things that crawl out of the darkness. And one day I probably will get myself killed. But that doesn't change anything. It's the job I've been given. I do it because no one else can or will. So far my skills have pulled me through and I'm learning new ones every day." Bianca rested, working at catching her breath as she said;

"You've got skills, special ones. Maybe you see them as a gift, a curse, maybe both, I don't know. Whatever, they're yours to use. Why should you help me? Because it's the job you've been given. It needs to be done and no one else can do it."

Lai Wan did not bother to reply to the small detective; the woman was already falling asleep in her chair. She was a fool, the psychometrist knew, but one aware of her foolishness.

And that, thought Lai Wan, puts her eons ahead of most of the human race.

The officer was also brave and determined and would no doubt pursue the matter which drew her to Lai Wan's foyer even if she did not acquire the psychometrist's help. And most likely get herself killed. And, Lai Wan grimaced as she accepted the thought, if the woman died because she was refused the help she asked, then her death would be the psychometrist's responsibility. The deaths of drug users and dealers did not bother Lai Wan but, she thought;

There really are too few brave women in this world.

Lai Wan allowed Bianca to sleep. She had spent the drive from Baltimore working herself into a state of frenzy, part of her normal modus operandi apparently, the psychometrist realized from their moment together. The officer's stress levels had been frazzled when she arrived. Lai Wan had felt them through the door when first she had gone to answer it. Staring down at the quietly sleeping officer she thought on what else she might be able to do for the woman. A sudden spot of cold against her wrist brought her the answer she needed.

"Stranger, how did I maintain my life before you arrived?" The dog looked up at his mistress as if to say such monstrously difficult questions were beyond him. Understanding, she told him;

"Be a comfort for this one, will you?"

Without hesitation, Stranger moved next to the small but comfortable chair Bianca had chosen and put his large body against her legs, and then draped his muzzle across her legs. Instinctively her hands encircled his head, drawing it closer. Satisfied that the officer was in capable hands, Lai Wan took the shoulder bag Bianca had brought with her and headed for her dining room table, saying quietly;

"Very well, detective, let us see what you have brought with you. And what I might possible do to help you."

***

Bianca awoke in the darkened hallway, a sleeping dog pressed gently against her. The hound came alert seconds after the officer, responding to the voice of his mistress as she called,

"Bring her, Stranger."

Carefully, the dog caught Bianca's hand in its mouth and tugged at her to stand. When she did, the hound released its grip, then lead the woman down the hallway and around the corner to Lai Wan's living room. There she found the psychometrist studying the contents of her bag. The crime scene photographs were close to useless to Lai Wan. She needed reality; a photo, the image captured on film or electrons then printed on paper, was twice removed from her tactile requirements. Still, she studied them, getting a more objective idea of the crime scene than the one she had from Bianca's mind. Then, of course, there was the blood.

"This is all that was recovered?" Lai Wan asked her question of the five swatches--dried stains, dark red, almost brown, all that was left of wasted lives--which she had taken from Bianca's bag.

"Just a representative sample," the officer told her. Deciding not to say anything foolish about invasion-of-privacy, wondering why she had been allowed to sleep, then wondering if she had been somehow put to sleep, Bianca shoved all questions from her head and added,

"Back in Baltimore a lab tech is doing DNA work on the rest."

"Then we shall work with what we have. I waited for you to awaken before trying these." As Lai Wan reached out to touch the first sample, Bianca stopped her, exclaiming;

"Wait. Hold out your hands." She examined Lai Wan's fingers. "No open cuts or sores. It's safe to touch without gloves."

"What would it matter," asked the psychometrist. "Safe or not, it must be done." And so saying, Lai Wan put a finger on the first swatch.

Tyrone Davis, never had a job, or a girl, or a chance. Straight from school to using, jacking any fool he found to get money for a buy. The house was a good place, a safe place, had been a safe place. No buying or selling, just using. Ty had scored a tester down on Sweet Air, most of 'em had, and went to the house to try it out, see if was worth getting regular. The sweet, warm glow had just hit when a scream broke the peace. It was Richie, Richie was screaming. There was red and Fatboy went flying past him, a sick thud when he hit the wall. Gotta see what's happening. Who's that? My arm, leggo my arm, fool. My arm, Oh God, Momma, my arm, my ar--

Lai Wan broke contact, falling back against her sofa.

"Are you okay?"

"No, Detective Jones, I am not okay. Dying, as I would hope you could imagine, is not an easy thing. That this was not my first time does not make it less difficult. However, unlike the unfortunate Mr. Davis, I will recover. And before you ask, I learned nothing but the name of one of the victims. I, or rather I should say, Mr. Davis caught a fleeting glimpse of the killer before the end. But the basement was poorly lit. Give me a minute and I will try again." Lai Wan reached for her tea cup even as she said;

"Stranger, attend."

Sensing Lai Wan's distress, the big dog was already at her side when she called. Rubbing against her, sharing his unconditional warmth, he cast a suspicious eye towards Bianca, giving her a brief snort of disapproval as if to say she was the reason for his master's dark mood.

The tea helped calm the psychometrist, but her faithful hound's concern washed over completely, cleansing her nerves and banishing the desperate waste of Tyrone Davis's life. After a moment, Lai Wan reached out once more.

Line's forming down Sweet Air. That's the word Markia got. Easy pickings tonight. She didn't use, never had, don't mean she didn't have no needs and wants. Junkies get all doped up, they don't miss what little they have. Follow the crowd, most of 'em down to the house on Vista. Fall in with 'em, make like one of 'em, wait 'til they start nodding. She'd be careful going through the pockets--don't want a stick, catch the damn AIDS that way. Nothing on the first one, second one got a few bills--fives, damn fifteen green, some unused rubbers. She'd use them too, tricks never brought their own. Fifteen green and rubbers--things lookin' up. She knew the third one, Darryl something, supposed be doing federal time. Under the light Markia saw he was awake, alert, like the stuff had no effect. His eyes, they looked funny, he looked funny, twisted and bigger. She moved past him then was grabbed. A growl and then snapping noises--sound of her own limbs, legs first then arms. The pain was late and she didn't feel it until she was in the air. Then she was on the floor. Fifteen green, damn, fifteen ... then there were shouts and screams and a noise like someone's piece and...

Again Lai Wan broke away. "This one, she was maybe the first. And she knew the one responsible as Darryl, possibly just out of federal prison. Possibly escaped; her thought was that she believed he was a federal prisoner, not that she knew he was one." Pouring herself another cup of tea, she asked;

"Was someone shot?"

"One of the second floor victims. He wasn't on the roll we were able to save." Lai Wan nodded, then held her hand over the third sample.

"Do you want to rest first?"

"No, I want to try something while Markia's last thoughts are still with me."

Lai wan brought her palm as close to the sample as she could without touching it, catching what sensations she could without contact, the name and image of Darryl foremost in her mind. After a moment she said "No" and moved on to the fourth. As she did, she found what she was looking for and, after only a moment's hesitation, dropped her hand flat, covering the bloody swatch.

Darryl, Darryl Armitage--messed up--got caught with product and a gun. Too much product, and a piece with bodies on it. Straight to federal time, hard time. Deal was thirty in PA instead of life in Kansas. Shit-ass deal but better than dying in Kansas. After a year come a better deal. Drug tests they called it. Time off he called it. They poked and prodded and took more blood then he knew he had. Then they put him to sleep and he woke up with something hard behind his neck. He walked out after two. Beat the hell out of thirty.

Back in the city. Two years without was long enough. Darryl needed to get messed up. Heard about free product, joins the line, winds up in a vacant house with everyone else. A bit up his nose and everything starts looking fine.

And then--every muscle in his body burns, bones hurt. He feels his skin start to stretch and there's a buzzing in his mind and a stinging in his neck. The pain gives way to rage. My eyes--what with my eyes? They did this to him, but he don't know who they are. Some bitch looks him over, walks past him. It's her fault--and he breaks her. Someone screams and he breaks them and what little humanity he has fades away as all is anger.

A popping noise--he feels nothing but knows someone's trying to hurt him. He sees that someone, takes away their gun and the arm holding it. How easy that was, he beats and strangles and tears. He follows movement up the stairs. Weaker, but strong enough to stop two more from fleeing before blackness overwhelms him. Just before death comes a moment of clarity and Darryl wonders if there's a hell for something he didn't know he was doing.

Abruptly Lai Wan broke contact, dropping back onto the sofa. Ministering to herself with another cup of tea under the watchful eye of her canine physician, the psychometrist told Bianca the high points of what she experienced.

"Bastards."

"Bastards are merely people with improper parentage, Detective Jones. This is the work of monsters. Understand the implication of my words--men are manufacturing these creatures and turning them loose. We must stop them."

"We?" Bianca's eyes narrowed to slits. She had been told the woman before her was a mercenary. Thinking that perhaps her English was faulty, she said, "You're a civilian, a noncombatant. You didn't understand; I wouldn't ask ..."

"You did not ask and my English is, most likely, superior to yours. Listen to what I am telling you--if you try to do this alone ... you ... will ... fail."

Bianca reeled. Even as she realized the psychometrist had somehow heard her thoughts, she dismissed that intrusion over the larger problem of a civilian looking to intrude in police business. Assisting as she had, much like an informant calling in a tip, that was one thing, but going out into the World, taking her into a combat zone--

"Put aside your misgivings, Detective," said Lai Wan coldly. "I can handle myself. Like Mr. Armitage, I have known bars. And I have known what it feels like to have those in authority play with your fate as a cat does dust in a shaft of light--attracted to its delicacy, with only brutality to offer in return."

"I know about your imprisonment before your escape from Communist China, ma'am, but please ..." Bianca managed to get out that much before Lai Wan cut her off, snapping coldly,

"I was struck down by a bus, and I died in the hospital. I was in the process of floating toward the light, knowing that my time in this hellish world was over and that eternal joy was to be mine, when something decided I needed further testing. I came back to life on the operating table, and I awoke with my new abilities in a hospital bed--one that had known cancer and third degree burns and rape." By this point Stranger had taken a defensive position between the two women and was close to baring his teeth. As Lai Wan took the massive dog's head into her hands, comforting him as he had her, she added,

"Detective, you feel cheated because you did not get to be the tallest girl in class. You are not the only person on the planet who did not get what they want for Christmas."

The psychometrist turned Stranger's head toward hers, signalling to him that stepping up into her lap was permissible. Throwing his front legs only up onto her legs, he delighted as she rolled her eyes upon his impact. Using his ears to shake his head back and forth, Lai Wan dropped her tone several degrees, then added;

"In any case, someone needs to accompany you to keep you from doing foolish things. Since no one in your department is willing to do so, that job too must fall to me, Detective Jones."

"In that case," the policewoman replied, "call me Bianca. Detective Jones works the pawnshop detail. He's fifty-five, overweight, and smells funny."

"Very well, Bianca. How do you wish to proceed?" Bianca outlined as much of a plan as she had for Lai Wan her plan. The detective admitted she did not much like the idea, but it was the best she had. The psychometrist agreed with her on all points, recognizing that hunting their prey would take too long. But that with fishing one's prey came to them. Bianca nodded, adding;

"Yeah, too bad I'm the bait."

"You are half the bait," Lai Wan corrected.

"And when we catch something?"

"I suspect you will have to take out your gun and shoot it. Do please bring enough bullets."

***

"I had intended to do this at the Baltimore crime scene," Bianca explained as the two drove to the site of the Brooklyn murders.

"This will be faster. Several members of the New York Police Department are in my debt. I could easily call in a favor or two. Are you certain you do not want a police presence large enough to attract attention?" Bianca shook her head, saying;

"Won't be necessary. The feds still have someone watching the house back home. They're sure to have someone here. I'll park in front so whoever that is can see my plates. Thanks to that call I made before we left, right about now the Baltimore Crime Lab is entering Darryl Armitage's DNA profile into the federal databanks. That should cause all the bells to go off that we need. Trust me; by the time we leave here we'll be targets."

"Now there is a sentence no girl can hear often enough."

The house they approached was much like the one Bianca had been in back in Baltimore--vacant, abandoned and left to rot by an owner who made more money from it as a tax write-off than he ever could by repairing it and renting it out. It was now home only to insects, rats and those whom society had forgotten. The two stood at the front entrance, the door open before them.

"Lai Wan, are you sure you want to go in?"

"No, I do not want to go in. Even from here I can smell the acrid stench of too many deaths. But it must be done."

Bianca nodded, and the pair walked in, Lai Wan holding her mental shields tight against the anticipated physic onslaught. As expected, the house's story flooded her senses. Had she wanted to, she could have told Bianca how it had come to be built, who its first owners were, the names of all those who had been born there, lived there, died there. Four murders had been committed in times past and there was still a body yet to be discovered behind a bedroom wall. But he had deserved his death and nothing would be accomplished by revealing it now. It was the tired building's more recent tragedy in which she was interested.

"It began here," Lai Wan said in slightly more than a whisper. "The condemned had just gathered, only three. Others were in the front. There were homeless upstairs -- men, women and children with nowhere else to go." Her hand touching the edge of a timeworn table, the psychometrist added;

"One of the ones in here, he changed, transformed ... in minutes he destroyed everyone within these walls. Then ..." Bianca followed Lai Wan as she walked to the back door and out into a small yard. Pointing, she told the detective;

"He then left through here. This time there was no one waiting to stop him."

"So he's still out there."

"Or with his keepers, being studied or dissected."

As she listened to Lai Wan, Bianca's trained eye scanned the surrounding houses. A flash of light, a reflection from a lens. No doubt there was another watcher out front. Whatever, her instincts told her the hook was baited. It was time to leave.

"What is next?" Lai Wan asked when they were back in the car.

"A nice leisurely drive in the country. That will give them time to track and find us." Bianca noted a change in Lai Wan's mood. Realizing something had amused her, the detective asked,

"What?"

"You are in New York City. You do realize the nearest countryside is at least an hour away?"

"Sorry."

"And even that would still only really be a suburban area."

"I said I was sorry."

"I do hope your plan does not depend on our being in the country."

"Would you like to drive?"

"Why, no," answered Lai Wan with a smile. "I brought some crocheting I was hoping to finish." Quoting one of her father's favorite lines from the Three Stooges, Bianca snapped,

"Remind me to kill you later."

"Considering what we are attempting, there could very possibly be no need for such a reminder."

"Now," joked Bianca in return, quoting the psychometrist back to herself, "there's a sentence no girl can hear often enough."

"Turn left up ahead," answered Lai Wan. "That will put us on the Belt Parkway. If you squint, some of it will actually look like countryside."

"Thought that's what they said about New Jersey."

Both women smiled briefly, and then settled in to see how long it would take for the fish they were after to rise to the only bait they had to offer.

***

When the two women had driven out of the city, they had no destination in mind. They simply pointed their vehicle toward Long Island and followed the road. Bianca did not think it would be long before someone came after them. She did know something of the federal government's resources. They were no doubt under satellite surveillance, that is, if one of the watchers back at the house had not taken the opportunity to plant a GPS tracker on their car.

As she followed the road, the policewoman wondered just how intelligent her actions had been. A nagging voice from the back of her head kept reminding her of how good a chance there was that possibly no one would ever hear from either of them again. The back-up messages she had left with Morgan and Russo in the event neither heard from her in forty-eight hours would be of little comfort to either of them if they were lying in a ditch somewhere.

Not that she would go down easy. She had her service pistol and under the seat was a special toy, a sawed-off shotgun, just in case the feds brought something extra to the party. No, her overwhelming thoughts were of the woman sitting next to her. How would she be if it came to a fight? Could she use a gun? Would she?

"I have my own resources, but thank you anyway." Bianca glanced at Lai Wan.

"I bet Watson hated it when Holmes did that to him."

"Forgive me, Bianca, but given the situation it is impossible not to sense what you are thinking."

"Can you guess what I'm thinking now?" Bianca asked, looking away from Lai Wan and into the rearview mirror.

"That the car that has been following us for the last mile or so is speeding up now that it is getting dark and we have so conveniently turned onto an isolated road."

"Exactly. Looks like it's show time."

"Just remember, if the agents are men, they will treat us as women first, and anything else second. And do remember I will need at least one of them alive." Bianca reached under the seat, then handed Lai Wan the shotgun, saying;

"Take this. If we bail out make sure it goes with you. Just drop it on the ground where I can see it."

"I believe I can do that," Lai Wan agreed, placing the weapon next to her on the seat.

As their pursuers sped up Bianca fed her car some gas, trying to make their charade look good. As the trailing sedan came closer Bianca pulled away just a bit, searching for a good spot to get rammed. A curve up ahead, then an open field. Good enough. She slowed just enough to let the other car catch her.

"Get ready," she warned Lai Wan then braced for the crash.

The cars hit, a right front fender into her left rear fender. Expecting the collision, Bianca had pulled slightly away at impact. Then she let her car roll into the field and to a stop. The dark blue sedan pulled off the road close to them. Two men got out, one from the front, another from the back.

The two women had gotten out of their car. Bianca paused a bit to look at her crumpled fender. She hoped the department would pay for the damages. Then she looked at the advancing government agents and tried to forget the gun tucked away in the small of her back. As Lai Wan had reminded her, she needed at least one of them alive.

"If you boys wanted a date all you had to do was ask." She smiled sweetly as she said this. Anyone knowing Bianca would have known what that smile meant and taken precautions. Fortunately, she was a stranger to these men.

One of them held up something bright and shiny. "Federal agents," he announced with practiced self-importance. "We have a warrant to take you into custody for violations of the Homeland Security Act."

Bianca and Lai Wan looked at each other then back to the men. This was no time for idle chatter or witty banter. As Lai Wan remained still, Bianca tensed as if about to offer resistance. The two men prepared for a fight but were not ready for what happened next. Together, both women extended their arms with palms and wrists turned upwards.

"You are making a mistake, officers," Lai Wan said, speaking for them both, "but that can be taken up with your superiors." She walked towards the men, their willing prisoner, all her will focused on keeping their concentration on herself. Bianca, too, slowly advanced. Having not expected this sudden surrender, the two agents allowed the women to get closer than they might have normally.

"Want to frisk me," Bianca offered, gyrating her up-raised her arms in open invitation. The federal man hesitated, only a moment, but it was long enough.

Police officers must be able to take down people taller than themselves. A police officer just over five foot tall must be able to take down many people taller than herself. In a much practiced move, Bianca kicked out and struck the man in front of her in his knee, shattering the joint and dropping him instantly to the ground. The sudden attack caused him to cry out, distracting his partner, which gave Lai Wan her opportunity.

Self-confidence, self-importance, raging feelings of superiority radiated from the man in front of Lai Wan. As she had approached him, she had sent her senses through the ground, making contact with him from afar to probe past his walls of assurance. When Bianca sent his partner to the ground his attention was diverted for an instant. It was enough. Reaching out, Lai Wan caught hold of his exposed hand with her and invaded his mind. The man fell to the ground screaming.

"I only need one of you alive," said Bianca, her gun out and pointed at the chest of the man with the broken kneecap. "Don't make it too easy a decision."

Lai Wan she asked,

"What did you do to him?"

"He was something of a track star in high school. The glory of those days has sustained his ego for nearly two decades. At present, he believes me a suicide bomber who has taken his legs. He will be catatonic with despair for some hours." Before Bianca could reply, a cry of anguish roiled outward from the government car.

"Time's up, you goddamn slits." Despite his ruined knee, the man near Bianca was smiling. "We have back-up in the car. Extra-special back-up."

"What's that mean?"

"Means, bitch, I gave him the shot just before we got out of the car, just in case. And there's no time for the antidote now." As the metal of a door lock was torn loose, the agent sneered,

"Enjoy your trip to Hell, girls."

And then, a murderous roar shattered the night as a horribly misshapen parody of the human form pushed its way free from the suddenly confining car. Its arms twice normal size, the skin rippling and stretching, tearing then healing, as its muscles bulged beneath it. What skin was exposed was deeply reddened and Bianca thought she could actually hear its heart beating faster and faster to keep up with its body's changes.

The most horrible of those changes were to its face. One eye had become hideously enlarged, burying its nose, almost overwhelming the other eye as well. Veins pulsed in its forehead and neck, blood leaking from minute ruptures. Its ears seem to be withering away, even as its teeth began to melt. All of it emphasized the terrible pain coursing through the mutating body-- agony so intense, Lai Wan could feel that the thing's only relief would be to hurt others--soon.

"You can try running," offered the man on the ground, "but that only makes them madder."

Bianca did run, drawing the creature away from the men but, more importantly, Lai Wan. Racing to the other side of the car where the shotgun lay, she prayed for extra seconds as she suddenly realized how quick the maddened thing actually was. She wasted no effort turning to look, could hear it coming up fast behind her. Knowing she would get only one chance she dove, caught up the weapon and then rolled. She turned to find the thing almost on top of her. The policewoman desperately slid her one hand around the trigger guard, finger sliding home, the other into a bracing hold. Bianca knew she did not have enough time, but continued to struggle, knowing she only needed an extra two second --

Then, just as she knew the creature was about to slash her throat with its clawed hands, the thing's eyes grew wide. It hesitated, then threw itself at

Bianca--a second and a half too late. The detective fired point blank, the close range discharge taking off the creature's head, spattering her with bone, blood, and gore.

Shoving the still thrashing carcass off of her, Bianca scrambled to her feet, then came around to the highway side of her car to find the wounded agent trying to take out his gun. She fired a quick shot beyond the effective range of the cut-down weapon, but the noise and the few pellets that struck the agent convinced him to cease his attempt to resist. Reaching him, Bianca pointed her weapon at his crotch and growled;

"I have no mercy left, you disgusting son of a bitch. You so much as blink I will blow your dick off and let you bleed out." A dark stain appeared on the front of the agent's trousers. The detective was too angry to smile. Instead, she shouted to Lai Wan,

"How's the other one?"

"Unconscious."

"Can you get what we need from him?" The psychometrist bent down, placing a hand on the man's chest. A few minutes later, she stood up, giving Bianca a nod. The detective nodded back, adding;

"Good, let's got the hell out of here." The two women returned to their own vehicle, but not before Bianca stripped both men of identification, weapons, and cell phones, and used the last of her shotgun shells on their tires.

"If we find him, we'll tell your boss where you are," the detective told the conscious agent. As she drove off, her words were little comfort to the wounded man lying in the gathering darkness.

"Did you get it?" Bianca asked Lai Wan after they'd traveled about a mile.

"I did, but I doubt that you will believe it." Lai Wan told the detective all she had found in the man's mind. Bianca answered;

"That's it, no cut-outs, no middle man? You're right, I don't believe it. While we're discussing things I can't believe, you know, I can't believe I actually got to my shotgun in time. You know anything about that?" Quietly, her voice almost sounding embarrassed, Lai Wan said;

"The creature was greatly agitated, and did not make a great deal of contact with the ground. When it did, however, I managed to slip within its mind and find a memory of its mother, screaming at it to 'Stop!' I replayed that memory for it as loud as I could. I do not think it bought you more than a second or two."

Bianca shuddered, not knowing how to thank the woman sitting there with her. As they sped down the highway, the detective merely said, "Well, since your place might be watched and mine is too far away, let's find a motel with a vacancy and we can finish this up tomorrow."

"If you do not mind, Bianca, I would prefer sleeping in the car at a rest stop.

Motels--too many people, too many sad memories in the pillows, mattresses--everything."

"Considering what some people do in motels, sad is probably the least of it. Rest stops are one of the places they'll be looking for us, but I'm certain we can find some place to pull over. First things first, though, let me call the State Police and tell them about our friends back there in the field."

"You are kinder than I."

"Not really, I left the shotgun I used on the monster under the guy you took out. With no ID they'll be in for a rough couple of days before things can be straightened out."

***

It was one of the first exits off Interstate 81, just after the roadway crossed into Pennsylvania from New York. The ramp bore no name, only a number. Poorly marked, it came up fast--a thing one would drive right past unless they knew what to look for. Only those who were lost or had business in the mostly vacant corporate park it led to would have any reason to pull off there.

Bianca and Lai Wan did. They had found a small town in which to hide for the night, sleeping in the detective's car under a darkened streetlamp in a suburban neighborhood. They left close to seven in the morning, having washed up the best they could with only the water remaining in a bottle Lai Wan had in her bag. Nether had slept well, Bianca suffering from nightmares that pitted her against tentacled creatures and headless monsters that would not die. The frightening dreams spilled over into Lai Wan's sleep, causing her to wake several time during the night. Neither woman was in a good mood when Bianca finally found the exit for which they were looking. At just after nine o'clock they pulled up in front of a business labeled "Banner Enterprises."

"Cute," remarked Bianca. She explained the comic book reference to Lai Wan.

"Ghastly. Not only are they making monsters but are bragging about it. It ends today."

The front door was not locked. They walked into a waiting area and were greeted by a young man who looked more like a clerk than the mastermind of a sinister plot. The man brushed back his thinning hair and adjusted his glasses;

"Ladies, welcome. I wasn't expecting you so soon."

"You were expecting us, Mr. ...?"

"Byron, Byron Shelly."

"And what is your real name, Mr. Shelly?"

"Does it matter, Ms. Jones? Although I'm sure your companion here could discover it quite easily, it would mean nothing to either of you. And to answer your question, yes, I was expecting you. There was a tracker not only in your car but also in the one of the men you, ah, disabled. When your car left and their's remained, it was apparent what had happened. Of course I sent them help immediately. So while your call to the State Police was appreciated, it was not necessary."

"And what happens now, Mr. ... Shelly?"

"Yes, now. Please come this way." Shelly led them to an inner office. "Please have a seat." When the three were seated, he continued. "Whatever our original intentions towards you two, after yesterday evening's, ah, incident, I spoke with my superiors ..."

"Who are?"

"Who are quite out of your reach, Detective Jones. Even if you were to extract that information from me, you would find them quite untouchable."

"Pennsylvania is an avenue as well as a state." Despite his control, Shelly turned a shade paler at the quiet comment from Lai Wan.

"It goes that far?" Nods from Lai Wan and Shelly answered Bianca's question.

"Not that you could prove it, ladies. I'm as high as you go. But as I was saying, I spoke with my superiors and we decided to go with Plan B. I'm going to tell you the truth." Both Lai Wan and Bianca were shocked at this pronouncement, one which neither expected.

"Are you sure you're with the government, our government?" Bianca wanted to know. "Isn't that against policy?"

Shelly smiled and shrugged. "These are difficult times, ladies. Difficult and dangerous. What has worked before against the enemies of our country has proven less than effective these days. New weapons are needed. We had hoped The Berserker Project would be one of them."

Seeing that Bianca was about to interrupt, Shelly held up and hand. "History tells us that the Vikings of old, and some Celtic warriors, would sometimes fly into a battle rage so fierce that one man would fight as twenty, killing dozens, maybe hundreds in battle before collapsing from exhaustion or dying from the multiple injuries he'd been able to ignore. It was thought that if that rage could be chemically induced, it would prove useful to us."

"I understood," Lai Wan said, "that these berserkers killed as many of their comrades as they did their foes. Why then would you wish to turn your soldiers into such?"

"Oh no, we would never do that. The plan was that once we perfected the process we would start releasing all those insurgents and terrorists we have in custody and sending them back home, after a full physical of course."

"And once they were back home and among their own people?"

"Well then, detective, we would trigger the process and there would be far fewer insurgents and terrorists then there were."

"That is horrible."

Shelly nodded in agreement with Lai Wan. "That is war, and yes, most war is quite horrible. Under my supervision, scientists developed a drug that quite effectively combined human growth hormone, adrenaline, and a psychotropic chemical similar to LSD. Of course it had to be tested, so we thought, why not see if it could be used to combat the drug problem as well? We used heroin as a chemical trigger for those experiments and, well, you know the rest."

"And now what?"

"And now, nothing. The project is being dismantled. The drugs destroyed, the scientists reassigned, all paperwork shredded. The banners did not perform as expected. Some died or were killed right away. On others the drug had little or no effect. Only in Brooklyn and Baltimore did things proceed as expected and even then we lost one. And then there was last night. It was, in a way, the final test. If a banner cannot defeat two women, only one of whom is armed, then it's not an effective weapon. Project Berserker has been cancelled."

Bianca looked over at Lai Wan, who nodded to tell the detective that Shelly was telling the truth. Still, neither woman believed him. While what he said may have been the literal truth, shades of falsehood and deception were certain to be hidden behind his words.

"If there's nothing else, ladies, I have an office to close."

"One other thing, Shelly," Bianca said. "Why bother telling us? Why not just wipe us out? It seems your style."

"Very tempting, yes, but although you could be disposed of without much of a ripple, Ms. Wan here has too many powerful friends. With the project terminated, it's so much easier to simple give you your 'victory' and send you on your way." After a moment of silence, Shelly asked it there was anything else, to which Bianca answered;

"I won't argue it, you've got all the cards for the moment. Which means you've won, this time. But if I hear of this horror happening again ..."

"Killing me won't make it stop."

"No, but it would make me feel so good."

"In that case, Detective Jones, you will not hear of it happening again. I so terribly hate to have to dispose of beautiful women. Even the short ones."

"Just so we understand each other."

Bianca held out her hand, Shelly took it, then automatically shook Lai Wan's when it was offered. He then walked the two out to their car.

"We did what we could," Lai Wan said as they drove away.

"Not enough. Project Berserker may be cancelled, but you know as well as I do that in six months, a year, it'll begin all over again under a new name."

"And so it goes, Bianca. Until then, we have done all we could."

"Still, if I ever see that Shelly again…"

"There is little chance of that. Obviously you remember that I shook his hand. In two nights, three, maybe in a week, he will begin to dream. Not good dreams, but dreams of what it is to be an innocent, to be a plaything for forces beyond his control. Eventually, every night, then his naps, finally even when he blinks, he will experience the despair and fear and terror of Tyrone and Darryl and all others forced into lives not of their choosing. Most likely it will drive him mad. If not, however, if he comes to realize why he dreams thus, perhaps then there will be justice for his victims."

There was little further conversation between the women for the rest of the trip. When Bianca pulled in front of Lai Wan's building, the psychometrist gathered her crocheting as the detective said, "Take care, and give Stranger a scratch for me. He's a nice dog."

"It is the only kind to have. You take care as well, Bianca." And then, Lai Wan handed her needlework to the detective, adding,

"It is a scarf. I made it for you. It will not stop a bullet, but when you wear it, please allow it to remind you that there are those of us who will care if you end up stopping one."

Bianca froze for a moment, completely caught off guard by the unexpected warmth coming from the psychometrist. Almost numbly she wrapped the gift around her neck, making a weak joke about how well it fit. Lai Wan nodded, then watched as the detective drove away.

She stood at the curb for some time after Bianca's car disappeared from sight. Finally, however, the street began to fill with people leaving the psychometrist with little choice other than to go inside to hug her dog.

21 DOORS

Bianca Jones is dreaming. Somehow she knows this, but that doesn't make things any the less real. She's seen enough to know that wherever you die it's for keeps.

She's at the top of a long stairway, not quite sure how she got there. There's a long hallway in front of her, a hallway lined with doors. Ten on each side, one at the far end. All the doors are shut. She tries the first one on the right.

It's a bedroom, dark oak furniture and a high posted bed. Nothing else. Another room, first on the left. Another bedroom, this one a girl's room -- all bright and pink, a canopy bed, and lots of frills. The kind she wanted when she was a girl, the kind she'd set up for the daughter she'll probably never have. She moves on.

The next door is locked, but there are sounds coming from behind it. A loud crash, a heavy thud, a muffled scream. She thinks to force her way in to help however she can, but then dream logic tells her that whatever's behind that door is someone else's nightmare.

She's closer to the end now. In one room there is a crying woman, rocking back and forth, holding something that might be a baby. In another two men argue. About what she doesn't know, but both agree that something must be done.

Four doors away from the end, two on each side. Two are bedrooms. In one are a man and woman moving together under the covers. She gives them their privacy and crosses the hall. The next room is dark, with just a small light. Suddenly a boy sits up, looks at her with eyes wide with fear. He's afraid of something -- of the dark, of her, of whatever waits in the house.

Two more locked rooms. From the sounds coming from them she hopes the locks hold. The end of the hall, the last room, the final door. It opens easy, and she steps into darkness. There's a flash of light, bright and quick like a camera. And in that brief instance she sees the room in red and black. Somehow she knows that the red is blood, and that the black is coming for her. The door closes behind her. Someone calls her name.

***

Bianca thought about her dream as she drove to the crime scene. I haven't had that one in a while. That particular dream was a familiar one, going back to childhood. When she was ten, she and a friend played "21 Doors," a game where one girl tries to go into a trance while another guides her through an imagined mansion. Behind each door of the mansion was something to be discovered, something to be described out loud. To Bianca, the game wasn't much fun, but it had somehow stayed with her, and that night she had dreamt about the long hallway with ten doors on either side and one at the end.

The dream reoccurred over the years, each time changing slightly, different people and things behind the doors each time. Once it was a school, each with a class she had to take. Sometimes lovers awaited her, sometimes there were rooms full of books to be read, shelved or copied. There were dangers as well -- men or beasts lurking, waiting to do her harm. The one constant was, or had been, that the room at the end was always locked.

Weird, she said to herself, although not surprising considering all the crap I've faced -- old gods, haunted books, bloodsuckers, ghosts -- it's a wonder that I have normal dreams anymore. She'd been having bad dreams ever since her first encounter with the unknown. But Morgan taught her how to deal with the really nasty ones. He'd no doubt call this one an omen or warning. It would have been nice to know how it came out. Now thanks to Russo I never will. He better have a good reason for waking me up.

Joe Russo was a criminalist in the Baltimore Crime Lab. Usually he worked inside, but a personnel shortage had him processing crime scenes. It was his call that had interrupted her dream, his voice that had called her name, waking Bianca up only in time to hear him leave his message. A murder in Brewer's Hill, an address, the need for urgency, then a quick cut off as if he was interrupted.

Bianca forgot all about her dream as she turned off Conkling on to Foster Avenue and saw the flashing blue and red lights. She counted at least eight marked cars, the whole sector, four of them blocking access to the 3600 block.

Parking as close as she could, Bianca hung her badge holder around her neck and approached the scene. As she ducked under the yellow tape she heard a voice call out, "Hey kid, other side."

Bianca showed her badge to the approaching officer. "That's okay, I work here." After getting her name and ID number, he pointed to a house in the middle of the block.

"Right over there, Detective."

"Thanks."

As Bianca walked away, another officer came up. "Who was that?" he asked.

"Bianca Jones. Works out of Special Investigations."

"Isn't she kinda short for a cop?"

"Don't let her hear you say that," the first cop warned. "She may not be much past five feet, but she thinks she's six-eight. And from what I've heard, she's taken down guys that big and more."

As Bianca came up to the murder scene she saw Joe Russo getting equipment from his crime lab van.

"What have you got for me, Joe? And whatever it is better be good, or you're going to pay for getting me out of bed."

She expected his usual smartass reply, something like "Actually, I'd pay to get you into bed." Instead, the usually smiling crime scene man looked at her with a pale face and said, "I wish it was good, Bianca, but it's bad, as bad as it gets."

"How so?" If Joe thought it was bad, it was. Crime scene people saw the worst that one human being could do to another on a regular basis, and their idea of bad was far beyond the average person's.

"The victim's Anita Dixon. She's a young girl, she's …" Joe couldn't get the words out. "Just go in and see for yourself."

The air around Bianca chilled. It suddenly occurred to her that there was only one reason Joe would have called her specifically. She put it down to an early morning following a late night that she hadn't thought of it sooner.

"This involves … what I do, doesn't it?"

Russo nodded. Bianca's actual role in the Department was little known. "Special Investigations" covered a wide area and for the most part she handled mundane crimes. Sometimes, however, something occurred that had no earthly explanation. When that happened, Bianca was handed the case, and was expected to handle it quietly and with finality. Few people were aware of this. Joe Russo was one of them, having assisted Bianca enough to realize that, at times, reality was multiple choice.

"Just one thing before you go in, Bianca. Don't tell Beasley I was the one who called you."

Great, Bianca thought, Detective Earl Beasley was the primary. Beasley was a hump of the first order, doing the least amount of work and always going for the easiest explanation. If it wasn't for the crime lab and phone tips, he'd never solve a case. He also wasn't found of women cops in general and Bianca Jones in particular. This ought to be fun.

"Who the hell sent for you?" was how Beasley greeted her as she climbed the stairs to the second floor. He stood on the top step, blocking her way.

"Who the hell do you think? Now move aside and let me see the victim."

Beasley shook his head. "I don't think so, Miss High and Mighty Special Investigations. The last time you interfered in one of my cases you cost me a collar."

"The man was innocent, Beasley."

"Oh, I see. His prints, his DNA, and him getting caught holding the bloody knife made him innocent?"

No it didn't, Bianca thought, being demonically possessed did. But she couldn't tell Beasley that.

"And what about that serial killer you let get away, Jones? That open case is still on my desk."

"Where I'm sure it has lots of company. Now if you'll please just let me look over the scene I'll be out of your way asap."

"No." There was a firmness in Beasley's voice that told her he was making a stand. "I'm the primary and this is my scene. I'm in charge, and I get to say who stays and who goes. And you, little lady, may leave."

Bianca was uncomfortably aware of her situation. Two steps above her, Beasley had the advantage of height and position. He was trying to make her look small in front of the other officers present, both literally and figuratively. Her choices were to either back down or make a scene. Be a coward or a bitch. Either way he won.

If that's what he was thinking, Beasley was wrong. Bianca made the third choice. She agreed with him.

"You know, Beasley, you're right. Command's got no cause to wake me up at two a.m. and send me out to your scene. Screw them. When Major Williams asks for my report later today I'll just tell him I couldn't get a look at the body. That you quite properly sent me packing, and that you'll be glad to brief him and the Chief when you get back from the Medical Examiner's after the autopsy. You have a good day. I'm going home and back to bed."

She turned, not waiting for the reaction she knew was coming. Three, two, one -- she wasn't halfway down the stairs when Beasley called to her. "Jones."

"What?"

"Take your damned look and get out."

Bianca climbed back up the stairs, Beasley stepping to let her pass. "She's in there," he said, pointing to the back bedroom.

Bianca paused at the partly open door, her dream and Joe's warning coming back to her. On the other side was something bad, something out of nightmare, and she'd be the one to deal with it. She went in.

It was worse than she'd expected. The victim, or what was left of her, was laid out on the bed. She'd been eviscerated, her abdomen torn open and organs removed. Blood was everywhere, and bits of what had been inside her spattered the walls and ceiling.

Bianca had seen such a thing before. A vacant house in Federal Hill, kidnapped women used as surrogates for demon spawn. The children ripping their way out of their mothers' wombs, feasting on the remains. Bianca had killed them and then confronted their true parent, returning her to the blackness in which she dwelt.

Could she be back? "Shub-Niggurath."

Bianca hadn't realized she spoken the name out loud until the officer with her asked, "What was that, Detective?"

"Nothing," Bianca said absently, looking around the room, under the bed, in the closet -- at everything except the body on the bed. Satisfied that she and the officer were the only living things there, she turned to the victim. Now that the initial shock was over, she was able to examine her more dispassionately.

Something or someone had ripped this girl open, from the outside judging by the appearance of the wounds. Why? There were easier ways, less messy, of killing a person. Or were the blood, guts and gore a message to someone? The parents?

When she left the room Beasley was waiting outside. "I've seen enough," she told him. "I'm going home. Send a copy of your report to Special Investigations as soon as it's done."

Passing Russo on the stairs, Bianca whispered to him, "Outside," then went out and waited by her car. Thirty minutes later, he came out to meet her.

"Done with the scene?" she asked him.

Russo nodded. "Just waiting for the M.E. So, the girl? Is our old friend back?"

"You mean Shub-Niggurath? No, if that was her work the body would have been partly devoured and there'd be a baby monster running around the house. As horrible as this seems, it might be just everyday human cruelty."

"Except ..."

"Except what, Joe?"

"No signs of forced entry. The windows were locked and the doors bolted. The parents were asleep two doors away when she started screaming. It took them maybe three minutes to get to her room. By then it was too late -- she was already dead. Whoever or whatever did this worked quick and somehow escaped with the parents just outside the door. Which is not humanly possible."

Bianca thought for a moment. "If all you have is a hammer, you see everything as a nail," she finally said.

"What's that mean?"

"It's something I read somewhere. Given what we've seen, it's easy to assume that anything weird or strange has a supernatural connection. Let's not ignore the human factor."

"You mean the parents?"

"Yes, I mean the parents."

Russo shook his head. "Maybe, but I don't think so. It's too clean, there's nothing, and I mean nothing, anywhere outside the bedroom. No blood, no hair, nothing. Besides, the neighbors heard the screams too. The parents didn't have time to clean up after themselves. I hope I'm wrong, Bianca, but this one looks like it's yours."

***

"Anything from the autopsy?" Bianca asked Russo later that same morning. At her request, the crime scene tech had attended the autopsy with Beasley. Now he was in her office with the results.

"Nothing we didn't already know, Bianca. Something ripped her apart and removed her internal organs."

"What kind of weapon was used?"

"The M.E. said that her flesh was torn, not cut. Thinks it's some kind of animal."

"And the Dixons don't have pets, do they?"

Russo handed her the autopsy photos. What had been done to Anita Dixon had been horrific, far beyond anything Bianca had seen on normal scenes.

"I don't think a dog or cat could have done this, Bianca."

"The missing organs, they weren't found on the scene?"

Russo shook his head. "Just the spatter. Beasley got a warrant and he's going to do another search this afternoon -- the drains, the pipes, the backyard, the basement -- but we both know he's not going to find anything."

"Damn!" Bianca threw the photos on the desk in front of her. "Damn!" she shouted again. She had been lying to herself since last night, telling herself that the monsters in this case were human, that whatever terrible things had been done to this girl had been done by her parents, or an intruder, or by someone with origins based in this world. But now, after what Joe had told her, after the autopsy, after doctors had cleaned the body, examined it in a clinical setting and cut into what was left, she couldn't deny it any longer. She slumped back in her chair.

She did not want this, did not want to go back into the darkness. She wanted to stay where, if all went wrong, the worst that could happen was that the guilty were freed or the innocent convicted. Matters of importance, true, but correctable -- mere matters of individual life and death. But on the other side she battled against creatures that saw humanity as playthings and cattle, and if she failed or fell, the cost would be measured in souls.

She wanted to say to Hell with it all and let someone else do it. But the Hell of it was there was no one else. "Who does the hard things?" someone once asked. Those who can. "Bianca, anything I can do?" she heard Joe ask.

"Maybe later," Bianca said, her smile telling him how much she valued his support. She grabbed the photos from the desk. It was time to see Morgan.

***

Fells Point is an historic area of Baltimore, full to bursting with antique stores, tourist shops and more bars per square inch than anywhere else in the city. Demand for retail space was so great that back rooms of existing businesses had been converted and rented to new merchants, with new streets being made from alleys.

Morgan's Rare Books & Collectibles was one of these alley shops, located on the newly-created Lisbon Street. From the outside the store did not appear very large, but the inside seemed to go back forever, causing casual browsers to wonder just what had become of the clothing store that fronted the address.

Morgan himself was no less an oddity. A small gnome of a man, he resembled some of the books he sold -- old and well used. But Bianca knew him to be in fine condition, and that he had stood many times on the same battleground on which she found herself. That he had won all of his fights went without saying. In this war you lost only once.

With the store closed and the door locked, the pair went back into Morgan's private office. As he looked at the crime scene and autopsy photos, Bianca browsed his shelves. Morgan's stacking system seemed to change with her every visit. This time he had Prinn's *De Vermis Mysteriis* alongside Holmes's *Practical Handbook of Bee Culture*. Marlowe's unpublished *The Redemption of Faust* was next to the script book for *Damn Yankees*. And as she always did, she made sure that *The Ravings of Abd el-Hazred* was locked securely in the safe.

"I wish you'd let me burn that book," Morgan said, not for the first, or last, time. "Its very existence is a danger to us all."

"And I've told you, it'd even more dangerous to destroy it. Now what can you tell from the photos?"

Morgan handed the pictures back to her. "Look at them," he said, gesturing towards his books. "There are five hundred, maybe one thousand volumes on these shelves. All of them are rare and collectible. Blood had been spilled for some of them and on some of them. Many are banned in most civilized countries, and for good reason. They describe horrors and nightmares and tell of monsters most men have not even imagined. And while I have not read them all, I am familiar with their contents."

"And which one will tell me what kind of a beast I'm looking for?"

"None of them."

Bianca looked at him in surprise. "You're telling me this is mundane?"

Morgan shook his head. "No, from what I see in the pictures, and the evidence, or lack of it, from the scene, I do not believe that we are dealing with an earthly entity. And the way that girl died, there are things that could do such a thing, would do such a thing. Many of them, but which one, and why? We can't proceed until we know more."

"Then can you at least tell me how this thing got in and out?"

The bookseller thought a bit, then nodded. "A door was opened. It had to have been. Either from one side or the other. Miss Dixon may have done something, consciously or not, to unlock it. Were there any occult symbols or artifacts in her room?"

"Nothing like that," Bianca replied idly, thinking of doors. The family was Protestant, just a plain cross in each room. "I dreamt of doors," she added suddenly. Then she told him about her reoccurring dream. "Coincidence?" she asked when she was finished.

"More likely your recent experiences are making you sensitive to the worlds around you. You see more, you know more, you sense more."

"So the thing at the end of the hall, behind the last door, was that the monster?"

"It was your monster. We each have our own. But this doesn't bring us any closer to finding out what killed Anita Dixon. Talk to her friends, her classmates. Find out who she's been dating, what movies she's been watching, what games she's been playing."

***

They held a memorial service for Anita at school. Nothing religious, but some students and teachers talked about what a good friend and hard worker she had been, and how much she'd been missed. There were grief counselors there, for those of her friends who wanted someone to talk to. At the end of the assembly, the principal asked anyone with any information to call the police and tell them.

No one did. There were those that could, girls who could have linked Anita's death to words whispered in the dark and what was happening to them at night.

***

It had started out as a game, just something to do at the party. While in the attic, Janice had found a Ouija board, or at least that's what her mother called it. After a bit of a search, they found the planchette that went with it. After her mother explained how the game was played, Janice thought it the perfect thing to have at her sleepover.

It was ten o'clock. All the girls were in their nightclothes, the s'mores had been eaten but the gossip and bragging about boys hadn't started. That's when Janice brought out the Ouija board. It was time to tell fortunes and see the future.

Two girls at a time, both sitting on the floor, the board in front of them, they asked questions about what was to be. Will I go to the spring dance?

When will I get married? How many children will I have? Does Jared really like me? These and other questions of similar importance to girls just into their teens were asked and answered by the mysterious brass planchette as it moved down to one corner to "Yes", then, in answer to another question, over to "No," then up to the letters in the center of the board to spell out the first name of someone's future true love. Of course, each of the girls swore that the pointer moved on its own, that their fingers merely guided it to where it wanted to go.

Then Anna took a turn -- shy, quiet Anna, who had surprised everyone, including herself, by even coming to the sleepover. Anna had just transferred to their school, and so far had not joined in with anything. Her invitation was more a matter of politeness than anything else. But she accepted, and now she and Janice had their fingers on the planchette, and it was spelling out the name of Janice's future husband. "K-A-R-L" the pointer revealed, to no surprise to anyone in the room, since they all knew that that was the name of a boy Janice really, really liked.

Then it was Anna's turn. Anna, the new girl, who had come to the sleepover hoping to make friends. It was up to Anna to ask a question.

Her question was going to be like the other girls', something like "will I be rich and famous when I grow up?" But before she could speak up, the planchette started moving. She and Janice looked at each other, each silently asking the other, "Are you doing that?" Neither was. Slowly the pointer moved. "B" then over to "L" and then to "A." It went on, and when it had finished it had spelled out:

BLACK AGGIE

"Black Aggie?" Janice said. "Who the hell is Black Aggie?" Anna shook her head, she didn't know.

"Black Aggie?" Janice's mother had just come into the room. "Where did you hear that name?"

"The board spelled it out," Anna said quietly.

The room suddenly got chilly, if not for the girls, then at least for Janice's mother. She knew the name Black Aggie, back from when she was a teen. Even then the legend was fading, there was no way these girls should have known it. She looked down at the board. Her chill returned. Maybe bringing it out wasn't such a good idea. "Tell you what, girls," she finally said. "Why don't I make popcorn while you put in the movie?"

The mood broken, they quickly agreed. Original or not, the mother thought as the girls started to watch *Titanic* for the twenty-eighth time, tomorrow that board goes out.

***

He had waited, waited for the door to open, for someone to use the key. It had been too long, and he was hungry. The woman waited too. She would always wait, such were her sins. And then, a minute later, an hour later, a day later -- for him there was no time, only need and hunger -- he felt it. Power, unshielded and uncontrolled. It was faint, though. He extended himself. It would cost, it would only add to his hunger, but he extended himself and found a thread, a thread that led him to its source. He did what he could before the power faded. His thoughts sent the name, the name that was the key. It was all he could do.

***

The Monday after the sleepover, Anna hesitantly approached the table where Janice was eating lunch. Anita, Brenda, and Liz, the other girls who were at the party, were with her. They all looked up at her.

"Can I sit here?"

Three heads turned and looked at Janice. The weekend had been a test of sorts for Anna, to see if she fit in. There was the weirdness with that board, but they had been tired of that game anyway.

Janice shrugged, "Sure, why not?"

Anita and Liz moved to make room for the newcomer.

For a while they ate in silence, Janice and her friends waiting for Anna to speak first, to pass yet another test. If she said something stupid or uncool, they'd pounce on it, make fun until they drove her away. Anna knew this, it had been that way in her old school, so she waited, let the suspense build, before she said, "I know who Black Aggie was."

"So you did spell that out," Janice accused.

"No, I just googled it when I got home Sunday morning."

"So who was she?" Liz asked.

"It was some kind of statue over a guy's grave in a Pikesville cemetery. It was supposed to be haunted. Some people said by the ghost of a nurse who had killed a baby. Others said that Aggie's eyes glowed red at midnight." Anna paused, looked at the girls to see how they were receiving her story, not wanting them to be bored or worse, giving her the "what a geek" look. No, they were all listening to her, waiting for the rest. "If her eyes glowed and you looked into them, you went blind. Not only that, there's a story that to get into a fraternity, this college kid had to spend the night with Aggie, sitting right on the grave. They found him dead the next morning, not a mark on him." She stopped to eat part of her sandwich.

"What else?" Brenda wanted to know.

"It's said that if you stand in front of a mirror at midnight, in a dark room, and say 'Black Aggie' three times, something will happen."

"What?" both Anita and Brenda wanted to know.

"You'll see Black Aggie, or you'll see Hell or" -- Anna waited for effect -- "you'll die."

"Let's try it," Janice said suddenly, taking the attention away from the newcomer and back to her.

"Try what?"

"What do you think, Liz? Tonight at midnight, we'll all stand in front of our mirrors and say 'Black Aggie' three times. Then we'll see what happens."

None of the girls replied at first, then Anna spoke up. "Sure, let's do it."

"I'm in," Anita agreed.

"Me too," Brenda added.

That left Liz. "But what about, you know, seeing Hell or dying?"

Janice rolled her eyes. "It's just a story, Liz. Nothing's really going to happen. Right, Anna?" Janice turned to the new girl, waiting for her to admit that she was just telling a tale.

Anna shrugged. "Probably not. It's like Janice said, it's just a story. But remember …" just then the bell rang. Lunch period was over. Anna waited for the ringing to end. "…Aggie's statute was moved and hidden away. Something bad must have happened for them to do that."

Janice wanted the last word before they all went back to class.

"Tonight, midnight. We say the words."

That night, five girls just into their teens, all them innocent of the flesh and the evils of the world, waited for midnight. And as clocks chimed, timers dinged and parents shouted, "It's tomorrow, go to sleep," each of them stood in the darkness of her room. And, since no two clocks keep the exact same time, each of them, one at a time, faced their reflection and recited, "Black Aggie, Black Aggie, Black Aggie." And they waited, and waited, and waited. And nothing happened. Nothing appeared in the mirror. No one crept up behind them. No visions of Hell or Death appeared. And so, the five girls, still innocent of the world and the flesh, went to bed. Some were relieved, others disappointed and four of them resolved to tell the fifth just how full of it she was.

***

How much more time went by, he could not tell. The hunger, the need had gotten worse. Not for the first time he looked at the woman and wondered if … No, some things were forbidden, even to him. Then he heard it, the faint echoings of the key. And the one who used it was strong, and ripe, and untouched. But no, she did not believe, and the power faded before the lock could turn. Yet, again, there it was, from another, and then another, and finally, two more. And they were all like the first. None of them believed, not truly, but there was strength in their youth and innocence, and that was enough. Soon, the door would open and he would be satisfied.

***

That night, each of the girls dreamed. Of what they couldn't say. There was something that wanted them, needed them. And what it -- no *he*, definitely *he* -- wanted and needed from them was not something they wanted to give. But he would have it anyway. There was pain, and pressure, and a sense of loss. And then, suddenly there was pleasure, of a kind none of them had ever sensed before. And then the dream faded, and left them to their sleep. And elsewhere, the thing that was the dream, that which the words had released, was for now satisfied, having fed well that night.

***

"Well," Janice asked in homeroom the next morning, "Did you all do it?"
A chorus of "yes" and "yeahs" answered her.
"And did anything happen?"
"Nothing," said Anita. Liz shook her head no. Janice was about to ask Anna when Brenda said, "I had this weird dream."
"What about?" Anna asked before anyone else could.
"I don't know. It was one of those dreams where you know something's happening but you don't know what. It felt bad and good all at the same time."
And each of the other four remembered her own dream, and how it made her felt and thought about dark rooms, and mirrors, and the words "Black Aggie."

***

Each night after that he fed well. Not as he had on the first, when he sated himself, but well enough. Each night one, sometimes two of them said the words, used the key and opened the door. And since he stayed in their dreams, their innocence and strength remained. But there was still the woman, and he would soon have to give her what she needed.

***

At midnight, in her darkened room, Anita Dixon stood in front of her mirror. "Black Aggie, Black Aggie, Black Aggie." She wanted the dream, and it came only when she said the words. Why, she didn't know. What she did know is how the dream made her feel. And each time was better -- less pain, more pleasure. There was a part of her that said it was wrong, that there'd be a price, but this she ignored. So she said the words, got into bed and fell asleep.

And the dream came, more vivid this time than before. She was in her bedroom. A door opened where there wasn't one before, and something man-shaped stepped through. Large, hairy, naked, and quite definitely male. As he got into bed with her Anita thought to scream but he was on her before she could. Then came the pain and the pressure and a true sense of loss. Pleasure, too, but less than before. It was over quickly, and Anita's awareness faded as the man left and the door that wasn't there closed behind him.

The next morning, Anita woke up stiff and sore. Her whole body hurt, especially her legs and thighs. She didn't remember her dream, nor did she see the blood on her bedsheet. Her mother did later that day, but only thought about how quickly girls become women.

*****

Soon, he told the woman in unvoiced words. Soon you will have what you want, what you need. The woman, a sad smile on her face, said nothing.

*****

"I thought the police had made an arrest," the principal of Belford Middle School told Bianca.

"We have," Bianca confirmed. "Anita's parents were taken into custody last night." With no signs of forced entry, and no explanation of how an intruder may have entered their house, Beasley had arrested Anita's mother and father.

"I'm doing background," she went on. "I'm hoping to talk to some of her school friends, to find out what Anita may have told them about her home life. The Department sent me because they thought the girls might feel more comfortable talking to a woman."

One by one, Anita's classmates were brought in to talk to Bianca. Most knew her only from school, and knew little if anything, about her home life or outside activities. Then Brenda came in.

Bianca introduced herself and explained why she was there. After some preliminary questions she asked the girl, "Did Anita ever talk about her parents, complain that they were mistreating her?"

"Well, I guess she complained, like how they wouldn't let her go out on a school night, and how, like, there were shows she couldn't watch, and music she couldn't buy and movies she couldn't see. But, like, she never talked about abuse or anything. And in gym, where you see almost everything, she never had no bruises or anything."

That agreed with what the other girls had said, and with the autopsy results -- other than what the murder caused, there were no signs of past trauma, no other injuries, old or new, were on the girl's body.

"Did Anita ever talk about the occult?"

"What?" Was there hesitation before the girl replied?

"The occult -- black magic, the goth scene, that kind of stuff?"

Again, Bianca noted some hesitation before Brenda answered. "She … I mean we … I mean … it really wasn't anything … "

"It's okay, Brenda. What ever it is probably doesn't have anything to do with what happened, but tell me anyway."

And Brenda told her about the sleep-over, about the fortune telling board, and about its spelling out Black Aggie.

Bianca knew that name from when she was young, had heard some of the stories from her aunts. None of the tales had ended happily.

"What about Black Aggie?" she asked the girl.

Brenda shrugged. "Nothing, really. After that we kinda stopped and watched a movie."

Brenda wouldn't answer anymore questions after that, except to tell Bianca who else was at the sleepover. The detective asked for Anna, Janice and Liz to be sent down to the office.

Janice arrived first. "Tell me about Black Aggie," Bianca asked directly. The girl repeated what Brenda had already said.

"My mom really, like, freaked when that happened. She tried to cover it up but I could tell she was really bothered and stuff. She put the board out with the trash that night."

Anna told Bianca about her Internet search, and how all the girls agreed to say the name in front of the mirror. She denied anything happened, but her body language and tone of voice told a different story. Bianca didn't press the issue. This was neither the time nor place.

"I don't like the way it makes me feel," was Liz's surprising answer to Bianca's question.

"How what makes you feel?"

"When I say Bla -- that name in front of the mirror then go to bed. I have dreams that make me feel cheap and used. Like when you're with a boy and he tries to feel you up. It sorta feels good, but you know it's wrong. That's what the dreams are like. They feel good, but they also feel wrong. That's why I stopped."

"And the other girls, do they have these dreams?"

Liz shrugged. "I guess so, we never talk about it. I mean, they all said that nothing happened. I did to, but I was lying. Maybe they were too."

***

"They probably were lying," Morgan told Bianca when she returned to his shop. "The five of them were, however unwittingly, playing with dark forces, and somehow opened a door to them. What did the mother say about the Ouija board?"

"What Janice told me. When the mother learned that the board had spelled out Black Aggie, she got rid of it. It was picked up the next day and by now is probably ashes at the bottom of the city incinerator."

"But the board itself, Miss Jones, where did it come from?"

"According to the mother, it's been in her family for years, supposedly one of the original talking boards made right here in Baltimore by the Ouija Novelty Company."

Morgan thought for a moment. "The first boards were used for serious fortune telling, not just as a party game. That use, plus being in its place of origin, would have given the board enough power to wake something up. And from what you've told me, this something may be an incubus."

"What's that?"

"A male demon, one that gets its sustenance from having intercourse with sleeping women."

"I thought that was a succubus, and anyway, wasn't that just the medieval explanation for erotic dreams."

Morgan shook his head. "A succubus is female, and lies with men. The incubus lies with women. Erotic dreams aside, both are very real." The bookseller got up, went to his shelves, his eyes scanning for particular volumes. When he found one he wanted, he touched it, as if to remind himself of its contents. "Milton learned of them in his vision of Satan's fall and Man's redemption, and wrote of them in 1671. Reginald Scot's *Discoveries of Witchcraft* discussed them back in 1584 as did Walter Scott's *Demonology and Witchcraft* in 1885. They are, indeed, very real."

"And obviously dangerous."

Morgan shook his head. "To the soul, perhaps. In dreams they'd lie with their victim, draining their strength, tempting them to licentiousness in their waking lives. But there is no record of such harm as was inflicted on poor Miss Dixon."

"Then I think the answer lies with Black Aggie," Bianca offered.

"Possibly, what do you know about her?"

Surprised that there was something that Morgan didn't know, Bianca took a moment before answering. "A local legend, or she was thirty years ago. Most people have forgotten her. I remember something about her, and looked up the rest." She told Morgan about the glowing eyes, the boy found dead, and the summoning ritual. At the last he nodded his head, as if expecting something like that.

"Aggie was originally a monument over the grave of a newspaper publisher, the design stolen from a statue called 'Grief' by Augustus St. Gaudens. There was trouble almost as soon as it was erected. About the same time, an African-American nurse had charge of an infant. Somehow the baby died, and the nurse was blamed for it. She was lynched by an angry crowd. After her death, she was said to haunt the Pikesville cemetery where Aggie was erected."

"I don't see a connection."

"Neither did I, until you told me about incubuses."

"Incubi," Morgan corrected absently. "Aren't people taught Latin anymore?"

Bianca ignored him. "One of the stories about Aggie is that a virgin who laid in her arms would lose her virginity within twenty-four hours. Another is that any pregnant woman who walked into Aggie's shadow would miscarry."

"I see," said Morgan, then was quiet. Bianca watched as the small old man considered what she'd told him. "Where is the statue now?" he finally asked.

"It was removed from the cemetery in 1967, and placed in storage. Later it was moved to Washington D.C."

"Where its evil would no doubt go unnoticed," the old man said dryly.

"So you think the statue is evil, Morgan?"

The bookseller shook his head. "The statue? No. But the stories that grew up around it? There are things out there, Miss Jones, evil things that have no name, no form. Merely a malevolent existence. And they wait. They wait for foolish people to summon them, to shape them with their beliefs. Stories were told about this Black Aggie. True or not, they were told, and in each retelling became more and more real, at least to some people. And when enough people believed, a door was opened, a door that allowed one of these unformed demons to come through into being."

"But Aggie's all but forgotten. Shouldn't that have killed the demon?"

"What you said, Miss Jones, 'all but …' As long as someone remembers, it, or they, still exist. Weak and hungry, but still they exist, the hunger making them all the more desperate and dangerous, ready to seize the slightness opening."

"So when the girls used the Ouija Board …"

"This thing used its power to send a message, and that message was 'Black Aggie.'"

"And when the girls used the summoning ritual …"

"They combined to open the door for the creature to have its way with them, at least on the dream plane."

"But, Morgan, Anita Dixon wasn't killed on the dream plane."

"The loss of virginity was only part of the legend, Miss Jones. We've been through this before, I believe. What is the possible result of sexual intercourse?"

"He leaves before you wake up, sends flowers the next day, but never calls you back."

That earned Bianca a stern glance. "We're speaking of serious matters, Miss Jones."

"So am I. At the very least I expect breakfast."

"Nevertheless, the purpose of sex is pregnancy. Imagine the wronged nurse haunting the cemetery, stalking mothers-to-be, then having her revenge by taking from them that which they hold most dear. She could do so only by removing the souls of developing children, causing their bodies to die. Black Aggie, at least her statue, has been gone these forty years. The nurse might still be waiting for another soul."

Morgan gave Bianca time to consider this. "And now imagine," he went on, "these two, the incubus and the nurse, working together. He enters the dreams of innocent young women and grows strong off them. And when he's strong enough, physically creates what the nurse needs, what she craves, and just as physically removes it."

"He makes the baby, then steals its soul. But where's the body?"

"The demon, Miss Jones, no doubt has appetites other than sex. Once the soul is gone, the body is merely flesh."

Bianca shook her head. "Good idea, but the parents would have mentioned the pregnancy."

"It may not have been advanced enough for anyone to notice, not even Miss Dixon."

"So he, they have got what they want. What next?"

"Consider this, Miss Jones. Without its body, a soul cannot long exist. It fades, and returns to the Source, to be united with another new life. And that brings us to the real horror."

It didn't take long for Bianca to realize what Morgan was saying. "With the child gone, the nurse will need another. And the demon will gladly create another, and another. The two of them will prey on these girls until they're all dead."

"And possibly beyond. Who's say that one of the girls hasn't told someone else about what happens when you stand in front of a mirror and call for Black Aggie, of the dreams that come and how they make you feel. And each time, with each victim, the demon grows stronger."

"Not if I can help it." Bianca's previous despair was now gone, replaced by a dark fury. Innocents had been seduced, Anita Dixon butchered, a child killed and its soul taken. She would exact payment. "How do I stop this son of a bitch?"

Morgan sighed. "I am not sure. Apparently thirty years ago the only solution found was to remove the focus of the belief and let the legend fade. We do not have that option."

"We know how to summon him."

"Yes, but to invite him willingly into your dreams leaves you as vulnerable as those young girls."

The answer came to her slowly. It came to her as Morgan again went to his books, mentally browsing them, looking for an answer. Dreams, he had said. The monster walked in, worked in dreams. But to enter, he had to be invited -- a key given, a door opened.

If that was the only way, so be it.

Bianca had a dream for him.

When she told Morgan what she intended the bookseller shook his head. "Too dangerous," he said. "We'll find another way."

"There is no other way," Bianca replied. "If there was, it'd be in one of your books. And there's nothing there, right?" She took his silence as agreement. "So my way it is. And it may not be as dangerous as you think. Let me tell you about a little game called '21 Doors.'"

***

That night Bianca lay in her own bed. Morgan was there as well, to put her in a trance then guide her through her dream.

"Are you sure you want to wear that?" he asked as he sat alongside her bed. He was referring to her nightgown. While it covered her from neck to feet, it was sheer enough to more than hint at the charms it hid. Morgan had blushed when he'd first seen it.

"For the third time, yes. What I wear to bed I wear in my dreams. And I want to entice this thing, make it want me. Now if you're ready, I am. Let's take this bastard down."

"Very well, close your eyes. Now then, you are standing in front of a large mansion. Slowly, the front door opens. You step inside. In front of you is a long flight of stairs. You ascend ..."

Eyes shut, Bianca concentrated on not on Morgan's words, but on the rhythm of his voice. She felt herself drifting off. With images of a long hallway in her mind, she dropped away from the world.

She was dreaming, she knew this. And she reminded herself that dream or not, what she faced was very real, and that dead was dead, no matter where or how you died.

A long hallway, ten doors on either side. And she thought of the red and black that waited at the end.

Slowly, she walked the hall.

Going past the first few doors, she looked for just the right room. As she walked the corridor, she again heard the sounds of men arguing, people making love, a baby crying. There was the dark room with the frightened boy. No, not that one. Nor did she want the bright pink girl's room. Too much innocence there, and this was no longer a game for the innocent.

Coming to the end of the hall she tried a door on the left, one nearest the final room. The door opened easily into a bedroom. It had the look of a room that was rented by the hour, and saw many guests every day. The bed was small, covered with used, dirty linen. The single dresser was tilted, and had one drawer missing. The carpet was soiled with stains better left unidentified. But there was a mirror hanging on the wall alongside the bed. And that made the room perfect.

Bianca walked up to the mirror, studied herself in the reflection. She paused, waited, then heard the distant sounds of church bells tolling midnight.

"Black Aggie," she said slowly, intoning each syllable slowly, belief in every word.

"Black Aggie," she said again.

And then for the third time,

"Black Aggie."

When she turned from the mirror things had changed. The tawdry hotel room was gone. Instead she was in a cemetery, just inside its gates. A cold wind blew. As she had believed, she was beyond dream now. Accepting this, she walked the only path, keeping the memory of the gates behind her.

It wasn't long before Bianca came to a clearing in which was a statue of a seated woman, robed and hooded. "Do you know what's being done in your name? Do you care?" She didn't expect an answer, and didn't receive one. Whatever power the bronze sculpture had was gone, lost when it was moved from its base, usurped by darker things.

A baby cried in the distance, and Bianca turned to the sound. There stood a woman not much bigger than she was, but very much older. In her arms was a ghost of a baby, the soul of Anita Dixon's child.

"That's not yours," Bianca told her.

The woman glared, saying nothing in reply.

Bianca looked into her reddened eyes, seeing first hate and envy, and then something else.

"All you have to do is give it up," she said quietly.

Again there was no reply.

A musky odor filled the air, the smell of passion and desire. From behind the woman came the figure of a man, or at least, something manlike. Whatever it was, it was large, unclothed and clearly male. She found herself drawn to it, despite knowing its nature. Without a word it promised her pleasures she'd never had in ways she'd never thought of. And a part of her wanted to yield, to let this thing take her and use her as it would.

Bianca welcomed this temptation, used it. As she felt her body responding to the incubus, she projected her desire back toward it and felt its need for her.

The incubus moved toward her. She turned and ran through the cemetery gates which she'd kept close behind her, knowing the creature would follow.

Gates are merely doors, and Bianca passed through them to emerge into the familiar hallway. With the creature close behind, she ran to the end, opened the last door, and entered.

Again she was in darkness, and again sudden bursts of light showed red and black, blood and death. Standing there was the hardest thing she'd ever done. If she waited too long …

She heard the door open and close behind her and the smell of passion and desire filled the room. Another bright flash, and the incubus was revealed. It grabbed for her, and she snapped a kick at its groin, doubling it over, rendering it helpless.

The room went dark again as Bianca rushed to the door. Behind her were the sounds of torn flesh and severed limbs as the nightmare that lived in the room, the one that Morgan had called her monster, found the defenseless incubus.

The sounds of carnage followed her out into the hallway as the door slammed behind her. It's over, she said to herself, and thought to wake up. But no, there was one thing left to do, one more soul to save.

Bianca remembered a room where a crying woman rocked what might have been a child. She went to it, and, as she expected, found the nurse holding the ghost of a baby.

"He's gone," Bianca told her, "back to whatever hell he came from. This is your last chance. Give me the child." The woman only held the infant tighter. "I'm not going to take it from you. You can keep it until it returns to be reborn. But then you'll be alone forever. There won't be another one. But give up the child, give up your hate, and maybe there's a chance for you too, for your own rebirth."

The old nurse looked down at the baby and then at Bianca. With sorrow in her reddened eyes she held up the child.

As Bianca reached out to take it, someone called her name.

***

Bianca awoke to a room full of light. It was morning. "Why did you wake me up?" She asked the waiting Morgan.

"Miss Jones, I know enough not to wake a lucid dreamer."

"Then who called my name?"

"Perhaps the part of you that knew it was time to awaken. How did it go?"

"I was right. Saying the name while in a dream was enough to take me to them."

"And?"

"I fed him to my nightmare."

Morgan said nothing, but his face expressed deep concern.

"What?" Bianca asked him.

"Nothing, for now. What of the nurse?"

Bianca thought back to the end of the dream. As she gave up the child, had Bianca seen peace replace sorrow on the nurse's face?

"I think she'll be all right."

"Of course, now the hard part comes."

"Tell me about it. I have to convince Major Williams to release the Dixons. And I have to get some teenage girls to stop fooling around with the occult without making it sound exciting or glamorous."

"That is not what I meant, Miss Jones. The creature, that which you sought to destroy, by your actions it is now a part of you. You must learn to contain it."

"Morgan, it's a part of all of us, the dark part that most of us keep safely locked away. This is just a piece that got out. If need be, I'll deal with. But for now, I may not have been awake, but I had a busy night. If you don't mind showing yourself out, I think I'll crash 'til noon."

Without waiting for Morgan's reply, she curled up into dreamless sleep.

The old man didn't leave right away. Instead he stood there and watched the sleeping woman, hoping the doors of her mind had very strong locks.

IT'S THE THOUGHT
THAT COUNTS

"**S**ince when does Special Investigations do missing persons, Major?"

"Since now." Major Williams handed Bianca Jones a case folder.

"Damn," she swore after reading half a page. Two more "Damns" quickly followed. "I guess this is ours," she conceded when she'd finished the file.

***

"Philip's not home right now, honey, but if you know where he is …"

Just five foot and slender-built, Bianca should have been used to being mistaken for someone much younger. She wasn't. Sighing, she flashed her badge.

"Police, Ms. Howard. Detective Jones. I need to see Philip's room."

"But the other officer already looked through it."

"I need to see it too."

The room was as described in the report. Mystic symbols and posters covered the walls, an inverted cross hung over the door. The bookcase was filled with horror fiction and books on the occult. The computer screen saver was a goat's head in a pentacle. The files the boy had saved were a collection of demonic images and downloaded spells. As the Baltimore Police Department's unofficial expert on the supernatural, Bianca knew most were bogus. But some were real, horrifically real. She only hoped Philip hadn't yet learned which ones.

***

"He's been in." Morgan handed the photo back to Bianca. Morgan owned a Fells Point bookshop. He was also Bianca's mentor in things supernatural.

"Sell him anything?"

"Lovecraft, Carter, some of the new writers like Henderson and Chambers."

"He ask for the real stuff?"

"They all do at his age. Like always I lied and told him I don't stock it. But there are others that do, and there's always the Internet."

***

Anna recognized Bianca as soon as the detective walked into her classroom.

A few months ago, fun and games had led to something much more serious for Anna and her friends. One girl died, then this detective somehow ruined it for the rest of them.

She knew why the cop was there -- Philip. As she waited for her to make the connection, she thought back two nights ago.

***

A circled star is drawn on the cement floor, candles at each intersection, charcoal burning in the middle. In the near darkness, someone giggles.

"Brenda, we need quiet."

"Sorry."

Anna sighs. "Get on with it, Phillip."

"I still think …"

"We are not getting naked. Now start."

Geek, Anna thinks, just wants to get into my panties, not that he'd know what to do. If only I could do this. But I need him, he knows the magic, or says he does.

She had once known magic. So had Brenda. They'd chant the words, and a demon lover would come to their bed. No more. When Anita died, so had the magic.

She wanted it back. So did Brenda. So now they sit in the dark waiting for Fat Philip to read from what he called a "grimoire."

Philip begins chanting in what might be Latin, Greek or gibberish. Now and then he throws incense on the coals. Smoke rises and grows thick. A cold wind blows through the garage. The candles go out.

In the almost total darkness, someone starts coughing, then wheezing, then gasping for air. There's a thud as someone falls hard on the cement floor.

"Philip? Anna, he's not breathing."

"We're out of here."

"We can't just leave him."

"He's dead, or will be. You want to explain this to our parents, to the police, to that bitch cop who took our magic?" No answer. "Let's go then. No one knows we were here. And it's not like anyone will miss him."

Brenda leaves. Anna moves to follow, then stops, turns, watches as Philip Howard struggles for life-giving breath. She smiles as a thought comes to mind and a prayer leaves her lips. An offer is made. The boy falls silent and she's gone.

***

"We're not talking to you," was the first thing Bianca heard when the girls walked into the principal's office.

"Philip Howard, where is he?"

"We don't know him."

"Is that true?" Bianca asked Brenda.

The girl almost answered but a glare from Anna shut her up.

"He knows you. Your names are in his journal," Bianca lied. "It told me everything but where."

"We don't have to stay here. We have rights."

"You have the right to silence. And if I find Philip dead you'll have the right to sit in juvie lockup until your parents come for you. If I call them."

"May we go?"

Bianca waved them away. "Go. When you get home maybe you can explain to your parents why detectives with search warrants ripped their homes apart today."

Before they left, Bianca dropped her card in each of their purses. Late that night someone called, giving an address. "Thank you, Brenda," Bianca said as the caller signed off.

***

Now the garage was brightly lit as crime scene investigators photographed, sketched and searched the area.

"Dust everything," Bianca ordered. "Those girls' prints have to be somewhere." To the M.E. "Cause of death?"

The Medical Examiner looked up, shrugged. "CO poisoning, smoke inhalation -- either way, accidental."

The crime scene tech came up to Bianca. "Leaving the scene, failure to report. Nothing you can bust her for, Bianca."

"I know. Joe, I've faced monsters, vampires and ghosts. So why do I feel this one teenager is going to be more trouble than any of them?"

***

That night in her bed, under an inverted cross she's hung on the wall, Anna sleeps. In her dreams there's a man. His skin is cold but his touch burns. In her dreams he does that which she's missed for so long, giving her the pleasure she's yet to experience in the flesh.

"So you were pleased with my offering?" she asks.

A Voice that once sang with angels replies. "The boy? He was mine already, but I thank you anyway. After all, it's the thought that counts."

A RARE MOMENT

Damon LeVaey looked out the window of the Inner Harbor condo and surveyed his kingdom. Soon all of Baltimore would his. His master had promised it to him. As Supreme Magus he would have the power of life and death over the pitiful fools who called the city home. Poor souls; poor damned, blind souls. They went about their mundane lives little realizing what sinister forces were at work, ignorant of the war being waged between dark and light.

The dark would win, of this LeVaey was certain. Those who fought for what they called "good" could hold out for only so long. They had to win every time and each of their victories only postponed the day of their inevitable defeat.

That day had been near, so very near. LeVaey had built his circle and had found the tome he needed to summon a creature to do his will. Then he was betrayed. That he could have dealt with, and the deaths the traitors would have suffered would have only enhanced his reputation and strengthened his power. But he never got the chance.

Those who had fled his coven and stolen his books met a different fate, fate in the form of a policewoman who, his sources told him, dared to stand against the dark in defense of the light. She was rumored to have fought monsters and banished demons and may have even destroyed one of the undead. LeVaey did not know how much of the rumor was fact, but he did know that she had killed his former followers and now had his books.

He sought her identity in a private ritual and she was revealed to him. His master, it seemed, had a special interest in this one and charged him with her destruction. His reward was to be great power and dominion over others.

In a dream induced by drugs and incense LeVaey was taken to the top of a large building. There all of Baltimore was spread out before him. From the shadows came the voice of one LeVaey dared not look upon.

"Do this for me and all will be yours. Bring her low and leave her broken body for the rats to gnaw upon and you will be rewarded with wealth, women, and power."

LeVaey agreed and when he awoke the woman's name was burned into his mind and there was a new mark on his hand. It looked like a burn and LeVaey know it for the sign of the infernal pact between him and his lord.

LeVaey put the word out among his followers and soon learned that this detective, this Bianca Jones, was also looking for him. She had been asking about him at various clubs that catered to the disciples of the dark. In one of those clubs someone had taken her picture.

The quality of the cell phone photo was poor, the lighting was dark and the woman was in disguise but still it was enough for LeVaey to mark her, to put a face on his quarry. Detective Bianca Jones. Such a little thing Detective Jones was to cause such trouble. LeVaey took comfort in the knowledge of how easily little things are crushed.

***

They left the club and ran towards the beach. This was the night, Donna realized, the night she lost it. She had somehow stayed a virgin through all of high school, but she was free of that now. It was senior week and time to get busy.

Long ago Donna had decided that she didn't care who got her cherry as long as he was cute and reasonably nice. She had also made up her mind that when the time came it would be on the beach at Ocean City.

She saw him at The Tidal Wave, an under-21 club off the Boardwalk at 31st Street. He had sandy blonde hair, not a bad build, and the kind of face she pictured when she heard the word cute. He said his name was Jason but she assumed he was lying, just as she had told him her name was Ann.

She made the first move, and they danced a few times, moving separately to the music until a slow song brought them together. He held her awkwardly and when she finally pressed against him she felt him grow hard against her thigh.

Jason backed off quickly, blushing and mumbling what might have been an apology. From this Donna assumed that he was probably no more experienced than she. She found that sweet and the thought of being his first appealed to her. She pulled him close and as they finished the dance suggested they go outside. Jason readily agreed.

They walked a few blocks on the Boardwalk. With Jason's arm around her, Donna scanned the beach looking for just the right spot. She also kept an eye out for the Beach Patrol. She didn't want her first time interrupted by a cop with a flashlight. She saw an outcropping of rocks down by 41st street that seemed just right --on the beach yet with the privacy needed for the perfect intimate moment. She slowed, pointed out the rocks to Jason and made her suggestion.

The boy's eyes widened as he stammered, "But, but, we hardly know each other."

"Exactly," came Donna's reply, "and when we're done let's keep it that way. You go your way, I go mine and we each leave with a sweet memory."

With hormones racing and not believing that it was actually, finally happening to him, Jason eagerly agreed and the young couple headed toward the rocks for a very special first time.

On a balcony with an oceanfront view sat a man with binoculars. He had been watching the same rocks to which Donna and Jason were walking. He had been watching them for three nights now, having reasoned that sooner or later a young couple would make use of them. He picked up a cell phone and speed-dialed the only number programmed into it.

"Now," was all he said before disconnecting, then watched again through his binoculars, wondering which one would be chosen. Not that it mattered, he reflected. Either one would do. All he needed was the body.

***

Tongues in each other's mouths, Donna and Jason inexpertly groped at each other. Shirts came off, then pants.

This is it, Donna thought. Watching Jason's face, she shifted slightly to peel off her panties.

At first she took his reaction for admiration or possibly amazement. Then Donna realized that he wasn't looking at her but rather past her, out at the water and the look of his face was one of terror. She turned and saw black, oily things coming towards them. She screamed but even had there been anyone to hear her, her cries would have been lost in the noise of the surf.

Donna felt herself pushed aside as Jason bravely put himself between her and the attacking creatures. One grabbed him then both headed back to the water.

Donna sat stunned for a few minutes, wondering if what she had just experienced had really happened. She looked down at the clothing in the sand, Jason's clothing, poor, brave Jason. Then horrible reality came rushing in and she ran screaming from the rocks toward the bright lights of the Boardwalk.

A naked teenager was not a rarity to Officer Joelson. Patrolling the Boardwalk he saw at least one a week. But the girl on the bench outside The Purple Parrot did not seem high or drunk and bore no signs of assault. As she sat there shaking in panties and a T-shirt someone had provided, she kept repeating that "black things" had taken her boyfriend. At first Joelson thought she was talking about African-Americans, but when he pressed her for a better description she shook her head. "No, not black men!" she cried. "Black things! Monsters!" She pointed to the ocean. "Monsters from there!"

Another crazy was Joelson's first thought as he again checked her for signs of drink or drugs. Then he remembered a roll call briefing from a few days ago and what had been found floating on Bayside. A cold shiver ran down his back and he knew without having to look that when he checked the rocks he'd find drag marks to the sea.

***

Bianca Jones reported to work on a Monday following the roughest week of her life. She was tired and looked it. She had flown back into Baltimore the Friday before and despite the weekend break had not rested at all. Her dreams, when she could sleep, were full of zombies, revenants, and other undead things that lurched through the night. And despite several showers, she imagined that she still smelled of fetid water and decaying flesh.

Major Chester Williams, chief of the Special Investigations Unit, was waiting for her.

"I see you survived the Big Easy."

Bianca dropped unceremoniously into the chair in front of William's desk. "Not many of us did. At the end it was just me, some of London's people, and two guys from Cincinnati. I ran out of shells for my Mossberg and was down to one clip for my nine. Some of the others didn't even have that and were just clubbing the zombies with empty guns. We almost didn't make it."

"But you did."

"Yes sir, somehow we did. We held them off just long enough for the big guns -- the magicians, the priests, the mambos and oungans -- to replace the charms and wards that Katrina washed away. New Orleans is safe once again, or at least until the next big storm. And when that hits and the army-built levees fail again you can damn well send someone else."

Williams shook his head. "That's the trouble, Detective, there's often no one else to send. Not many people are willing to risk their lives and more to fight an evil that most people believe exists only in horror fiction. That's why when your, shall we say, counterpart in New Orleans called for help we allowed you to go."

"Allowed? You mean I had a choice?"

"You still would have gone."

Silently Bianca agreed with her boss. Ever since she found out that there existed monsters and creatures that saw mankind as their prey and playthings she had been fighting against them. She hated her job but she had no choice but to do it. She was the only one who could. And to ignore evil was to allow it to triumph.

"If I bother writing up a report will you read it or just shred it?"

"This is the BPD, Detective, I'll read it, then forward it to the Commissioner. He'll read it and then I'll shred it. But there's no hurry. It can wait until you get back."

Bianca was suddenly alert. "When I get back from where?"

"How does Ocean City sound?"

"For some reason it doesn't sound like a vacation."

"It won't be." Williams took a case folder out of a desk drawer and passed it over to Bianca. "Young boy went missing a week ago, his body washed up Bayside two days ago."

Bianca looked at the autopsy photos. The boy, teenager really, had obviously been in the water a few days. Crabs and other aquatic scavengers had fed off his body. But he hadn't died by drowning, not judging from the deep knife wounds on his arms, torso and neck.

There were more pictures, close-ups of the boy's injuries and of ligature marks around his ankles. Behind these were two more sets, one of a young man a little older than the first, the other of a teenaged girl not much older than Bianca was when she made her first solo trip down the ocean. Both had wounds similar to the first except that the ligature marks on the second male were around his wrists

"Cause of death in all three cases was the same," Williams explained as Bianca studied the pictures. "Exsanguination. The first one and the girl from the neck; the other had his genitals cut off and bled out from there."

Bianca closed the case folder and shook her head. "Please tell me that this is the work of your usual, everyday, sexually obsessed but very human sadistic serial killer."

That's when Bianca learned of the black things than had come ashore and dragged Jason, the subject of the first set of photos she'd looked at, off the beach.

"And how did I get involved?"

"OCPD requested you." In answer to Bianca's obvious next question Williams added, "Word gets around, Detective. You're too valuable a resource to keep to ourselves."

"So now I'm the monster hunter for both Baltimore and the Delmarva peninsula?"

"And parts of Pennsylvania."

Sighing in resignation, Bianca laid back in her chair and closed her eyes. She was exhausted, physically and mentally tired to her soul. She had not had a decent rest in weeks and could not remember when she any serious downtime. Briefly she thought about how nice it would be if she could simply walk a post in the most violent, drugged plagued part of Baltimore. It would a welcomed break.

"Detective, detective, Bianca, are you okay?"

Williams's voice called her back from her unplanned rest. "Sorry, sir. Haven't had much sleep."

The chief waved it off. "We've all been there. Every week we take bets on who's going to nod off in Comstat."

Bianca again looked through the case folder. "I may need some help on this one."

"Whatever you need, Detective, whatever you need."

What she needed was Joe Russo. Joe was a criminalist and crime scene specialist with the BPD crime lab. She and Joe were close friends, though not as close as Joe would have liked. In New Orleans Bianca had found herself missing more than just his crime scene expertise and advice. Joe, Bianca had realized, wasn't the only one who wished they could be closer.

The chief had told her that she could have whatever she needed. And this case looked like there was a lot of forensic evidence to review. She'd have Joe detailed to Special Investigations, take him to Ocean City, and to hell with the inevitable gossip. They'd work the case and when it was closed take a few days to themselves. A little R&R would do them both good.

Bianca called Joe when she got back to her office. "Pack your bags," she told him, affecting her best Baltimorese accent, "cause we're going downy oshun, hon."

"What?"

"You and me, Joe," she said in her regular voice, "we are going to Ocean City for an indefinite period of time."

"That's what I thought you said, but why?"

There was confusion mixed with disbelief, happiness, and no little anticipation in Joe's question. As much she hated to, Bianca had to bring him down to earth. She needed him to focus on the case at hand instead of being distracted by her.

"Don't get your hopes up, Russo, or anything else for that matter. This one's business so pack your camera and crime scene bag along with your swimsuit and sunscreen. I'll pick you up at your place tomorrow morning and brief you on the way down. Plan on several days' stay."

The next day Bianca drove east on Route 50 towards Maryland's Eastern Shore with Joe riding shotgun. On the way he reviewed the case folder provided by the OCPD.

"The two with their throats cut were hung upside down going by the rope marks on their ankles. The other one had the same kind of marks on his wrists. He was right side up when they mutilated him."

"Any forensics from the bodies?"

"Let's see, silt that matches the area they were found. I suspect that it would match just about any place Bayside. Nothing under the nails, no foreign body fluids or DNA. No signs of sexual assault or trauma other than the obvious."

"So nothing to tell us who or what killed them."

"Just the description from our only witness -- two large black things that dragged her Jason off."

"Is that it, Joe?"

"Investigators got more out of her later, in bits and pieces. She went into hysterics early on and never quite came out of them. From what the detectives were able to put together, Jason was taken by two man-shaped creatures with large eyes and shiny black skin. Crime scene photos show a scuffle near some rocks then drag marks to the water."

"What does that sound like?"

Joe thought a minute, reviewing what he knew of Bianca's involvement with the supernatural and extra-normal. She'd gone up against vampires, shape-changers, and living nightmares. Then he thought about the books he had read on those same subjects, books that only a short time ago he would have passed off as fiction.

"Could be disciples of Dagon or those things from Innsmouth."

"Joe, you're thinking zebras instead of horses."

"What do you mean … oh, right." He sat back embarrassed. He was supposed to be the scientist, the rational one. "Just the same," he said, "There was seaweed recovered from the scene. I'm going to have it examined to make sure it's indigenous to the area."

"And if it's not?"

"Then I'm sending it to Arkham University for further analysis. Sometimes it is zebras."

"You know what a zebra is, Joe?"

"What?"

"The largest size a girl can buy."

And that got them talking about things other than crime until they crossed the bridge over Assawoman Bay.

Ocean City is Maryland's only seacoast. It is an ocean resort town about eleven miles long and a mile wide extending from the southern tip of Delaware, with the Chincoteague Bay on one side and the Atlantic Ocean on the other. It's been Baltimore's favorite vacation spot since its founding in 1870.

Modern Day Ocean City is one long line of motels, hotels, condos, souvenir shops, restaurants, and miniature golf courses. On any given block of the world famous Boardwalk one can buy beach toys, fried foods, or T-shirts with your choice of tacky or sexually suggestive phrases printed on the front. Adults love it for the beach and the bars, kids for the rides and arcades, and teens for the sense of freedom and license in the air.

And it was in this family vacation getaway that something evil was lurking, preying on its visitors, taking them in the night, cutting them open and draining their blood.

Bianca had made reservations at The Barbary Coast, a mid-priced motel location on Coastal Highway near the Convention Center. Despite the name, the décor had nothing to do with either North Africa or San Francisco in the late 1800s. It had instead a piratical theme loosely based on a series of popular movies.

Joe was disappointed as soon as they checked in.

"Separate rooms?"

"What did you expect?" Bianca asked in her most business-like tone. Then she added, "Of course there is a connecting door. I figure we can work in one and sleep in the other."

"That's more like it," Joe said with a smile. The smile faded when they got to the rooms. There were two double beds in each.

"That bed's yours," Bianca pointing to the one closest to the window and throwing her suitcase on the one near the door. "Now let's get settled and start working on who killed these kids."

By mid-afternoon Joe had both beds in what they were calling the workroom covered with documents sorted by victim, autopsy reports, lab results and crime scene photos. After arranging things in chronological order he began to study all of them in the hopes that a new line of investigation would come to mind.

Bianca had disappeared. After unpacking she announced, "I have a meeting with the OCPD and then I'm going shopping," then added, "I'll bring back lunch." With that she was gone

"Here I thought," Joe said to no one in particular, "that going to OC with a good looking woman and not leaving the room would be a good thing." He went back to reading reports.

An hour later Joe heard the door to the other room open and close. Hoping it was Bianca and not some creature in black who had somehow managed to track them down he cautiously looked around the connecting door. It was his partner, loaded down with bags. Some were from boutiques or clothing stores. Others, judging from the smells that suddenly filled the room, contained his long awaited lunch. When Bianca produced sandwiches from Bull on the Beach and French fries from Thrashers he decided to forgive her for leaving him alone.

"How did the shopping go?" Joe asked between bites of a pit beef sandwich.

"Good," Bianca mumbled, her mouth full of a London Jack she'd bought herself from The Dough Roller. "I got all of what I'm going to need."

"A new bikini?"

Bianca gave Joe the smile that women use to answer that kind of question, the one that says, "Maybe" and "You wish" and "You might just get to find out." She followed it up by saying, "Mostly disguises. I'm going out tonight -- alone."

"Disguised as what?"

"You'll see."

That evening he did.

They went to eat at a 24-hour pancake house, "There's nothing like breakfast for dinner," Bianca had told him, then went straight back to their rooms where Bianca vanished into the bathroom for what seemed like forever. Joe had put the reports aside, there would be time enough for them later that night, and was watching cartoons on cable when Bianca emerged.

"Well, what do you think?"

Joe's mouth fell open. The detective he worked closely with, the woman he had grown to care about and was starting to love, was gone. In her place was what looked like a seventeen-year-old girl.

Bianca's normally dark hair was frosted with blond tips. She was heavily made-up, like a young girl would be if she were trying to look older. She was wearing hip-hugging jeans selectively torn in all the right places and tight enough as to leave little to the imagination. Above these a tattoo of an inverted pentagram encircled her navel. She completed her outfit with a sleeveless belly shirt on the front of which was printed "Future MILF."

"I'd love to." As that thought raced though Joe's mind he realized he couldn't picture her as a mother.

"Wh-why the get up?"

"The victims were all under twenty-one. I'm going to hit the kiddie clubs the next few nights and I have to look the part. I'll see if I can get a line on alternative night spots, ones with, shall we say, a darker theme."

"If I didn't know you would certainly fool me." Joe meant it. If anyone in the BPD could pass as a teen it was Bianca. Her small size, slim build and youthful appearance made her perfect for the roll.

"Do you think the shirt's all right?" she asked him. "I have one in black that says 'Witch in Training.'"

"Considering why we're here," Joe said as Bianca dug through a shopping bag, "that one might be better, especially with your tattoo. Is that, er …"

"It's henna, it will wear off." Bianca came up with the other shirt and studied it. Then she nodded, took off the one she was wearing and put the black one on, giving Joe a brief glimpse of the red padded bra she was wearing.

Seemingly unconcerned that she'd given Joe a flash Bianca studied her look in a mirror. "You're right, that is better." She fixed a make-up smudge and grabbed a small purse.

"I'm out of here. I have my cell but don't call unless another body washes up or those 'monsters' grab another kid." With a "Don't wait up" she was gone.

Joe tried to get back to work but found it hard to concentrate. Bianca as a teen, Bianca in a bra. He knew he would not sleep well that night, especially with her in the next bed over.

***

I should have come here sooner, Damon LeVaey thought as he looked out at the ocean. So many young people on their own for the first time, alone, adrift, looking for the next good time, searching for the new, the different and the thrilling. How easy it was to lead them down the dark road.

Like the two in the bed he had just left. They had done things tonight they had never dreamt of, especially the boy. LeVaey smiled, thinking of how his cries of pain had turned to whimpers of pleasure.

Pleasure was what it was all about. "Do what thou whilt." What other creed was needed? Pleasure in this world and power in the next. How could anyone resist what his master offered?

The thought of his master reminded LeVaey why he was in an overpriced condo on the Atlantic Coast and he wondered where Bianca Jones was. She was here in this city, of course. There were monsters killing children, where else would she be? Stopping them was what she did, who she was.

His followers were waiting and watching in all the right places, places she had to visit. They had her picture and sooner or later he would get the call that she had been found. Then LeVaey could do that which would please his master. Until then, LeVaey thought, he would please himself.

He went back to the two young people in the bedroom.

***

The boy Jason had last been seen at the Tidal Wave, so Bianca decided to start with that under-21 club. As she walked down Coastal Highway toward it, Bianca realized that the mental and physical fatigue she'd been feeling was mostly gone. This assignment was what she had needed. Away from the city, breathing fresh sea air, working with Joe, teasing him a bit -- okay, more than a bit. And she was doing police work. While it might lead to something more at the end, something dark and evil, right now it was pure procedure. Search for the crime scene, look for suspects, develop and follow the leads. And when it was over, with her and Joe still in Ocean City, who knew what would happen next.

Bianca knew what she wanted to happen, and she was sure that Joe did as well, but she had a secret, something dark and evil of her own. Something she had almost loosed in New Orleans when it looked like the undead would overwhelm the last of her small army. Joe needed to be told about that. Before they spent their first night together, Joe needed to know.

Bianca put that thought aside for later. She was close to the Tidal Wave and could already hear the pulse pounding music every time its doors opened. She made one last check. She knew she looked the part and had her fake ID at the ready as she prepared to enter a club filled with young people most of whose thoughts were to party, enjoy themselves and maybe get lucky. It was up to her to find the ones with other motives.

Her ID passed inspection. There are worse places I could be, she thought as a blast of dance music hit her. She looked around for a likely partner and reminded herself that this was supposed to be work.

***

She returned sometime after midnight to find that Joe had fallen asleep watching a movie. He woke up at her touch.

"How did it go?" he asked.

Bianca shook her head. "I have never been grabbed, groped, and felt up more in my life. And since when did 'slow dance' mean grinding yourself into your partner?"

"Well, teenage boys are like that."

"It wasn't just the boys."

Joe was suddenly torn between not wanting to hear anymore and dying to know everything that had happened. Rather than say the wrong thing he changed the subject.

"Any leads come out of your ordeal?"

"A few propositions, several cell numbers, invitations to a rave, and a hotel key card. A guy and his girl did stop to read my shirt while checking out my boobs. Then their eyes stopped at my pentagram on their way to my crotch."

"And?" Joe asked, doing his best to keep his eyes from drifting to those areas mentioned.

"He asked if I 'followed the dark lord' and she wanted to know if I was 'in a circle.' I dropped LeVaey's name and their eyes widened."

"You think he's involved?" Bianca gave him a vague nod. "You've been after him haven't you? That's a lucky break."

"Yeah, it could be luck, maybe. Anyway, before they left they suggested I meet them tomorrow night at some place called the 'Black Cat.' It's near here off the Boardwalk. I told them I might and as they left I heard her ask him if they should bring me to the house."

"What house?"

"That they didn't say. But it's a start."

***

LeVaey's followers began to call in. Jones had been spotted. She had been seen dancing at the Tidal Wave, drinking at the Purple Parrot and shopping at the Inlet -- all at the same time. She was also said to have been at three other clubs and four different bars sometime during the night. Two men and a woman even reported "close contact." One insisted she was asleep in his bed.

He wanted to know if he should sacrifice her right away or wait until LeVaey came over.

Damn fool! To think that he could actually seduce the woman. Or maybe she seduced him, to get close to his circle. Not likely but possible.

LeVaey decided not to take chances. "Kill her," he said. "Slit her throat and paint the walls with her blood."

To his follower's eager "Yes, Master," LeVaey added, "Kill yourself as well. The bitch will need someone to escort her to Hell."

This time the "Yes, Master" was far less enthusiastic. LeVaey wondered if the fool would actually do it. Without a doubt he would kill the woman, but would he take the next step? Doubtful. No matter, one body or two, if found in time it would give the police one more thing to think about.

LeVaey knew that one or two of the Jones sightings could have been genuine. It didn't matter which of them it was. All of his followers had been given the same instructions, all would have said the same thing, let slip just enough. Soon the final snare would be laid.

***

The Black Cat was a Goth club, full of teens and young adults for whom daytime was something to be endured and slept through until the sun went down and they could feel alive again. The band on stage called themselves "Zombie Boogaloo," dressed like rejected extras from a Romero movie, and played self-written songs they called "Undead Rock." They were not very good and most of the patrons ignored them.

Dressed entirely in black, Bianca had done little to disguise herself. She remembered the last time she had been in such a place. It was a club much like this one. That night had not gone well. Like now, she had been looking for a lead on Damon LeVaey. She had instead encountered his master. She stole a soul from him but had lost others and made an infernal enemy.

Trying very hard not to listen to the music, Bianca was thinking of that encounter and considering certain possibilities when she was joined by her friends of the previous night. She pretended to be surprised.

"Staven, Mordica, good to see you again." Bianca motioned them to join her at the too small for three people table.

"What do you think of the band?" Staven asked her.

"If there is music in Hell, they should play there."

"It is torturous, isn't?" agreed Mordica, putting her arm around Bianca, who shifted to keep the girl's hand off her breast.

They listened a few more minutes then Bianca said, "Isn't there someplace better then this?"

Staven reached under the table and began to caressing Bianca's inner thigh. "Are you truly one of us?"

Bianca squeezed his hand, seemingly in interest but really to keep it from going higher. "I've ridden the Goat, and been ridden by him. I have the mark. Were we closer, you would see it -- eventually."

Staven and Mordica looked at each other, as if they were coming to a silent agreement. Finally she said, "Tomorrow night, there's this house on St. Louis Avenue …"

Bianca sat through one more set, a hellishly awful heavy metal cover of Sympathy for the Devil, then left. As soon as she did, Staven took out his cell phone and made a call.

***

Soon, thought LeVaey, it will be over. He made his calls, laid his plans and made his preparations. Tonight, one way or the other Bianca Jones will be destroyed and the Master pleased. LeVaey thought about what power and privilege would be his once the job was done and smiled.

***

One way or the other, Bianca Jones thought, by tomorrow it should all be over. Again she reviewed her plan. She didn't like it, but saw no other choice. For the third time she checked her guns. They were ready, oiled and ready for the night. Looking at the cold pieces of metal on the desk before her, flashes of Federal Hill and New Orleans came back to her. Why, she wondered, does it so often come down to this? She was a cop. She should be arresting people, not killing them. But what is jail to a monster, human or otherwise? How can prison intimidate those who look forward to Hell? And why is it that too often the only answer is to send them where they want to go?

Bianca heard Joe in the other room, getting things in order, gathering reports, but mainly staying out of her way, giving her time to prepare for the night. She longed to go to him, pull him down on the bed and let their passions take over. But it was not the time. If things went bad she would rather he miss her as a friend than mourn her as a lover.

It was time to go. She gave Joe final instructions, said her goodbye with a light kiss on his lips.

"Be careful," he told her. It was killing him, staying behind. He had offered to go with her, but Joe was a civilian, a noncombatant, an innocent. Bianca was determined to keep it that way.

"I will," she assured him.

"Remember what I said, this could be a trap."

Bianca smiled and was gone.

Walking south down Coastal Highway hoping to pick up a bus down to the 20's, Bianca thought about Joe's last words.

"Joe," she said to herself, "it always was a trap."

And a well-laid one she had to admit. The first two bodies could have been anything. The witnessed abduction of the second boy by what were probably men in wetsuits, that was a nice touch, one clearly designed to draw attention to what was going on and to bring her in on the case. And she had discovered the St. Louis location far too quickly, as if she were being led. A lamb to the slaughter, a sacrifice come willingly. Of course it was a trap, but one that could spring both ways.

She had to walk into it; there was no question about that. The water had done its job on the bodies, there was no physical evidence tying anyone to the murders. Only accomplice testimony or a direct admission would get LeVaey into court. As a detective it was her duty to do whatever she had to bring him to justice.

LeVaey was no doubt counting on that. But he probably had not considered what else comes with being a cop.

She picked up a tail just as she was getting on the bus. Bianca spotted him right away. He was young and not very good. She sat in the back. He took a seat on a front side bench and kept looking back her way. Bianca pretended not to notice him, looking out the window instead and counting the streets until her stop.

Bianca got off at 20th St, walked west to St. Louis then backtracked to the address she'd be given at the Black Cat. She approached slowly, looking for the watchers she knew were hiding in the darkness. There were probably four or five, maybe as many as a dozen. She imagined their red eyes checking her out, anticipating the night's activities, waiting for the signal to pounce.

Staven was waiting for her at the door.

"Detective Jones, we've been expecting you."

That confirmed the trap. I could back out now, Bianca thought, bring an end to it. But that was not how this game was played.

She stopped expecting a search, Staven's roaming over her body, relieving her of her guns, but instead he just opened and held the door for her.

"Enter freely and of your own will."

Bianca stepped inside.

The first floor had been gutted to form a large meeting place. About twenty young people, most of them in their teens, stood in a half-circle facing her. Before them was a man in red robes in back of a low table. Damon LeVaey no doubt.

Bianca was struck by how young LeVaey looked -- late twenties, early thirties at a stretch. He didn't have the years on him she had expected. He was tall and blonde, somewhat well built and good looking. Even at first glance Bianca could see why impressionable minds seeking a different way would follow him.

Bianca thought about her gun but knew that the crowd would be on her before she could draw. A door slammed. Staven came up behind her and held her tight.

"Good evening, Detective Jones." LeVaey's voice was mild and pleasant and had the tone of one quite pleased with himself. "So good of you to join us on this special night." He reached behind her, found and removed her pistol. "Tonight you will have the honor of being sacrificed to our lord Lucifer. At His request I designed a special ceremony just for you." He stepped in close to her. "It's quite lengthy and very painful. But there's some pleasure in it as well." His hand cupped and squeezed her breast. "For us at least. I'll be going first, but all will have a turn and after your body has been used up your soul will be sent to Hell."

As LeVaey continued to grope her, Bianca's dark secret began to stir. She pushed it back down and resisted the urge to break Staven's hold and both his arms. There was no need, not now. She was close, just one thing more.

"I've been looking for you for some time now, LeVaey. A word in some of the wrong places was all that was needed. You didn't have to kill three people."

"But it would not have been as much fun, and this way I was sure to have your complete interest."

Confession was good for the soul and even better for the prosecution's case. It was over.

"This ends now," Bianca said, loud enough for the small microphone sewn into her jacket to pick up.

The lights went out. Aided by surprise, Bianca kicked back and broke free of Staven. Falling to the floor, she swept her leg outward, hoping to drop LeVaey.

Doors and windows exploded inward and into the hall rushed members of the State Police Special Weapons Team, closely followed by Ocean City officers. All were wearing night vision goggles and the sound of the struggles in the dark as the cult members were rounded up was music to Bianca's ears.

As soon as the house was secured the lights came back on. Bianca stood to find all of her would be assailants sitting on the floor, their wrists secured with plastic cuffs. She quickly scanned the group. LeVaey was missing.

As she was about to ask "Where's the one in the red robes?" an OCPD officer led LeVaey in through the front door.

"This one made it as far as the front porch," the cop said. He marched

LeVaey over to Bianca. "We heard what he said he was going to do to you. If you want some 'private time' with him we got stairs back at the barracks we can say he fell down."

Bianca declined the offer. "No thanks, this one's going to suffer enough, both in this world and the next. His boss doesn't like failures." To LeVaey she said, "It was a good plan, and might have worked with some people. But you forgot that I'm a cop and we never work alone."

****

Alone in a cell in the State Police barracks in Berlin Maryland, Damon LeVaey laid on a cot and considered his fate. That bitch Jones had been right; his master was not one to condone failure. As he started to think of ways by which he could appease his lord, the shadows in his cell spoke to him. The silent conversation was brief and one-sided. When it was over, LeVaey understood that whatever he suffered in this world for his crimes, the price of his failure in the next would be much worse.

And before it faded away, the voice added "And lest you think otherwise …"

The screams from LeVaey's cell lasted all night and into the afternoon.

****

To celebrate the closing of the case, Bianca took Joe to dinner at Dumser's Dairyland on 124th Street. It was everything Bianca wanted for the occasion -- a family atmosphere, good simple food and plenty of it, and high backed booth for much needed privacy.

"I just wish I could have been more help to you," Joe said after Bianca finished telling him about the St. Louis Avenue raid.

"You were there if I needed you, Joe. Knowing that helped a lot."

"Yeah, but the way it played out you never needed me at all."

"Not yet."

"What do you mean?" The look Bianca gave him said it all. "Oh! You mean …?"

"If you want to?"

"Why wouldn't I?"

Bianca then told Joe of her dark secret, the creature of nightmare she had inside her.

"The girl on Brewer's Hill, the one you called me in on. It killed her, Joe, and would have kept on killing unless stopped, and this was the only way. It's under control, but one day I may have no choice but to set it free, and God help us all if I do."

"Then I better stick around to make sure things never get that bad."

"You're sure?"

"Bianca, I …"

Gently, Bianca put her hand to his lips, stopping what she knew he was about to say. "Tonight, Joe, save it for tonight."

He did. That night, when she came to him, he told her of his feelings, his hopes and his dreams and how much of a part she played in all of them. In turn, she told him how he was her one bright spot in a world of shadows and for that she would always love him.

It was early morning when Bianca awoke, Joe still asleep beside her. She thought about waking him but decided against it. Instead she laid back in a darkness that was, for once, comforting rather than threatening and savored a rare moment of happiness and peace.

SOUL SEARCH

There was a monster inside her, an ancient thing formed when creation began. Sometimes late at night, when her defenses were down, she felt it aching, begging to be released. It had to beg, it could never free itself. It was a part of her and she had control over it.

Bianca Jones knew that one day she would have to free the beast. Probably when her back was to the wall and the price of failure was not just her life but also the death of those she loved and the destruction of all she held dear. Only then would she free it and pray she had chosen the lesser of evils.

That was she why she had accepted the monster. It was the price of the lives of some foolish young girls and the soul of an unborn child. And all it cost was a small piece of herself, a place inside of her for the monster to live and wait.

Tonight, it was awake. Bianca was inside an old church, one whose congregation had grown from a handful of worshippers to a standing room only Sunday crowd. But over the years the crowd had slowly shrunk until finally the diocese closed its doors and scattered the remaining faithful among other parishes. Now it was an empty shell -- pews broken, altar shattered and stained glass replaced with plywood.

Not that it wasn't being used. Worshippers of a different sort were there, intent on profaning what holiness still remained. To this end they had an innocent woman tied to what was left of the altar. They intended to sacrifice her to their dark purposes, first carnally then physically. Over her lifeless body they would drink her blood in hopes that this communion would win them favor with their god.

Bianca Jones was there to stop them. A detective in the Special Investigations Unit of the Baltimore Police Department, her job was to investigate anything having to do with the occult or supernatural. When the threats were real she was authorized to do whatever it took to contain them.

Bianca had heard whispers of a Black Mass in the making. Investigation led her to the church just in time to watch the cultists file in. Thirteen in all entered the church, the last two carrying a large, bulky duffel bag. Bianca thought that the bag probably contained vestments and needed items of worship until she noticed that something inside the bag was struggling.

That changed things. Bianca had thought merely to observe the night's proceedings to determine the level of threat these people offered. She adjusted her plans and slipped into the church after the last two entered.

Hiding in the shadows of the darkened vestibule, it pained Bianca to watch the coven's victim pulled from the bag, stripped and lashed to the broken altar.

She had worked sex offense for five years and knew the horror and trauma the woman was suffering. But she could not yet intervene. She needed time, time she may not have, before she could act. She'd wait; wait until the victim was in even more danger before she acted.

"You don't have to," said a voice from a small piece of herself. "You have the power, use it, use me. Destroy them and save the girl."

"Shut the hell up," Bianca told it, checked her watch and looked towards the altar. The person posing as the priest was chanting in something that might be Latin. If so, it was not the language she had learned in school. This was corrupt and profane and she loved every minute of it, for as long as it was spoken the woman on the altar was safe.

The chanting stopped. The cultists dropped their robes. All stood naked, the men erect, the women with strap-on devices. All planned to participate in the sacrifice and lined up accordingly, the priest in the lead.

No time left. Ignoring the voice that reminded her how easy it could be, how much these rapists deserved to die, Bianca drew her pistol.

"Police," she shouted, still in shadow. "Don't move."

The victim on the altar forgotten, some of the coven backed away. All but one of the men lost his erection. That was the priest, who turned towards the sound of Bianca's voice.

"And if we don't, officer. What if we continue our worship?"

"Then I will kill you."

"Then I will die." To his flock the priest said, "Form a shield, protect me while I complete the ritual and remember, if you die for Satan, you will live with Satan and be rewarded by him."

The cult members gathered in front of the altar, protecting their priest. Great, she thought, true believers. She had just resigned herself to sending a few of them to their infernal reward when her cell phone vibrated. Finally.

"Your unholiness," she shouted, "time's up."

Bianca dove for cover as the plywood-covered windows exploded inward. Flash-bang grenades were thrown in, followed by black-clad members of the BPD Quick Response Team. The disoriented devil worshippers were quickly taken into custody by the QRT officers.

Clad again in their robes, the handcuffed cult members were led to waiting patrol wagons.

"As always, Sergeant Greggs, thanks for the help."

The head of the QRT took Bianca's outstretched hand. "Glad to help, detective. At least this time you caught some live ones."

"Yeah, the dead just aren't any fun."

"Not when they don't fall down when you shoot them."

A wagon man came over. "What are we doing with this bunch, detective?"

"Take them to Central Booking. Charge the lot with burglary, abduction, sexual assault and attempted rape. I'll get working on the statements of charges when I get back to HQ and send them over as soon as possible."

***

"I thought busting rapists was my job now."

Bianca had just finished sending the last of the charging documents. She looked up to see Earl Beasley standing in her doorway.

"What are you doing here, Earl? I thought you sex offense detectives only worked daylight."

"Yeah, right. Lately I feel like one of those undead you keep chasing. I haven't seen the sun in nearly a week. We've been after the Park Ave Peeper, the perv who's been bothering all those nice rich people in Bolton Hill. Finally caught him after four days of patrol and stakeouts. So how's it with you?"

Bianca told him about busting the coven, then added, "It wanted out tonight."

Beasley nodded, he knew about the monster and how she'd acquired it. "Ignore it. It's just a small, annoying voice."

"Speaking of which, how's your boss?"

"Moran? He's okay." Beasley held up a hand. "I know, he didn't like you and you hated him. But I knew him when he was a rookie. I got dirt on him and the pictures to prove it."

"I wondered how you got into Sex Offense so easy after being booted out of Homicide."

"I asked for that transfer and you know it. You were there. In fact, you were the reason. Anyway, Moran leaves me alone and I clear cases for him. Perfect arrangement."

"It suits you, Earl."

It did. Beasley had been an average homicide detective, one whose clearance rate was barely good enough to keep him in the unit. His success working sex crimes had surprised everyone, including himself.

"Actually, little girl, it's your monster I came to talk about." Seeing her surprise, he added, "Your other one I mean, the young one." He laid a case file on her desk. Bianca read the name.

ANNA BURGESS

"Shit."

"Thought that would cheer you up."

Anna Burgess was the reason Bianca had accepted the monster, one of them at least. At a sleepover Anna and some friends had played with the occult, the game getting out of hand and leading to the monster invading their dreams and their bodies. One girl died. Bianca saved the rest at the cost of a little piece of her soul.

But some people will not be saved. Anna had come to crave the power, the thrill of the forbidden. Another young person died, this time in a failed attempt to raise a demon. Again Anna was involved but the death was ruled accidental and there was little Bianca could do.

"What's the little bitch done now?"

"Bianca, please. We're talking about a child here, a sweet innocent barely in her teens who deserves our love and protection."

"What's the little bitch done now?"

"Went and got herself knocked up. Parents called it in as soon as she started to show. We were handling it as statutory case."

"Were handling it, Earl? Who did the father turn out to be, one of her classmates who talked his way into her pants?"

Beasley shook his head. "Miss Burgess wouldn't give him up. We decided to wait until the child was born. Then we'd get the court order for the kid's DNA and run what we had through the system."

"Right, standard procedure. What went wrong?"

Beasley tried to look offended. "Who says something went wrong?"

"You're here, talking to me about a routine case. A routine case for which you just happen to have the case folder. The case folder that I suspect you're planning to leave on my desk. So tell me, Earl, what went wrong?"

"She's not pregnant anymore."

"What happened? Abortion, miscarriage, stillbirth?"

"None of the above. One day she's bulging out at five, six months; the next she's got her youthful figure back. And ..." Beasley took a breath, a deep one. "... we had a doctor examine her, one who didn't know her medical history. There's no indication that she was ever pregnant. In fact, there's no sign that she was ever sexually active. She's still a virgin, physically at least."

Having delivered his news, Beasley stood and watched the young woman behind the desk take in what he'd told her. She seemed so small to him, almost a child herself. He had once been fooled by her, dismissing her as a real cop because of her small size and slender frame. That was before he knew what horrors she faced, what terrors she confronted to protect the city from the things that lurked on the other side of reality.

"Oh, Anna," Bianca said as she picked up the case file, "what have you done and with whom, or what, having you been doing it?"

"Well, little girl, you can ask her that yourself. She wants to talk to you."

***

Given its probable nature, it was decided that Bianca's conversation with Anna should not be held in her home. With Beasley talking to her parents in one interview room of the Sex Offense Unit, Bianca met with Anna in another.

"I want my baby back."

A simple demand, one Bianca had heard before. But never was it said with such hatred and contempt toward her. The detective ignored the teen's attitude.

"What baby? The doctor says you were never pregnant, never even had sex, how could you have a baby?"

"You know how, bitch. It's your fault. If you hadn't stopped the magic the first time …"

"You'd be dead, Anna, just like Anita."

"Anita was weak, she couldn't handle it."

"Handle what," Bianca asked calmly, "being raped in your dreams?"

"It wasn't rape, I enjoyed it."

"Did you now? Is that why you talked Philip Howard into the ritual that killed him?"

"That was Fat Philip's idea. I just …"

The girl went suddenly quiet, as some suspects do when they realize they've said too much.

"Just what, Anna? Killed him?" No reaction from the girl. "Left him to die?" Again, no reaction. Something happened, Bianca knew that. She let it go, changed direction.

"You claim you were pregnant, that your child was taken. By whom and how? Or maybe you sold your child, sold it to something to get the magic back?"

"NO!"

Anna stood as she cried out. "That wasn't the deal. I offered Him Fat Philip. The geek was dying anyway. I offered him up and that night He came to me, came as often as I wanted Him."

"You traded a soul for cheap sex," Bianca goaded.

"It was better that that, it was magic. He told me I could have anything I wanted, but all I wanted was Him."

"And the child?"

"That was His idea. He gave me a baby, said it was finally His turn."

"His turn for what?"

"A virgin birth, of course."

That told Bianca who the father was and where the child could be found.

***

"Ghost child, no more real then the Devil himself." That's what Beasley said when Bianca told him what she had learned. Then he added, "Anyway, it's not our worry anymore. Last time I checked, Hell is outside our jurisdiction, unless you want to count certain parts of the Eastern District."

But Beasley was wrong. The Devil was real. Bianca had met him, tricked him, even kicked him in the balls. And as far as jurisdiction, the crime had occurred in the city, hadn't it? That made it theirs.

"So what are you going to do about it?" Bianca asked herself once she was back in her office. It was late. Everyone else in Special Investigations had gone home or was out on the street, leaving Bianca alone with her thoughts.

There was a child out there, taken from its mother. Under normal circumstances that would not be a problem. The child was at best half-human, its father demonic. Did that make its newborn soul less innocent, less worthy of protection? Did it have a soul? If so, was it in Hell with its father?

Hell, that was the real problem, Bianca admitted. Getting to Hell was easy; people send themselves there every day. It was the getting back that was the problem. Orpheus was said to have done it, so had Rugglesby.

But even if she could do it, should she? It was not just her life at stake but her soul. Was this child's soul worth so much more than hers that she should risk eternal torment?

It did not take her long to decide.

On the way home she kept telling herself that she had made the right choice; that sometimes there was nothing to be done, that the risk was too great, that her soul was as important as the child's. She was still telling herself these things as she readied herself for bed.

That night she dreamt of innocents in Hell. Hundreds then thousands of pure white souls behind burning metal gates, all begging for a release that only she could give. She stood before a gate, a key in her hand. She looked at it, then at all those suffering because of her. She turned from them and let the key fall to the ground as she walked away.

Morning brought no relief. There was still a sense of guilt, of having abandoned someone in need of help.

"That will pass with the dreams," Bianca told herself. She knew she'd suffer them for a week or two, until another crisis occurred with its own set of worries. In the meantime she'd have to endure. "Damned if I don't, really damned if I do."

The thought of the child stayed with her. "Surely Heaven will not permit an innocent in Hell. Something will be done."

"And what if you are meant to be that something?" asked the part of her still not convinced.

"But why should Heaven care?" the small voice continued. "The child is part demon. It belongs in Hell."

Maybe it did, maybe it was meant to be with its father.

"And why would that be?" asked the small voice. "Why would the Devil need a child?"

Bianca then remembered what Anna had told her. It was not just a child but the child of a virgin. A special child, to be raised in Hell and then, what? Returned to do its father's bidding? And that would be -- nothing good for this world, Bianca was sure.

That changed the odds. No more doubt, no more guilt. Bianca knew what had to be done.

"I hope The Love Zone sells asbestos bras," Bianca said to herself as she prepared for a trip to Hell.

When she got to police headquarters, Beasley was waiting in her office, a cup of coffee in his hand. He picked another cup off Bianca's desk and handed it to her.

"When do we leave?"

"Leave for where, Earl?"

"You're going after the kid. I knew that last night even if you didn't."

"Then you have more faith in me than I do. Look, Earl, if I don't get back, tell Joe and Morgan what happened. I'd tell them myself but they'd try to talk me out of it."

"Tell them yourself, Little Girl, cause I'm going with you."

"Like hell you are."

Beasley smiled. "You got that right. Listen, this is my case, so I got the right. And only a dumb cop walks into a bad situation without back-up. You ain't no dumb cop. I'm going, end of story."

"This is more than just a bad situation, Earl. This is Hell itself."

Beasley shrugged. "Over the years enough people have told me to go there. Time they got their wish. But I have to tell you, I find it hard to believe that there's really a Devil. I mean, I know there's 'Evil' with the big 'E,' we've faced that often enough, but Satan, never thought he existed."

"He's real, Earl," she said, taking a sip of coffee. It was strong and bitter. "I've met him. He doesn't like me."

Beasley nodded, looked down at his empty cup, thought about getting a refill and longed for the old days when it was okay to add a little something extra to the brew.

"I didn't think he liked any of us."

"He doesn't. He wants us all to suffer as he does. But I stole a soul from him; he doesn't like me a little bit more than the rest."

"So this might all be a plan to get you on his turf. Ever think of that?"

"Doesn't matter. I'm still going."

"We're still going, little girl. Just one thing, how do we get there?"

***

Bianca spent the rest of that week trying to answer that question. She read through copies of ancient tomes and grimoires that were old when Columbus set sail. She talked to those who might be considered experts in demons and devils. Finally, she consulted one who business it was to know about the afterlife.

Father Anton Lawrence was an agent for the Vatican's Office of Holy Orders, formerly the Inquisition. As such, he had confronted Evil in all its faces, fought it in its legion of forms. He was not pleased when Bianca told him what she planned to do.

"You both are putting your souls at risk."

"There's already one at risk, we're trying to save it."

"It is demonkind, best to leave it where it is."

"It's also part human, with one foot in this world. You would rather have it raised in Hell only to return and raise Hell on Earth?"

"If that happens, Miss Jones, we will deal with it and trust that Right will prevail."

"That's like saying we should allow a disease to become an epidemic and trust that the vaccine will work. The way to treat a disease is to stop it before it spreads."

Father Lawrence considered her words. He had had dealings with Bianca before, knew that there was little he could say to dissuade her.

"The way will not be easy," he finally said. "There will be danger and temptation. And should you reach the infernal city, you must still deal with the Enemy. That will be the greatest risk. Beware of whatever he offers, for he is the arch deceiver. And should you succeed, should you somehow free the child from Hell, consider this. Even if it is raised in the Faith, it may still chose to follow its father's path. What then?"

Rather than give an answer they both knew, Bianca said, "He or she will have the same choice as any of us -- good or evil, right or wrong. But let's make sure it has the choice."

Father Lawrence shook his head. "You are determined then?"

"Yes, I am. So tell me, how do I get to Hell?"

"You begin by turning your back on God."

***

Bianca and Beasley met on Cathedral Street a few minutes after midnight, the time that is both night and morning, when the old day and the new are joined until the light comes to banish the darkness.

"If God is anywhere in this city, it's here."

Beasley had to agree. They were in front of the Basilica of the Assumption, the first major religious building of the newly formed United States. A recent renovation had just restored it to its original grandeur.

"So what do we do now?"

"Like Father Lawrence said, Earl, we turn our backs on it and try to put all thoughts of God out of our minds. Think of all the bad you've seen on the job. Think of the Devil and really, really want to be in Hell."

"It's that easy?"

"Probably not. But I've a guide to help us along the way. And before I left, I called Anna Burgess and told her to let her boyfriend know we were coming. That might open a path for us."

Their backs to the grand symbol of faith, the two detectives started south towards Liberty Street. They would walk as far as the Inner Harbor and then if nothing changed, if there was no sign that they were someplace other than Baltimore, they'd give up their quest and try something else.

Bianca woke up the part of her that was the monster. It was neither demonic nor infernal, it had no real connection to the Pit or its master. Bianca wondered if may not be older than both, a malevolent presence left over from a primordial era when there were no gods or devils.

Still, it was a terrible thing and Bianca counted on like calling to like, the evil inside her being drawn to that which she sought.

Side by side, alert for the slightest change or threat, the two passed Charles Plaza when Beasley spoke, "Is it me or is it getting darker?"

"It's night time, Earl. It's supposed to be dark."

"Not darker, then, blacker. It's like the shadows are more solid and the street lights not as bright."

Bianca realized that her partner was right. The few cars that passed were somewhat insubstantial, their engine noises muted. She looked down Liberty. The way ahead was hazy, a heavy fog was moving in, obscuring their vision.

A small piece of her gave out a cry of joy.

"Looks like we're going the right way."

"Stay close, Little Girl. I have the feeling it's only gonna get colder and darker."

A few blocks more and there were almost completely enveloped by a dark grey, nearly black mist. Only their knowledge of the city kept them on their chosen path.

"One thing, Bianca," Beasley said as they marched carefully through the blinding cloud.

"Just one?"

"Yeah, once we get there, what makes you think the Devil will just hand the kid over?'

"He may not, this may all be for nothing. But if he does, he'll want something in return. He'll offer a challenge or a deal and leave it for us to decide."

"And we trust him?"

"Not in the least. He's the Devil, remember? The Father of Lies. Oh, he'll keep his word, but only to the exact letter of whatever agreement we make."

"And what do we do?"

"We pay the price, keeping our word to the exact letter." Bianca already knew, or at least suspected, what the price might be and who would pay it.

Liberty Street led them to Hopkins Place, past the federal courthouse. From there to Pratt Street where the two turned east towards the water.

"Why the Harbor?" Beasley had asked when they had made their plans.

"Because that's how it's done."

Against natural law, the dark fog lessened the closer they came to the water. By the time they were alongside the Pratt Street Pavilion of Harborplace, it had nearly lifted completely.

"There," Bianca said, pointing, "beside the Constellation."

Beasley looked into the water. Floating next to the Civil War era naval sloop was a black barge, its pilot dressed in a dark hooded robe.

"Jesu…"

"Don't say it, Earl."

Beasley shut up as Bianca approached the barge. A skeletal hand was thrust out and she dropped six gold dollars into its palm.

The hooded head came up and Bianca felt herself studied by cold red eyes.

"Round trip," she explained.

A spectral nod and the two were waved aboard.

The passage was made in silence. When the ferryman reached the other side, they disembarked onto a shore not of this Earth.

It was a featureless plan, one of brown dirt and grey skies and peopled by ghostly images. Wandering aimlessly, these barely visible shades took no notice of the living beings now among them.

"So this is Hell," Beasley said, affecting an air of nonchalance. "I'm not impressed. I was expecting something more dramatic. Thorndale and Pimlico is scarier than this place."

"This isn't Hell, Earl, just the outskirts. True damnation lies across this plane."

"So who are Casper and all his friends?"

"Uncommitted souls. Ones who never made the choice between good and evil. They're doomed to wander until they do."

"So which way do we go?"

"It doesn't matter, Earl. Hell's a big place. We'll find it soon enough, or it will find us."

They chose a direction and began walking.

Time passed -- a minute, an hour, a day -- it was impossible to tell in a place where time had no meaning. All Beasley knew was that it seemed he had been going on forever, and for what? So some little tramp could get her half-breed bastard back. Should have brought her along, he thought, and left her ass here. But no, we couldn't do that.

Beasley looked at Bianca who was now a few steps ahead of him and seemed to be moving further away.

It's her fault, he decided. Her fault I got kicked out of the Homicide Unit, her fault I'm the new guy in Sex Offense, her fault I'm in Hell. She has to have things her way, has to show how special she is, show off for the brass. We'll get back and they'll all say how great it was she went to Hell and saved a kid. How wonderful you are, Detective Jones, how great it is that you fight monsters.

She'll get the glory and I'll probably get busted back to patrol for letting the kid get snatched to begin with. Left behind again.

Left behind. Beasley suddenly realized that that was what was happening. Bianca was now walking faster and leaving him behind. She wanted the glory and to get it she was going to leave him in this wasteland.

Like Hell she was. Beasley stated walking faster, almost running. He'd catch up and then he'd show her what was what, just who the boss was. As he got nearer he decided how he'd do it. Knock her down, get those pants off her then take her every way a man could take a woman. That's what they were for anyway, wasn't it?

Earl felt himself harden, smiled, and hurried to catch the woman ahead of him.

Not caring if her companion kept pace or not, Bianca walked steadily toward Damnation. Things were good, she thought. No, not good, great. She couldn't understand why she had been so worried before. Everything was going according to plan. Her plan. She'd walk up to the gates of Hell, pound on them until something answered and demand to see the boss. If she was refused, she'd lay waste until he showed his face. She knew she could do it. Her cause was just, her anger righteous. Nothing could stop her.

But it could slow her down. She briefly glanced back to see Beasley lagging behind. "Why did you bring him?" she asked herself. "He's old and out of shape. Useless in a fight. Probably have to save his ass too." She thought on this for a minute. "Screw it. Let him watch out for himself. He would make a nice distraction, though, if things get tight. Throw Beasley at the demons while I make off with the kid."

The kid, how was she going to get the kid? No problem, she decided. I beat that old bastard once. He hands it over or I'll kick him in the balls again, have him crying like a baby. And if that doesn't work, well, Devil or not, he was still male. She'd make him the deal no male could refuse, no straight one anyway. As she remembered he was very good looking, probably packing a big dick too.

Bianca smiled and hurried on.

Somewhere inside her a dark thing chuckled. Soon, it thought, soon.

Trying to reach the woman ahead of him, Beasley couldn't quite do it. Even running flat out, he was no match for Bianca who just kept walking faster. As much as he wanted to rip her off her clothes and screw her until she bled, it just wasn't worth the effort. No pussy was.

He should stop, he thought. Just sit right down and let her go on. That's what she wanted anyway, wasn't it? To go it alone? So he'd just sit down and wait right there for her to come back.

And if she doesn't?

"Well," Beasley said to himself, "when I get tired of waiting I'll take the boat home. Tell everybody that we did our best but hey, shit happens."

Beasley stopped, watched as Bianca got further away from him. "Good luck, Little Girl," he thought, then sat down, not expecting to see her again.

How long should I wait, he wondered. To pass the time, he made a list of those people he'd have to notify about Bianca's death. The brass wouldn't believe him. Major Williams might, he was her boss. Her friend Morgan and that crime lab guy she was screwing would as well. Beasley imagined telling them.

"We went there with the best intentions but just couldn't pull it off."

Best intentions, there was something about that. No, not best intentions, good intentions, good intentions and the road to Hell.

Which is where they were.

Realization hit. "Oh shit," Beasley said out loud. Running faster than he ever had, faster than he thought he could, he raced to catch Bianca.

"If I'm going to use that asshole as bait," Bianca thought, "I should wait for him." She stopped and turned to see Beasley rapidly coming towards her.

What did he want? No sense taking chances. If he wanted to die in Hell that was okay by her. She shifted into a combat stance.

Beasley stopped short, just out of Bianca's range. He struggled to catch his breath as she started to advance on him.

"Wait," he was finally able to shout. She halted, but stayed in a fighting pose.

"Wait," Beasley said again, still breathing hard and almost unable to stand after his hard run. "He's beating us."

"Who's beating us? What the hell do you mean, Beasley?"

His words came in short bursts. "Exactly. Hell." He pointed off in the distance. "Him, he's beating us. We're not even there yet."

Bianca didn't back away but she no longer looked as if she were going to jump him, so Beasley rested. When his wind came back he said, "What are you thinking right now, Bianca? Better yet, what are you feeling? Pride, Anger, Lust maybe?" When he said this last Beasley couldn't help but look Bianca over and think about what almost happened, what he had wanted to do. Equal parts shame and desire washed over him.

"This is Hell, Little Girl, the Devil's playing field and we're the visiting team. He's got home field advantage and he's using it, hitting us where he can, in the dark part of our souls. Me, I was feeling, well, never mind, but I'm willing to bet you were ready to storm right in there and take 'em all down, sure you could do it. And I'm willing to bet that Pride wasn't the only deadly sin you were feeling either, was it?"

There is a moment between sleeping and waking when one realizes that everything that had been happening was a dream. Reality then comes rushing in. For Bianca this moment usually brought an end to horrible nightmares and came as blessed relief.

Standing on the Plain of Hell, ready to challenge the Devil himself, Beasley's words brought Bianca that same relief. It was as if she'd been asleep and was now awake and all that she'd been feeling had been experienced by a dream self.

"That bastard, he played us."

"He let us play ourselves. That's what he does, Little Girl, and he's very good at it."

"That son of a bitch, I'm going to …"

Beasley put a hand on Bianca's shoulder. "You're not going to do anything. We're cops, he's a perp. That's how we're going to play it. Anything more, anything less and neither one of us leaves here, at least not until the final trumpet and maybe not then. Okay?"

"Yeah, okay."

Humbled but even more determined the two cops again started walking towards the gates of Hell.

Their journey wasn't long. In what might have been minutes they sighted a long wall, one that came closer with every step they took.

"Get ready," Bianca warned and that fast it was upon them.

The wall was bigger than any they'd seen, taller than any structure in Baltimore. It was built of yellowed bones shaped into rough bricks and held in place by mortar made from blood. It reeked of death and decay and from within came the moaning of the damned used in its building. Looking left and right, the two detectives saw that it stretched to infinity in both directions.

Massive gates were suddenly before them, gates of iron that burned with an infernal heat. Slowly and with a creaking of a thousand nails on a hundred chalkboards, the gates swung open and invited them inside.

Beasley moved to enter but Bianca held him back.

"Wait, Earl. There are rules, even in Hell. 'Abandon All Hope' is more than just a line from a poem. We go inside and it's all over. We'll wait, make him come to us."

"What makes you think he will?"

"What makes you think he has a choice? We're here to challenge him. His Pride won't let him ignore us."

Bianca turned her face to the open gates and stared into the depths of Hell, waiting for its master.

Satan appeared as light, the star of morning, so brilliant that the two detectives had to shade their eyes or else go blind. And with the light came the sound of wings, the buzzing of a vast swarm of flies.

When it was again quiet, when she could no longer feel the heat on her back, Bianca chanced to look. Before her stood Lucifer, outcast from Heaven and Lord of Hell. He was clad in white, his nine-fold wings behind him. Fallen he might have been but he still retained his angelic nature.

Bianca tried very hard not to be impressed, reminding herself that before her was Evil Incarnate.

The Devil had all eternity to wait; Bianca did not. She finally broke the silence.

"We've come for the child."

"And what child would that be?" His voice was as soft as a whisper, as gentle as a mother's touch, the voice of a liar and seducer.

"You know which child," Bianca spoke as a cop, in a tone that said she would accept only the truth and she hadn't heard it yet. "The only innocent in Hell could not escape you, especially since you brought it here."

"I give you my word, Miss Jones, there are no innocents in Hell."

They were outside the gate, so that could mean only one thing.

"Then it's with you."

From beneath a wing Satan brought forth the child. It was a girl. She looked to be almost full term and was still as she had come from her mother's womb, clothed only in a newborn's innocence. The Devil smiled with a look that said all was going as he had planned.

"That's Anna Burgess's child?"

"It is, Detective … Beasley, isn't it? I recognize you. You walked the edge for so very long I always thought you would fall our way. But now.…" he directed his gaze to Bianca, "there's still time, I suppose. One never knows what may happen."

"Never mind that, give us the girl and we'll be gone."

"No."

Satan turned toward Bianca. "Tell him, Miss Jones, that it's not that easy. As you said, even here there are rules. Something for nothing is not one of them."

The infant disappeared behind a wing.

"What will it be? A test of strength, of courage? One of you against a champion of Hell? Or maybe a game of wits, mind versus mind. There must be something, if only a game of chess."

He was toying with them. Any game or contest would be played on his terms and would be rigged for them to lose. Bianca knew this, and he knew she knew, and both knew the only terms he would accept.

"How about a deal instead?"

Satan smiled again. "I've been known to make them. What have you in mind?"

"The simplest one, a soul for a soul."

"Bianca!"

"Stay out of this, Earl. I'm doing what I have to do."

"Yes, Earl, stay out of this. Anyway, you're too late. Offer made and accepted, Miss Jones, or may I now call you Bianca?"

"Call me what you like. Just hand the child to Detective Beasley."

Again Satan brought the girl into view and soon Beasley had her in his arms. She felt good, her innocence soothing amid the oppression of Hell. But whatever joy he had in it faded when he considered the price of her freedom.

He'd be back, Beasley resolved. He knew the way. He'd come back with an army if need be. And even if meant freeing every damned soul there ever was, he'd tear down the wall and save Bianca.

"I'd like to see them safely back," Bianca said meekly, as if asking permission. "And then you'll have your soul."

Satan smiled. "Of course, my dear. What are a few minutes now that we have all eternity? You'll find the ferryman," he pointed in a direction different then the way they had come, "that way. And Bianca," his smile faded and a terrible look of menace appeared on his face, "do not think to cheat me. If you do, I will come and claim what's mine, killing as many of your friends and loved ones as I can."

"You'll have what you were promised."

A master of lies, Satan read nothing but the truth in Bianca's words and so let her escort Beasley and the girl from Hell.

On the way to the dock, Beasley pleaded with her. "At least let me take your place," he offered. "You heard him, I was halfway his once, who knows what might happen when I get back? I could wind up here anyway."

"Enough, Earl, the deal's been made." She saw him starting to drop back, trying to get behind her. "And don't even think of trying to take me out and take my place. Old Scratch back there won't go for it."

They came to where the ferry waited to take them from Hell. Bianca saw Beasley and his chare safely on board.

"And now to pay what is owed."

And with that she reached down to a small part of herself, found the monster and loosed her hold on it. "You're free," she said.

That which was old when Heaven and Hell were made came forth into its new home. It was still as she remembered it, a creature of lust and desire and the need to act on its passions. It turned toward Bianca, as if to seek vengeance on it captor but the detective shook her head.

"We had a deal. Now do your part."

Without a word it started back toward the wall, the gates, and the waiting Lord of Hell.

"What the …"

"I promised Satan a soul, Earl. I never said it would be mine."

Their passage already paid, they climbed aboard the dark barge.

"So that's why it was six coins."

"Three souls going, three returning."

"Yeah, but, Bianca, are you sure it was smart to set that thing free in a place like this?"

The cloaked pilot would have begun the journey but Bianca's praised hand held him up.

"That thing holds no allegiance to anyone or anything but itself. As I'm sure someone is finding out just about now."

In the distance came screaming, the sound of an angel in pain.

"Let's go," Bianca said, "while he's too busy playing with his new toy to worry about us."

They had made half the passage when the boat slowed, then stopped. Bianca ran to the stern, looked back the way they had come. There was nothing to be seen, not even land.

"No sign of pursuit."

"Try up front."

She met Beasley at the bow. In the distance were two lights, high above them. They came closer and grew brighter. The sound of wings filled the air and again the two detectives had to shield their eyes.

There was no heat or the buzzing of flies and somehow Bianca and Beasley knew when it was safe to turn.

Hovering above were beings much like the one they had just left, only these retained the dignity and majesty that the other had abandoned.

You carry a burden.

There was no speech, but Bianca could hear them just the same. A single thought in two voices. She looked to Beasley who was just staring at the celestials. Did he hear it too, or was the message for her alone?

I bear it willingly, she answered without words, somehow not surprised she could do so.

There is no need. We will take the Fallen One's child from you.

Take her where?

There was a hesitation before the reply. *To a place prepared for her, where all will be safe.*

Are you acting on your own, or did your Boss send you?

Another hesitation gave Bianca her answer. She made her decision.

The child stays with me. She deserves a chance at life, a human life.

And should she choose her father's path?

I will do what is needed. As you say, it is my burden.

As you will and the beings were gone. The ferry resumed its travel.

"What was that all about?"

"Just some travelers, Earl, looking for direction. I set them straight."

"They wanted the girl, didn't they?" Bianca nodded. "So we gonna give her back to her mother?"

"You've read the reports, Earl. Anna Burgess was never pregnant so this can't be hers. I've already arranged with Father Lawrence to have the child adopted. He, or rather his order, will keep an eye on her."

"Little Girl, you're taking a big chance."

"Every child is a chance, Earl. Anyone of them could grow up to break your heart or make you proud. You never know."

"Yeah, and that's the hell of it."

***

Two nights later Bianca dreamt of a barren land of brown dirt and grey skies. A gated wall was in the distance and before her was a being clothed in white. He was battered and bruised and his face not as beautiful as it had been but there was an appreciative smile on his face.

"Well played, Miss Jones. It seems that it is part of my Hell to always underestimate you mortals. That creature and I have yet to come to understanding, but once we do …"

The rest was left unspoken. Bianca woke and allowed the threat to fade with the dream. He wasn't finished with her. This she knew. But she had been to Hell and had left the worse of herself there. When the time came she'd be ready. Until then it was a new day and she had work to do.

COLD IRON

It began in *Tir na nOg*, home of the Tuatha de Danann. Ages ago they left the land of their birth; some say they were fleeing the Milesians, others that they were driven out by the God of the Tree. No matter. What is known is that they left one land for another, and settled in an unchanging world of eternal youth.

They were not the only exiles. The Unseelie Court from the Northern Mists and the Plant Annwn from the Land of the Afternoon also fled the incursions of Man. They met in that which was called Fairie and there followed a time of strife and trouble as each tribe sought dominance over the other two. Alliances were made and broken many times over and for years the people knew only war. Brave warriors from all sides fell and the crows grew fat on the battlefields.

But at last there came a time when the people grew tired of battle. An uneasy truce was formed. Peace was declared between the three courts, a peace that balanced on sword's edge, its fall only the slightest breeze away.

With so much death, new life is rare in the Land. The birth of a child is cause for rejoicing. Even more so when a son is born to Finvarra and Donagh, king and queen of the Tuatha de Danann. Assured of an heir, Finvarra declared a month's celebration.

It was in the waning of that month that two men approached Finvarra's Keep. As late night grew to early morning they stood in the deep wood and watched the guards step through their paces.

"There, Carney, see it? A period of not less than five minutes when no one is on this side of the wall. The next time we make our approach."

Carney shifted the bundle he was holding. "And the door will be unlocked?"

"She said it would be, and I doubt that the Lady of the Queen would lie. Just make sure that one stays quiet."

"He didn't cry when I lifted him from his crib. He'll not cry now, Bran. Not with the touch of valerian I've given him. He'll sleep like a baby."

"Funny. Just make sure the other brat doesn't wake either. We must get in and out without being seen or it's all for naught."

"Not entirely. This one does seem a tasty morsel."

"And what would you use for the exchange? Keep your mind, such as it is, on the job."

The two men waited for the next passage of the guards, then moved quickly across the open land to the keep. As promised, they found the unlocked door and made their quiet way to the nursery and just as quietly left, bearing with them Finvarra's heir, a mortal child having taken his place in the cradle.

***

It had only been a small cry, but even in her sleep a mother knows the sound of her child. Diane Mohr woke to see what the matter with her son was. Her scream when she found his empty crib woke her husband.

"Devin's gone, missing." Frantic, she picked up the phone to call the police. But as she finished the call, a cry came from the baby's room. Her husband came into the room carrying their child.

"But I thought he was gone," Diane said, hanging up on the 9-1-1 operator.

"You had a bad dream," her husband said, handing her their son. "I think all new mothers have them."

"I suppose," she said, putting Devin to her breast. It must have been a dream, she thought as the child began to suckle, but it had seemed so real.

Outside, two men stood in a place between two worlds. "A fair exchange; all is in balance."

"Just so, Carney. Think the glamour will hold?"

"Long enough for them to forget their own brat. We've done them a favor, Bran. It's not every couple who gets to raise royalty."

And the two stepped back into their own world.

***

The sign on the door of Morgan's Rare Books and Collectibles said "Closed." Ignoring it, Bianca Jones entered the store. "It's just me," she shouted, letting the bookstore owner know she'd arrived.

"We're back here, Miss Jones."

We? That was odd. Morgan did not usually have company, not when he'd summoned her to deal with, as he put it, "a situation that has arisen." Bianca wondered what the threat was this time.

She walked to the back, past the shelves of history, sociology and political science. She went past general fiction, fantasy, and romance. Morgan's office was just beyond the horror section, something Bianca found oddly appropriate.

The bookseller was, as usual behind his desk. Morgan was a gnomish-looking man, apparently in the twilight of his life. Despite his aged appearance, Bianca knew there was a strength inside him, one that came from a lifetime of struggle against dark and evil forces, a fight into which he had enlisted her.

Morgan's visitor stood when Bianca entered the room. Her first thought on seeing him was that this was the second most beautiful man she had ever seen. This was also her second thought. He was well over six feet, well-proportioned, with muscles that strained the medieval style clothing he wore. His hair and features were dark, and one could almost get lost in his eyes.

But Bianca knew that beauty could lie. She could see that there was no joy or kindness in this stranger's eyes, and she suspected that his full lips never smiled except at the defeat of an opponent.

Morgan started introductions. "Calder, this is …"

"A child!" His hands resting on the sword and knife hanging from his belt, the man named Calder stared down at Bianca, obviously not pleased with what he thought he saw -- a slender young girl, not much taller than five feet. "I ask for your help and you summon a child. How dare you!"

Morgan did not see exactly what Bianca did to Calder. One second the man was towering above the young woman, the next he was collapsing like an imploded building. As he fell, Bianca slipped his knife from its sheath. When he tried to rise, she held it in front of his face, silently daring him to say or do anything.

"As I was saying," Morgan went on as if nothing had happened, "Calder, this is Bianca Jones, a detective with the Baltimore Police Department, what you might call The Watch. As you can tell, she is quite a capable young lady. Miss Jones, would you please let my visitor rise?"

Bianca reluctantly stepped away from Calder, allowing him to stand. She returned his knife with a smile that said "I took it once; I can take it again anytime I want."

For his part, Calder stepped away from her enough to show caution, but not enough to suggest fear. "My apologies, my lady, and to you, Lord Morgan, for not trusting your judgment." As he spoke he kept a careful eye on Bianca. She'd surprised him once; she'd not do so again.

"What's done is done, right, Miss Jones?"

Bianca nodded toward Calder. "Apology accepted. We both should have listened to Morgan. You're not from around here, are you, Calder?"

"Calder is from that land which is called Fairie."

As the BPD's investigator of all things occult and supernatural, Bianca had faced creatures from other dimensions, fought with ghosts, and redeemed vampires. So if Morgan said this guy was from Neverland, she was willing to believe him. "You're an elf?"

Somewhat offended, Calder replied haughtily. "Elves are from Scandia, I am of Fairie."

"I stand corrected. How can I help?"

And Calder told her of a stolen child.

"He is the son of Finvarra and Donagh, rulers of the Tuatha de Danann. As best as we can judge, one moon ago he was exchanged for a mortal child and brought to this world. I am charged with finding him and must do so without delay."

"After a month, why the rush?" Bianca wanted to know. "And why look here?"

"Our world is an unchanging one. There is little to do but play the eternal games of war, love, and intrigue. And in all three, any advantage must be seized and exploited. So Finvarra, who is my liege, has sent me on the hunt. I'm sure by now the other kings have learned what has happened and have done the same. And if one of them finds the boy before me …"

"Holding the heir of *Tir na nOg* would give them a definite advantage. But as Miss Jones asked, why here?"

Calder shrugged. "His path, as far as it could be traced, led me to this city. Once on this side, I lost the trail, but not before laying false ones for others to follow. So I've come to you, knowing the service you've done for Fairie in the past."

"That was in the past, Calder. What obligations there were have long since been discharged. Why should I aid you now?"

"Can anyone afford not to have a court of Fairie in his debt? Or if he can, why would he not want to return a stolen child to its mother?"

"I am past the age for questing, Calder. Any help must come from Miss Jones."

The Fairie knight turned to Bianca. "My lady, do you have the heart to seek a lost child?"

Bianca made her decision. "Two missing children, Calder. There's a human child involved in this as well." She was all cop now, investigating an abduction. "I'm supposing that whoever kidnapped the heir did so for this advantage you talked about. What was the boy's name?"

"He had not yet been given one. He now bears whatever name his foster mother has given him."

"By foster mother you mean the mother of the other child." Calder nodded. "That's the next thing, why the switch, why not take the child outright?"

"It is not the way. In all things there must be fair exchange -- favor for favor, blow for blow, equal value given and received. If the heir was to be hidden in the mortal world, a mortal child had to take his place."

"And what would become of this mortal child?"

Calder clearly did not want to answer. He looked to Morgan for help. "Tell her," was all the bookseller said.

"If he lives, he will be given to the servants to raise, to become one of them when he's grown."

"If he lives? Who wouldn't he?"

"My lady, there are those among my people who would consider a human infant, newborn and innocent, as … a delicacy."

There was a pause while Bianca considered his words. "I'll find this prince for you, Calder," she said, barely restraining her fury. "Find him and return him to his home. In fair exchange, I want the human child. And if he is dead, injured or has been abused in any way, I will hunt down those responsible. Their lives will not come close to the value of the child, but I will take them anyway."

"Your vengeance would come at a high price, my lady."

Her reply came in a cold voice that promised nothing but death. "One I would gladly pay."

"Let's find the changeling first," Morgan suggested quietly, "and hope for the best in the future."

"You said you tracked the child here. How did you do that, Calder?"

"I have a sort of hound that traced his scent from a gown once worn by the prince. He has tracked the scent this far. However, once on this side my barghest soon lost the trail."

"And you have no idea of where the child could be?"

"Obviously not or I would not have come to Morgan for help."

"Well, that makes it easy, doesn't it, Morgan? All we have to do find one child in a city full of them, assuming he's even still in Baltimore. Shouldn't be too difficult at all." Bianca did not try to hide the sarcasm in her voice

***

"Shouldn't be too difficult at all," Joe Russo said once Bianca explained the problem. Joe was a crime scene investigator for the Baltimore Police Department who had assisted Bianca in several of her more arcane cases. In addition, the two enjoyed a more personal relationship. Morgan had suggested calling on Joe for his advice. He was at the bookstore within an hour.

"Something growled at me from the shadows as I came in," Joe said after being introduced to Calder. "Your puppy, I assume."

"My barghest," Calder confirmed. "It was good you did not approach it."

"How do you know that?"

"You are still alive. How can you help me?"

"It would be nice to visit the crime scene, and to see this Fairie, but there's little sense in going there now, not after a month's gone by. Any evidence would be gone and the scene contaminated."

"Not a good idea anyway, Mr. Russo," said Morgan. "From my experience, time runs differently over there. Depending on how it is flowing, every day you spent in Fairie could be a week lost here, or a month, or maybe a year."

Just like Rip Van Winkle. Bianca's thoughts on how the time difference might affect the missing heir were interrupted as Joe said, "And I'm short on vacation time, thanks to that week in Ocean City." He looked over at Bianca, causing a rare blush to come to her cheeks.

"How good a tracker is that hound of yours?" Bianca wanted to know.

"Very, he was bred to it."

"Yet he lost the trail." Bianca thought she knew why. "What if he had something more personal than clothing?" She glanced over toward Joe. A nod from her friend told her that he was thinking along the same lines.

"Such as?"

"His essence, or rather, his parents' essence"

"I don't understand, how can one capture a person's essence? Is this one a sorcerer?"

"You two are talking about DNA?" When Bianca and Joe nodded, Morgan turned to Calder. "It is a kind of magic," he explained, "one that Mr. Russo does very well. But you have my word that it will cause no harm to either the king or queen." To Joe he said, "Tell him what you'll need."

"I'll need something from their persons -- hair, skin, body fluids. From this I can make, well, a potion that would allow your dog ..."

"It is a barghest."

"Your ... barghest ... to track that part of the king or queen that is in the missing heir."

Calder thought for a moment. "This can be done. I'll need to return to Finvarra's Keep. If time flows well, I shall be back within half a moon. Otherwise, when I can. Until then ..." He nodded to them in turn, "... Lord Morgan, Sir Russo, Lady Bianca -- fare you well."

Leaving through the back door, Calder walked into the alley. He turned, and where once was a wall there appeared a shimmering portal, behind which could be seen blue skies untouched by smog and a land untainted by chemicals. Calder stepped through and was gone. A large hound-shaped shadow followed and the portal closed.

"Now that was an exit."

"Yes it was," Morgan agreed. "Mr. Russo, do you think the DNA will enable the heir to be tracked."

"Do fairies even have DNA?" Bianca wanted to know.

"I think the switch would have been found out before now if they didn't have something close. Probably with the first check-up after the switch." Joe held up his hands as if reading a headline "Couple has alien baby. Mother gives birth to mutant child. I think it will work."

***

Eight days later, Joe was on a burglary scene when he got a call from Bianca. "You busy tonight?" she asked.

"Not too busy for you. What did you have in mind? Dinner, followed by a movie, followed sometime after that by breakfast?"

"How about a large man wearing leather and his nasty looking dog?"

"It's a barghest, remember? And how about you collect the samples and meet me in the serology lab later tonight."

"Which one are you afraid of -- the hound or the fairy?"

"Actually, it's Morgan. I've always been afraid of old men selling books."

"I think you just want to get me alone in the serology lab again."

"There's that. But the sooner I start the sooner I can extract the DNA and the sooner you two can start the hunt."

"Okay, Joe, see you later tonight."

***

At the bookstore, Bianca again found Calder and Morgan in the backroom, enjoying each other's company over wine. Each had his own. Morgan drank from a bottle Bianca had given him last Christmas; Calder poured his from a flask obviously brought from his own country.

"I would offer you a taste, my lady, but it is not wise to eat or drink of a strange land's fare. One might never get home, or else long for a place one can never see."

"I'm sort of on duty anyway, but thanks for the thought. Did you bring the samples?"

Calder stood and, bringing up a leather bag took out two cloth-wrapped bundles. "I supposed the wizard would have me keep them apart." He handed them to her.

"Good thinking. You supposed correctly." Slipping on a pair of rubber gloves, Bianca opened the first to find a hairbrush.

"Taken from Queen Donagh's own dressing table. Sir Russo did say he could make his potion with hair."

"He can," Bianca confirmed and opened the other package to find a piece of cotton linen which bore a light colored stain. "Is this what I think it is?"

"It is indeed, my lady. The night of my return, the king took a maid to bed. Not wanting to father a bastard, he spent on the sheets. Since it is the king's son we seek, I thought it the appropriate sample to bring."

"I think the brush a better choice."

"Why is that, Lord Morgan?"

"We are looking for the king's heir."

Bianca groaned at the pun. Calder merely scowled.

"Lord Morgan, were we at court you would have been pummeled with loaves and sentenced to drink nothing but weak mead. As it is, maybe more wine will make that seem a better jest than it was. My lady, will you find a bottle and join us?"

"Thank you again, Calder, but I'd better get these to Joe as soon as possible." And she left the knight and bookseller to their wine and their stories.

It took Joe the rest of the night and into the morning to extract the DNA from the two samples. "I'm going home and crash," he said, handing Bianca two vials. "The blue capped one is the king's; the red cap's the queen's. Call me later and let me know how things worked out."

"You're not coming?"

Joe gave Bianca a tired smile. "You're the action hero, remember. Besides, you've got Conan of the Mists on hand if there's any trouble. Which reminds me," he opened a cabinet and took something out, "take this." He handed her a fireplace poker. At her puzzled look he explained. "I did some research. I understand that where our new best friend comes from they don't like cold iron. You never know, you might have trouble with that hound of his, and I don't think hitting it with a rolled up newspaper would do any good."

Bianca accepted Joe's gift with a smile. "Gee, a new weapon. Some guys just give their girls flowers or candy. You know the way to my heart, Mr. Russo." She kissed his cheek. "Thanks."

Bianca, wearing a coat against the cold and to better hide the iron poker she had strapped to her back, stood outside of Morgan's shop as Calder allowed the barghest to smell the contents of the king's vial. The beast remained cloaked in shadow and she still had not gotten a good look at it. She could only make out its general form as it sniffed the air searching for a scent. Finding none, it sat back on its haunches and let go with a low moan that chilled Bianca more than the night air.

"He's found nothing," Calder complained. "It seems that your wizard's potion is useless."

Bianca shared a glance with Morgan. "Or maybe we've found the reason the boy was taken," she said.

The bookseller nodded agreement. "Try the queen's vial," he suggested.

Calder did, and after a brief sniff the barghest began straining at the leash Calder had him on.

"It seems the game is afoot. You two be careful. The others may not all have been fooled by Calder's false trails."

"We will take care, Lord Morgan."

"I'll keep him safe, Morgan. Thanks to Joe I'm ready for anything."

"I hope so," Morgan said softly as the beast led the two hunters away.

Calder slipped off the barghest's leash and let the best run free. Soon he was almost out of sight.

"Won't we lose him?"

"No, my lady, he will run ahead until he finds our quarry, then signal to lead us there."

"As long as no one reports a monster running through the streets of Baltimore."

"I doubt they will. He's one with the shadows and must he emerge, I've placed a glamour on him. To anyone else he will seem naught but a large hound."

"You know, Calder, once we find the prince you just can't take him back to Fairie. He has a life here."

"I assure you, my lady, I have no intention of taking the babe back with me. Just knowing where he is will be enough."

He still thinks of the prince as a babe, Bianca realized. He hasn't fully considered how time might flow between our worlds.

Jus then the night air was pierced by a horrendous howl, answered by the baying and barking of what seemed every dog in the city.

"He's found something." Calder began running toward where the howling had come from, leaving Bianca to trail behind.

She found Calder standing in back of a row house, the dark shape of the barghest pacing up and down the yard.

"What is this? Your wizard's potion has again proven worthless. I have been here before; this is the site to which the barghest first led me. There is no child here, no mother with babe in arms. I watched it for a day and night and saw no one leave or enter but a young man, a scholar of sorts to judge by the books he carried."

"You were led here twice, Calder. What does that tell you?"

He thought for a moment. "That the child lives within. But there is no child, only a ..." An embarrassed look crossed his face. "I have been several kinds of fool. A month in my world has become years in yours. The babe I seek has grown into a man."

"And as I said, he has his own life now, and may not be all that willing to believe in fairies."

"I would still like to meet him, is that possible?"

After a bit of thought Bianca said, "There is a way, but let me do all the talking. Later we can figure out the best way to reveal his true heritage."

"Yes, his true heritage is indeed important."

Bianca knocked on the door. It was answered by a young man who, like Calder, was much taller than average and well muscled. There was, however, an innocence about him that was lacking in the Fairie knight.

"Can I help you?" he asked.

Bianca was planning to ask the young man about a non-existent accident that he may have witnessed. She had her badge out and was about to identify herself as a police officer when Calder pushed her outside and slammed the door behind her. Before she could reopen it she heard a brief struggle, a single cry for help then nothing. By the time she was inside it was all over.

The young man was dead, a knife deep in his heart. Calder was standing close to her, his sword drawn and pointed at her chest. Bianca knew that were she to try for her gun there would be another corpse on the floor.

"Did you think, my lady, that I missed the meaning of why the barghest did not react to the king's essence? My hound tracked this one from Donagh's vial because there was part of the queen in him. That meant there was nothing of the king. This is but a bastard, and one who bears the image of the MacRoy of the Unseelie Court."

"You did not have to kill him."

"My lady, that is exactly what I had to do. If Finvarra discovered that he wore a cuckold's horns, there would be war. And I could not chance a bastard of another court taking the throne of the Tuatha de Danann. It would not bode well for my people. With this one death peace is assured, and only I will know the truth."

"I'll know."

"But you cannot follow where I am going." A shimmering portal opened behind Calder.

"And what of the mortal child?"

"It was to be returned in exchange for the prince. This," Calder kicked the corpse, "is no prince. There will be no exchange."

Calder whistled and a black shape came in through the still open door. "Fare you well, my lady. I doubt we will meet again."

Guarded by the barghest, Calder moved to step through the portal. Moving swiftly, Bianca shrugged off her coat and unslung the poker Joe had given her. Waiting until the knight had committed himself, she called out, "Calder, catch," and threw the cold iron his way.

Calder turned in time to see the poker come toward him. From the look on his face, it was clear he knew what it was and what it would do. He had time for a single "No!"

The entry of the poker into the rift between worlds was much like that of a radio into bathwater. The shimmer became sparks which crackled with loose lightning. Calder began screaming as his clothing caught fire and the flames quickly spread. There followed an explosion that blew the knight's charred body back into this world. Then the damaged portal closed tight and vanished.

Bianca did not see any of this. She was too busy watching the barghest, which she was now seeing clearly for the first time. Enraged by the death of its master, it came at her from the shadows, all teeth and claws. It might have been just another of Baltimore's strays, its mind ravaged by rabies. But feral street dogs don't have wings and horns and their eyes don't glow with the red of Hellfire. Bianca Jones drew her pistol and prayed that hot lead worked just as well as cold iron.

The two shots in the beast's chest slowed it down but failed to stop its charge. A third shot took out its eye and a fourth entered its brain, but to little effect. The barghest was acting on rage and instinct and would not be denied its vengeance. It was almost on Bianca, its jaws open wide to tear out her throat when she fired her last few shots straight into its mouth, blowing out the back of its head. The nightmare beast dropped at her feet.

***

"So what did you tell your fellow officers?" Morgan wanted to know. After leaving the house, Bianca had called Joe and asked him to meet her at the bookshop.

"That I heard an explosion, investigated and found two dead men. A vicious dog then attacked me."

"And what did they say about the horns?"

"Calder's glamour held, Joe, even after his death. We're okay as long as no one orders a necropsy."

"And we all know the department's too cheap to do that. Are you going to tell Major Williams the truth?"

"I suspect, Mr. Russo, that Miss Jones's commander is at the point where he longer wants to know the truth, just that situation in which she's become involved has been abated. Is that right?"

Bianca nodded. "He just asks, 'Did you make it go away?' I tell him I did and he's happy. Wish I could be."

"Why not? You beat the bad guy."

"At what cost? A human child still lost in Fairie, two others dead, three counting the barghest. Poor beast was just doing its job."

"As you were doing yours, Miss Jones. That's all that can be asked of anyone." Morgan's words were cold comfort. Bianca stared out at nothing at all as she tried to banish all thoughts of fairy knights, shadow hounds, and lost boys who would never find their way home.

A WARNING TO OTHERS

Hector Oxendine did not usually do his own killing. But sometimes a message had to be sent, an example made as a warning to others.

Bobby Lochlear had been skimming the take. That was no surprise. Everybody took a little something for himself; it was expected. But Bobby got greedy; he started taking a bit too much. Worse yet, he was stealing from Hector's cut. And that was something the gang boss simply could not let pass.

"You know, Bobby," Hector said to the man kneeling before him, "the first time you came up short I figured that maybe it was a miscount. Mistakes happen, right? That's why the keyboard has a backspace. The second time I had my suspicions, but I said 'No way Bobby steals from me. He's my boy. He wouldn't dis me like that.' So I let that one go too. But this time, that's three times in four months. So, Bobby, I gotta ask …" There was a click as the hammer of Hector's .380 locked into place. "You stealing from me?"

Bobby knew the rules, even if he didn't follow them. He knew this wasn't downtown court, where reasonable doubt and moral uncertainty were enough to save your ass. No, on the street suspicion was enough to convict, and only one sentence was ever handed out. The question was -- how clean were you going to die?

"Yeah." The one word confession was Bobby's only choice. To have said otherwise would be to invite Hector to start shooting him in non-vital areas and to keep shooting until a confession came. Better to get it over with.

"Why, Bobby?"

"Does it matter?"

"Not really."

The sound of a single gunshot filled the air. The body of Bobby Lochlear fell to the ground. Hector put the barrel of the .380 against Bobby's head and tapped him again -- just to be sure.

"Get the brass," he told one of the men who had witnessed the execution. "Lose this," he said to another, wiping the gun and handing it to him.

"What about Bobby?"

Hector looked at the man picking up the spent casings. "Leave him. This far into the woods, it'll be weeks before he's found, if ever. Ain't like anybody's gonna look for him. Won't nobody care but his mamma, and she never liked him that much anyway."

Now Hector made one mistake that night. It wasn't killing Bobby. That had to be done. And it wasn't killing him in front of witnesses. That was part of the message. There had to be somebody to spread the word about what would happen if you stole from Hector O. If he double-tapped one of his own boys just think of what he'd do to a rip-off man. No, Hector's mistake was the gun.

In Hector's world guns were a disposable commodity. Everyone knew from TV how the crime lab could trace a gun. That's why you picked up the brass. That's why you ditched a piece that had a murder on it. The word on guns was "use them and lose them," just like cell phones and women. That way you stayed clean. The cops could have all the snitches in the city point at you, but they wouldn't have the proof. Baltimore juries watched TV too, and they wanted to see the proof.

That's why Hector told Ray Chavez to lose the gun. Ray was a good soldier; he knew what to do. Find deep water, wait until things were clear, drop the gun in. Baltimore being a harbor city, this was easy to do.

From Leakin Park, Ray took the long way to the Hanover Street Bridge. From Gwynn's Falls to Monroe, all the way down Monroe to the Parkway, then the Parkway to Patapsco. He'd come up on the bridge from the south. A quick stop and drop and all would be cool. Then it was a short ride home.

It was a good plan. As Ray pulled on to the bridge he was thinking about a six-pack in his fridge, the game on ESPN, and how he was looking forward to enjoying them both. Then he saw the black SUV cross the center line and come right for him.

There was no time to stop and no room to swerve. Several tons of Detroit metal struck the driver's side of Rays' car, driving it into the abutment and crushing most of what was inside. Ray's last thought was of how unfair it all was. He was only eighteen. He thought he'd live to at least twenty-one.

***

"How's everything tonight?"

Joe Russo looked up to see Detective Bianca Jones standing in the doorway to the Crime Lab. Suddenly, working the night shift didn't seem so bad. "What are you doing here so late?"

Bianca shrugged and sat down in the chair Joe had just vacated. "I got pulled in for that murder on Franklin Street."

"Anything to it?"

She shook her head. "Not for me. The detectives saw three black candles, a crystal ball and a *Buffy* poster and right away thought it was a cult slaying. So they called me. Turns out it was the boyfriend. He gave it up before I even got to the scene."

"So no fun tonight?" As soon as the words left his mouth Joe knew he shouldn't have said them.

Bianca gave him a hard look. "What I do is never 'fun.' It has to be done and I'm the one who has to do it." Joe started to apologize but she waved him off. "Sorry, I'm just cranky and tired. I was sound asleep when they called me in and I'm still not fully awake."

Bianca raised her arms over her head and unselfconsciously stretched, trying to shake the sleep out of her system. As she did, Joe took the opportunity to admire the shape that was revealed by her tightened clothes. Bianca caught him looking.

"Enjoy the show?" she asked, smiling.

Joe smiled back. "Always." Not for the first time did he wonder how Bianca did it. Not more than five-foot with a slender build; she looked more teen than detective. Yet she was probably the toughest cop in the department, having confronted nightmares that most people could never have imagined. Her assignment to the Special Investigations Unit made sure that she was called in whenever a case seemed to involve the occult, unusual, or bizarre.

"So why weren't you over on Franklin Street?" Bianca's question interrupted his thoughts.

"There was only one murder, right? They only needed one crime lab guy."

"Well, Mr. Crime Lab Guy, if you've finished eyeing me up, how about buying me a cup of coffee to keep me awake."

"Sure, Bianca. And if you're willing to wait until I'm off duty, I'll even buy you breakfast."

Just then the radio on his hip crackled Joe's unit number. Joe answered and wrote down the information the dispatcher gave him. "My master's voice," he told Bianca. "I'm needed at a fatal accident on the Hanover Street Bridge."

"Isn't that the job of the Accident Investigation Unit?"

"Yeah, but there's a gun in one of the cars that needs to be dusted and recovered. There's goes the coffee, what about breakfast?"

"I might just go home and go back to bed." And before Joe could make the obvious offer, she added, "To sleep. Now go dust your gun."

Bianca watched Joe leave and, not for the first time, thought about the differences between them. Like most cops, she was almost always on the front lines, struggling to maintain order and sanity in a chaotic, crazy world. So what if the threats she dealt with weren't the usual kinds of bad guys. They were still a danger to her city and had to be stopped, most times with force and violence. As a civilian, Joe fought crime his own way, with science and reason. As far as Bianca knew, he'd never fired a gun, never thrown a punch in anger or defense. Despite the horrors he'd witnessed on crime scenes, his was still a kind and gentle soul. He was her complete opposite. Maybe that's why she was attracted to him.

***

The accident on the Hanover Street Bridge was first reported on the morning traffic alerts, as just another tie-up snarling the morning commute. The noon news had more details, but with Ray's name withheld pending notification of next-of-kin. Hector O. didn't learn about it until six that evening. He wondered briefly about whether the police had found the gun that killed Bobby, then decided it wasn't worth the worry. If they did, it wasn't likely they'd connect it to the murder, if and when the body was found. And if they did -- well, it was in Ray's car when he was killed. They'd put it on him. "Abated by death" was one of the cops' favorite phrases.

***

Joe Russo did not find any prints on the recovered .380 pistol. There was, however, a very nice thumbprint on the magazine that held the cartridges. He lifted the print with tape, placed it on a white card and sent it to the Latent Print Unit for evaluation and comparison. The gun he submitted to the Firearms Unit to be test fired and the results compared to open cases.

Joe's report to Latent Prints was just one of dozens that that unit received each and every day. And since his case was only one of recovered property, his report was assigned the lowest priority. Unless someone made a special request, it would be months, maybe almost a year, before an examiner looked at it.

The Firearms Unit did test fire the .380. No immediate matches were made to either the spent bullet or ejected cartridge case.

***

Two weeks after the deaths of Ray Chavez and Bobby Lochlear, a fourth-grader who attended Dickey Hill Elementary School failed to return home. Her mother called the police and told them that her daughter liked to play in the trees near the school. These trees made up the western edge of Leakin Park.

The Police Academy Class was called in to search the woods. While the recruits were searching the little girl came home. She'd gone to a friend's house after school and had forgotten to call her mother. The search was called off, but not before a recruit stumbled across Bobby's somewhat decomposed body.

***

Every organization has its systems, each one designed to start working under differing sets of circumstances. The discovery of Bobby Lochlear's body caused one of the BPD's more efficient ones to go into effect.

The recovered bullets, one from Bobby's head, the other dug from the ground beneath his body, were submitted to the Firearms Unit where a routine computer check caused them to be matched to the .380 pistol Joe Russo had recovered a few weeks earlier. With the recovered gun now involved in a homicide, Joe's report to the Latent Print Unit was given top priority, and by the end of the day the latent print lifted from the magazine of the .380 pistol was identified as the left thumb of Hector Tyrone Oxendine.

Hector O. had his own system. Part of it consisted of people willing to exchange information for money. Some of these people worked for the Baltimore Police Department. Twenty-four hours after his print was matched, Hector learned of the one mistake he'd made in the murder of Bobby Lochlear. He had dropped the clip of his piece to make sure it was loaded, and had forgotten to wipe it along with the rest of the gun.

It didn't take long for Hector to learn who had lifted the print that could convict him for murder. "Find him, bring him here," he ordered two of his band.

"Hector," the braver of the two spoke up, "you're talking about messing with the cops. Sure you wanna do that?"

"He ain't no cop, just some low-paid lab tech. And without his testimony about finding that print, the cops ain't got a case against me. So yeah, I'm sure I want you to bring him here. I want to see the piece of shit who thinks he can put me away."

***

Working the evening shift -- 2 p.m. to 10 p.m. -- Joe caught a late homicide call and didn't leave work until after two. He got home shortly before three. Two men were waiting for him just outside his apartment building.

They came at him before he could open the front door. Knowing that he would not have time to get inside, he ran, hoping to rush past them. Surprise took him by one, but the other grabbed him. He tried to resist, but the two-on-one odds were too much for someone not trained in fighting and Joe was soon beaten into unconscious and dragged into a waiting car.

***

This isn't good, Bianca Jones thought as her ringing telephone woke her up. No one calls at -- she looked at her clock-radio through bleary eyes -- three-thirty to give you good news. She checked the caller I.D. It was Earl Beasley calling from his cell.

"What is it, Earl?"

"Trouble, Little Girl, big trouble."

"Little Girl," Beasley was the only person in the department, no, in her life who could get away with calling her that. The first time he'd said it he'd meant it derisively, dismissing her size and sex with one curt phrase. But that was in the past. Since then they'd fought side by side through Hell and worse and now it was a term of friendship and respect.

Before she could ask about the kind of trouble, Beasley told her. "Joe's been snatched. A neighbor heard a disturbance and looked out in time to see him being put in a car. She didn't get a tag."

"Where?"

"His place, of course. You do know where it is?"

Of course she did, and he knew it too. "I've been there on occasion," was her understatement.

"Good, get there soonest."

As she rushed to the scene, Bianca played out possibilities in her mind, trying to figure out who or what could have targeted Joe. It was the what that worried her more. She prayed that it wasn't an old case coming back to haunt her -- literally -- by striking out at those she held dear.

When she got to Joe's building Bianca saw that it had become a full scale crime scene. Stadium-strength lights turned night into day and yellow tape was everywhere. Joe's co-workers in the crime lab were taking photographs, drawing diagrams and searching for evidence. Detectives and uniformed officers were canvassing for witnesses. Bianca found Beasley in the center of it all, barking out orders, directing the investigation. The ex-homicide cop might now be in the sex offense unit, but that hadn't stopped him from taking charge of the scene.

"Earl, what have we got?"

"Good and bad news, Bianca. The good news is that if whoever it was wanted him dead, he'd be under a sheet right now. And since there's no evidence he was eaten by some ghoulie, it probably has nothing to do with any of your investigations."

Beasley paused as the two watched a lab tech swab a red stain from the sidewalk. "His or theirs?" Bianca wanted to know.

Beasley shrugged. "We'll know if we find him."

"You mean when we find him, right?"

Putting his arms around her shoulders, Beasley drew Bianca away from the scene. "About that bad news. As soon as I got the word, I had the guys at headquarters start looking into Joe's cases, to see if he had worked on anything that might prompt this."

"And?"

"He got a fingerprint hit on Hector Oxendine for murder."

Beasley had said the name as if expecting Bianca to recognize it. Her blank stare told him she didn't. "Bianca, Hector O.'s a major dealer. He don't play around and he's more than half crazy. This sounds like something he'd do."

"Where is he?"

"If we knew that, Little Girl, we'd be sweating him in the box right now."

Forget the box; Bianca wanted the dealer there, in front of her. And she'd have him bleeding, not sweating. She wanted to strike out at whoever had hurt Joe, but right now all she could do was wait. She decided that the longer she waited, the worse it would be for whoever had taken Joe.

While waiting she thought. Why wasn't Joe killed outright? This Hector O. wanted something. Information? Joe wouldn't have any. Then what? One possibility came to her mind.

"Earl, where was the murder?"

"What mur … Oh, the one Joe hit Oxendine for. Leakin Park."

"Where in the park?"

"I can find out, why?"

Bianca was already dragging Beasley to a car. "Find out on the way. Let's go."

***

Regaining consciousness, Joe at first did not know where he was. Then the pain from his beating reminded him of what had happened. A moan escaped him.

"He's awake," he heard someone say.

"Too bad for him then," said another.

From the floor where he was lying, Joe looked around. As his vision came into focus he saw five men standing in a rough arc in front of him. Wooden cases and cardboard boxes were behind them. He was in some sort of storeroom. He looked at the men again. He could now make out their faces. They didn't seem to care. From this he knew they did not expect him to live to testify against them.

One of the men spoke. Joe figured him to be the leader. "You know why you're here?"

Joe stayed quiet. He wasn't going to give this guy the satisfaction of a reply. A kick to his side changed his mind. Once the fresh pain subsided he coughed out, "You're going to kill me."

"No, I'm not going to kill you." The man pointed to Joe's abductors. "These two are. I just wanted to look at you before they did."

"Why?" Joe had to ask. He didn't want to, didn't want anything from this man. But neither did he want to die without knowing the reason.

The man looked at him thoughtfully. "You really don't know, do you? You don't know who I am or why I want you dead. I should tell you, but I like it better that you'll die not knowing." He turned to the men. "Take him out. You know where. Oh, and no head shot. Make it nice and slow."

"You sure it's a good idea doing him where we did Bobby?" one of the two who had snatched Joe asked. "We do that, the cops are gonna know it was you."

"So what? When this punk dies, so does his evidence. No proof I killed anybody. The cops can put two and together all they want. Without proof they can't say four to a jury. But everyone will know what happens to anyone who threatens me."

He's wrong about the proof, Joe said to himself as he was being thrown back into the car. There's plenty of it. My blood's in that room and in this car. And I've touched the car door so it's got my prints. There'll be no problem putting me on this scene. But these thoughts failed to give him any satisfaction as he was driven to his fate.

The ride was short. Five minutes after being put into the car Joe was again dragged out of it. He was walked through the woods, one man holding him tightly from behind with the other in front. In the early morning it was just light enough to make out a trail. Soon they stopped.

"This it?" the one in the lead asked.

"Close enough, let's do it."

Joe started running as soon as he was released. He didn't get far. He heard a pistol crack then felt a searing pain in his left leg as a bullet entered and shattered the bone. He fell face forward to the ground.

Joe dimly heard one of them say "My turn" before there was another crack and a second bullet took him in his right thigh.

***

"You've got the light, intersection's clear."

"I see it, Little Girl."

On the scene, Bianca had commandeered a patrol car, and now she and Beasley were making a desperate drive to Leakin Park. Beasley was driving, running lights and sirens. He'd switch both off before approaching the park so as not to give any warning.

"Are you sure about this?" he asked Bianca as he weaved around a driver stopped in the middle of the street.

"No, I'm not. I'm not sure about anything except that Joe wasn't dead on the scene. Which means somebody wanted him for something. And if it was this Hector O., maybe it was to send some kind of a message. And where better to leave it than the scene of the first murder?'

"And if you're wrong?"

"Then I'm wrong, and Joe will still be missing, and we still won't know where he is. But if I'm right, I only hope that we'll be on time."

"Well, I've got Southwest patrol rolling to meet us at Windsor Mill and Wetheredsville Road. They'll know better where the murder took place."

Ten minutes later the pair was in the park. There was no patrol car in sight.

"Should we wait for them?" Beasley asked.

There was the sound of a gunshot, followed by another one a minute later.

"I don't think we have to," Bianca said, getting out of the car and moving towards the sound.

***

The two men with guns looked at the body lying still on the ground. "Think he's had enough?" one asked.

The other looked at his pistol and shrugged. "I got bullets left. What about you?"

"He's done, why waste them?" said the other.

"Two in the head then?"

"One from each of us."

The pair took aim. But before either could fire … "Freeze, police!"

They turned. Two cops -- both were in plain clothes, but what else could they be? -- were standing there, guns drawn.

***

Thanking God she was right, Bianca saw two men standing over what could only be Joe's body. She heard Beasley yell "Freeze, Police," not that his warning mattered to her. She was already aiming, preparing to fire when the two turned around, guns in their hands. She didn't give them a chance to surrender, couldn't take the chance that they would shoot it out.

Bianca started shooting, Beasley beside her doing the same, both detectives discharging their weapons in a calm, controlled manner. There was no thought of Joe, no thought of the man who'd had him abducted, no thought of anything but the moment. These were men with guns; they had to be put down. As their targets jerked with each impact, the detectives kept firing until both men had fallen.

"Cover," Bianca, slightly deaf from the discharging, barely heard Beasley say. She stood watch, pistol trained on the fallen bodies, as her partner dropped the clip from his piece, replaced it with a fresh one then slid a live round into the chamber. Beasley then stood guard as she did the same. Only then did the detectives approach the bodies.

Bianca rushed to Joe's side. Grabbing his hand, she put her fingers on his wrist, searching, praying for a pulse. Nothing at first, but then she felt the weak beating of his heart.

"Earl, Joe's alive!"

Beasley stood up from checking on the other two. "So's one of the suspects, at least for now. The other's already out of service. I've called it in, got an ambo on the way, along with everybody else."

"Which one's alive?" Beasley pointed out the survivor. Bianca left Joe's side to go over to him.

"Be careful, Little Girl."

Bianca ignored him, bent down over the surviving gunman. A few minutes later she stood up. "He's gone."

"He give you anything?" Beasley asked. Bianca shook her head. "Shame, a dying declaration putting this on Oxendine would have been nice."

"Yeah, wouldn't it?" Bianca said distantly, then went over to kneel by Joe until the medics came.

***

As an officer involved in a shooting, Bianca had been assigned desk duty, her police powers temporarily suspended. She didn't mind. It would only be for a few days. It was obvious to all that it had been a good shoot. Even if it wasn't, given the circumstances everyone was prepared to make it one.

Joe was still in the hospital; his condition critical and unstable, his survival depending on equal parts medical skills and divine intervention. Bianca had been to visit him several times. Seeing him lying there unconscious only deepened her resolve and reinforced the decision she had made in the park.

She had lied to Beasley; the dying man had given her something.

"Where's Hector?"

"Screw you, bitch."

Her body hiding her actions from Beasley, Bianca drew her gun; put it to the man's eye. "Screw you. You want to live, tell me where to find Hector." There was a siren in the distance. "Hear that? That's the medics. Talk now and you leave with them. Or you can leave in a bag. Nobody's going to notice one more hole in you." She racked the slide of her Glock for emphasis.

The man didn't hear it. Right then his whole world was the gun in front of him and the approaching ambulance. He was dying, he knew that. There was nothing anyone could do to stop it -- probably. That siren coming nearer and nearer was his last bit of hope. He couldn't let it go. He gave out an address.

The gun moved away to be replaced by the woman's face. It was the last thing he saw in this world.

Bianca had not known she was going to hold back Oxendine's address until she heard herself lie to Beasley. Back then, she hadn't known why. She did now.

The men who had abducted and shot Joe were dead. There was nothing to tie them to Oxendine. And without Joe's testimony, the evidence from the gun that had killed Bobby Lochlear could not be admitted. So while there was probable cause to arrest Hector O., there was no chance he'd ever be convicted.

Hector Oxendine would remain free, his freedom a warning to others that he was not a man to be messed with, that his power extended beyond the street. And with this warning came a message to all other criminals, that their freedom was just a bullet away.

Bianca was going to send a different message.

The address the dying gunman had given her was a warehouse on DeSoto Road. As soon as her suspension was over, Bianca staked it out. On the second day of her watch she saw four men go in, one of them matching the photo of Hector Oxendine she'd gotten from the Identification Unit. Four against one, she thought. I've faced worse odds and walked away. She checked her weapons. It was almost time.

She again asked herself if this was the right thing to do. She was risking it all -- her career, her freedom, her life. Well, it wouldn't be the first time, she thought. The man in that building had not just broken the law; he'd attacked the system she'd sworn to protect, and in doing so had brutalized someone she loved. He was as much a monster as the others she'd faced.

And it was her job to hunt monsters.

Without hesitation Bianca walked quickly from her car to the building.

The door to the warehouse wasn't locked. As she expected, there was someone just inside.

"Yeah?" He looked her up and down, his relaxed manner telling her that he didn't see her as much of a threat. With her size and apparent youth, why would he?

"Here to see Hector."

"Why?"

"I got something for him."

"What?"

Bianca let out a sigh. "Look, asshole, I don't have time for your bullshit. You gonna let me back there or not?" When the guard hesitated she gave him her best "I don't believe this" look. "Fine, next time I see Hector I'll tell him why he didn't get what he's due." She turned to go. "And I'll tell him why."

"Wait." The guard took a quick look outside. He didn't see anything he hadn't seen a dozen times before. "Go on," he told her, pointing towards an office in the rear. She nodded her thanks and went on back.

When Bianca entered the room she saw three men sitting around a card table in a mostly empty office. Whatever they were doing, there was no sign of any criminal activity. They had looked up when she opened the door and no doubt saw what she wanted them to see, a young girl in an unzipped hooded jacket. "Hector Oxendine?" she said in a quiet, nervous voice before any of them could ask her business. She knew who he was but she wanted him to identify himself.

"I'm Hector," the man at the left of the table said. "What you want, sweet thing?"

"I got something for you."

Hector laughed a dirty laugh. "You a little thing, but maybe you do." He looked at him men, inviting them to join in with the joke. "I hope you can share it three ways." His leer left no doubt what he meant.

As three shared a laugh at her expense, Bianca, in a practiced gesture, slipped off her jacket and let in fall to the floor. The men stopped laughing when they saw the badge clipped to the right side of her belt and her pistol to the left. They didn't notice that her left hand was behind her back.

"You a cop?" Hector's question was part surprise, part disbelief. Without waiting for an answer he asked, "What do you want?"

Before answering, Bianca took the time to size up the men in front of her, deciding which was likely to move first. "You're going to pay for Joe Russo and Bobby Lochlear, Oxendine, one way or the other. You can either confess, or …"

"Or what?" Smiling, Hector seemed amused by this pint-sized cop.

Bianca returned his grin. "Or one of us dies."

Hector's smile faded. "Waste the bitch."

Both of Hector's men stood up, their eyes watching the pistol still on her belt. Which is why they didn't see Bianca bring the .38 revolver from behind her back.

She shot the one opposite her first, her twin shots hitting him twice in the chest. Before he could fall she turned her gun on the second man and put a bullet through his eye.

Hector was on the floor. Unarmed, he was scrambling for the gun dropped by the first man. This gave Bianca time to deal with the guard who was then coming through the office door, gun out but lowered. She had by now drawn her 9mm pistol. She leveled it at his head. "This doesn't concern you. Leave." The guard took one quick look at the men on the floor. He dropped his gun and fled.

Bianca turned back to Hector. He now had a gun and was pointing it at her. She moved just as he pulled the trigger and his bullet struck the wall behind her. Returning fire with both her guns, she caught him twice in the left shoulder. Her next volley struck him in the chest. Hector wavered. The fight was out of him, but he was still standing, still holding his gun. Aiming carefully, Bianca took out his both knees and his left elbow. Hector fell. To be sure, Bianca used the last bullet in her .38 and shot him in the right wrist. He let go of his weapon.

"No more," he begged her.

Bianca stood over him, her revolver pointing toward his head. "Too bad, Hector, because I'm not finished." She cocked the gun. "Goodbye, Hector."

She pulled the trigger to his cries of "Please! God, no!" and the hammer fell on a spent casing. A wet stain spread across the front of Hector's pants.

"This one's loaded," she said, showing him the 9mm. Standing at a distance so as not leave powder burns, she got ready to fire. A simple head shot and it would all be over, Joe would be avenged, justice would be served. About to fire, she got a better idea.

"Here's how it's going to be," she told a surprised to still be alive Hector. "You're crippled. You're not going to heal right. Your arm and legs, well, if you don't lose them they'll never work right again. You'll be in constant pain."

"What's your point, bitch? Finish it or …"

Bianca moved the gun down towards his crotch. "Quiet and listen, or go through life as Hector No-balls." Hector shut up.

"You can confess, take a plea and go to jail for long time. Not as long as you should, but long enough. And in jail they'll use money that should be spent on honest folk to fix you up almost as good as new. Or you can keep quiet and walk, or in your case, limp painfully. How long you think you'll last back on the street, crippled and weak, a one-time player who got taken down by some dame?"

She let him think about it for a minute. "Those are your choices, Hector, and I don't really give a damn which one you pick. Either way you'll be my warning to others not to go hunting police."

She left him in his pain and walked away to call in the shooting.

CITY ON FIRE

In a dark room, close to the hour of midnight, a young girl stood in front of a mirror. Naked except for an inverted cross around her neck, she waited for the clock to strike. When it did she silently counted the strokes.

"One, two, three ..."

When she got to nine she looked deep into her reflection and said out loud, "Black Aggie. Black Aggie. Black Aggie." The words were timed so that the last syllable left her lips just as the clock struck its last.

She waited -- for a door to open, for a lover to appear, for death to come.

Nothing came, nothing happened, nothing but what might have been mocking laughter from the dark as she fell on the bed to cry herself to sleep.

***

It was supposed to have been a small ceremony held in the fifth floor conference room with only a handful of his closest friends and co-workers in attendance. But word got out and instead of retiring quietly, Joe Russo was getting full department honors and recognition.

"I still don't see what the fuss is all about, Bianca," Joe said, balancing on his cane in the waiting area just outside the auditorium. "All I did was get abducted and shot. You and Beasley saved me and then you caught the guy behind it. You're the ones who should be getting the medals."

Detective Bianca Jones reached up and adjusted Joe's tie for the fourth time that morning. "They don't give out medals of valor for shooting drug dealers, especially when they suspect that you deliberately hunted them down."

"Which you did," Joe said smiling, after making sure no one else was within earshot.

Bianca returned the smile. "They deserved it. Nobody shoots my boyfriend and gets away with it." She lifted her head, Joe lowered his and they shared a quick kiss.

"Joe, you deserve every award they give you. You were the one injured in the line of duty. You were the one who developed the forensic evidence on Hector O. And you were the one he tried to kill. And even then you made sure to leave behind enough evidence to convict him even if you didn't make it. No one in the department has ever done a finer job, especially no one from the Crime Lab. Now get ready, they're about to call your name."

Bianca left to take her place in the front row between Detective Earl Beasley and a man who called himself Morgan. The former had helped Bianca save Joe's life. The latter was outwardly the owner of a Fells Point bookstore but was in reality so much more.

Bianca took her seat just as Joe was called to the stage. As he slowly ascended the steps, she again said a prayer of thanks for his survival. Joe had been a long time recovering from his wounds. He had been shot multiple times and, despite the finest medical care that the City of Hope Hospital could provide, had not been expected to pull through.

"Don't despair, Miss Jones," Father Anton Lawrence, a priest of her acquaintance, had told her. Father Lawrence had rushed to Joe's bedside as soon as he had heard the news of his injuries. "The boy is strong; his faith is strong, as I know is yours. If it is meant to be, he will survive. The Lord looks after His own, and Joe is one of His special ones, as are you, I should add."

Bianca knew what the priest meant for hers was a unique position in the Baltimore Police Department. Assigned to the Special Investigations Unit, it was Bianca's job to investigate any occurrence that involved the occult, supernatural or the otherworldly. In doing so she had battled cults, fought monsters, and stolen souls from Hell. Joe had been with her from the start, providing both technical and emotional support. She had met Father Lawrence when she and Joe had sought his help in redeeming a vampire.

As she watched Joe cross the stage, Father Lawrence's words came back to Bianca. "He does look after His own," she thought as she recalled Joe's slow but miraculous recovery. He was now almost fully healed, but the damage to his left leg was such that he would always walk with a cane. When the department doctors had declared him unfit for duty he had no choice but to accept a medical retirement.

On stage, Joe handed his cane to the Lab Director to receive, in order, the Medal of Valor, the Silver Star, and his retirement plaque. Once these awards had been given and handed off to a cadet for safekeeping, Joe again took up his cane and made his way off the stage and over to the waiting Bianca.

Arriving in the Atrium for Joe's farewell reception, it was no surprise to either him or Bianca that Detective Earl Beasley had beaten them there and had already made use of buffet table.

"So what are you going to do now, Russo?" he asked, somehow managing to balance a ham sandwich, a cup of coffee and a chocolate doughnut all at the same time.

"I'm taking my two-thirds pension and going to work in Morgan's bookstore. He's going to, um, teach me the trade."

Having assisted Bianca in her "special investigations" Beasley was aware that Morgan in addition to being a book dealer Morgan was Bianca's advisor in her crusade against the darkness.

"So you're staying in the game."

"Once you're in there's only one way out. Besides," Joe looked over to the buffet table where Bianca was getting them both something to eat, "someone has to look after her."

"Joe, that little girl can more than look after herself. She may only be five foot nothing, but I've seen her take down things twice that, and I do mean things."

"It's afterwards I worry about, Earl."

"You and me both, friend. You and me both."

***

Some blocks away in the Maryland State Penitentiary, hard men were having their own meeting. They gathered in a corner of the prison's common room, away from the other prisoners. They spoke in low whispers so as not to be overheard but they need not have bothered. No one came near them; no one wanted to come near them. For within the walls that enclosed society's worst, men whose behavior was such that they had to be removed from the outside world, this group was feared.

Their leader was Damon LeVaey, a tall blonde man in his late twenties or early thirties. LeVaey was serving multiple consecutive life terms for the cult slayings of teenagers on Maryland's Eastern Shore and for the attempted murder of a Baltimore City Police officer. The latter was his one regret in his lifetime of evil. His failure to kill Bianca Jones had caused him to be arrested and convicted and he knew that once his life in prison was over he was damned to serve another sentence, an eternal one of torture and pain for having failed his hellish master, the one who had bid him to seek out and destroy the young detective.

LeVaey's first days were a taste of what awaited him in his afterlife. LeVaey was well built with rugged good looks and a manner that appealed to most women and a fair number of men. On the outside this was an advantage to a man who wished to seduce young people into following the dark path. On the inside, however, he attracted those who preyed on the weak and helpless and to whom new fish were especially tempting.

It was several of these men who confronted LeVaey in the shower room on his third night inside. With the correctional officers who were supposed to be watching them nowhere in sight, the men surrounded him and made their intentions known. LeVaey was given a choice of either surrendering his body or taking a severe beating, after which he would still be raped.

The ex-cult leader had been expecting such an assault but had no way to avoid it. Bereft of his followers and abandoned by Satan, he was without the power he needed to repel his assailants. Otherwise, with few spoken words, some gestures, a sign drawn in the air, he could have turned the five men against each other. As it was, he was helpless and he felt sure that sure his master was watching from down below and laughing.

Not wanting a beating, LeVaey suffered himself to be bent over a dirty toilet to be roughly penetrated by each of the men in turn.

They used him for over thirty minutes with two of the man taking him twice. When they were done, they threw him to the tiled floor, relieved themselves on him then left. The guards found him a few minutes later; his body spattered with cum and piss.

"What happened to you," asked the oldest of the uniformed men. "Were you assaulted or did you just … trip and fall?" By what the officer said and the way he said, LeVaey knew that his answer would set the course for his prison stay.

"I … I tripped and fell."

The two guards nodded as if expecting the answer. The youngest threw him some towels. "Be more careful next time, and clean this mess up. Light's out in twenty minutes."

The correctional officers left as LeVaey began to wipe the leavings of his assailants from his body. When he was done he looked at the towel in his hands, the towel containing the essence of the men who had raped and abused him, the men who were no doubt bragging of how they had made the fresh meat give up his ass.

Let them laugh, LeVaey thought to himself, let them have their victory for tonight. For he realized that in his hands he held both his means of revenge and of the return of his power.

That night, his cellmate asleep, LeVaey conjured in the dark. Like called to like as the stains on the towel he had taken from the shower room separated and reformed. When he was done, there were five distinct areas, one for each of the men who had attacked him. He then ripped the towel into strips, each containing one stain, and fashioned the strips into five crude doll-like shapes.

LeVaey now had what he needed, representations of his enemies with semen and urine from their bodies, fluids freely given. Using what little magic he had left, he charged the dolls, changed them so that in effect they were his enemies so that whatever he did to the stained cloth would be mirrored on his attackers' bodies.

He thought about doing it that night -- burning one, drowning one, crushing another beneath his heel. He'd shove a pencil in the rear of the fourth and the fifth would go under his pillow to cause the last man to slowly suffocate.

That would not do, LeVaey realized. As satisfying as their deaths would be, no one would know that he was the cause. By the morning his humiliation in the shower room would be public knowledge, and so his vengeance must be known to all.

Dawn was coming as LeVaey finished his work. He laid down for a brief nap before the morning wake-up call. As he drifted off LeVaey thought he heard an approving chuckle come from the long shadows cast by the sun.

At breakfast the next morning as LeVaey entered the cafeteria he felt the stares of those who knew what had happened to him the night before. A quick glance around showed him that all his abusers were in the room and coming towards him. He sat down and his table emptied. As he hoped, the five from the night before joined him.

"Hi ya, sweet cheeks," said one, loud enough for all those around him to hear. "You eat up good cause you're gonna need your strength tonight."

"Yeah," added another, "can't wait to get my dick in that tight ass of yours again, though it ain't as tight as it was." This prompted general laughter, shared by some at the other tables. LeVaey did not join in.

"Hell with his ass," said a third, "I want to try his mouth. You got a nice mouth on you, friend. You know how to use it?"

LeVaey answered this question with a cold stare, looking deep into each of the five men's eyes. They quieted and as he stood they tensed, wondering what he would do. They knew he had not had the time to make allies or fashion weapons, but a crazed man could do much damage even with his fists.

The mood was broken when LeVaey pulled one of his makeshift dolls from his shirt. The five men relaxed as one of them said, "Aww, you've got a little dolly. Guess you really are a little girl. Well, tonight, little girl, you got a date with five big men," he looked around at all those staring, "maybe more."

LeVaey held the doll gently in his hand. "I don't know which of you this is," he said, "but let's see what happens." He gave the doll a vicious twist.

There was a loud "crack" and the man who had called him "sweet cheeks" cried out in pain and fell to the floor. He tried to rise but found that with his back broken his legs refused to obey him.

The man's cry had attracted the guards. As they rushed toward the table LeVaey bent over the fallen man as if offering help. Instead he handed the man his doll and said in a low voice, "Take very good care of this. What happens to it, happens to you." At the orders of the correctional officers he then backed away and joined his other tormentors.

"You four are next," he whispered, confident that others heard as well. "One by one you will suffer and you will come to think that he," LeVaey nodded to the now crippled prisoner, "was the lucky one."

"Bullshit," said one of the remaining four, "you can't expect us to think that a fairy like you caused that."

"No?" LeVaey took another doll from his shirt and let it fall to the floor. "Let's see." He stepped on the head and walked away as a man fell dead, his brains having exploded inside his skull.

The other three died within the week. One slowly strangled as LeVaey tightened the piece of string he had tied around his doll's neck a little bit each day. Another died screaming in the night as his bones were broken one by one. And the last took the quick way out, cheating LeVaey of his vengeance by hanging himself in his cell.

Word spread. Five men dead by LeVaey's hand. The crimes he committed on the outside became known. His reputation grew and as he gathered to him a small band of followers so did his power.

One night the shadows spoke to him.

"You have done well," came the voice of his master.

"Then am I forgiven?"

The Devil laughed. "It is the Other who forgives. But I will allow you to serve me once more and if you please me I may remit some of the tortures that await you."

And Satan told his disciple what he must do to earn his favor and why he must do it. LeVaey eagerly agreed.

It was in furtherance of his master's wishes that LeVaey had called his followers together in the common room. He told them what he needed.

"Anyone in particular?" asked one of the men.

LeVaey thought for a minute. "One of the Aryans. Try to make it look like it was done by one of the black or Hispanic gangs. The retaliation murders should liven things up around here."

"What should we do with the body?'

LeVaey shrugged. "I don't really care. Just hang him and bring me his left hand."

***

Bianca Jones took a few days off to help Joe Russo celebrate his retirement. No sooner had she returned to work then she was summoned to the office of Major Chester Williams, chief of the Special Investigations Unit.

"A new case, Detective Jones," he said, handing her a folder, "one that might be in your line. There was a murder last week. The victim was killed on Highland Avenue. Patrol found the gun that was used in an alley off Jefferson. The Latent Print Unit matched a thumbprint from the clip to a suspect."

"What's strange about that, sir, other than actually getting a print match off a gun?"

"The suspect's been dead for over a year."

"That doesn't mean this is one of *those* cases, Major."

"Dead men don't leave fingerprints, Detective."

"Before they die, they do." Bianca looked through the case folder. "From what Joe's told me, unless they're wiped off, prints stay around forever. The print that the Latent Unit matched was from the pistol's magazine. It's quite possible that it's a year old." She read further. "Our dead suspect, um…Devon Maran, got dead by being shot. Whoever killed him probably robbed him of his gun afterward."

"That's possible, it makes sense and it's probably what happened, but …"

"But you want to make sure that Maran didn't get up and walk away."

"Vampires, ghosts, and rapists from other dimensions. I think it's best we make sure."

"Yes sir. I'll get started right away."

"What's your first step?"

"What else? We dig him up."

***

It was the phone call everyone in the Crime Lab had been waiting for, ever since they got word that Joe Russo was retiring. It was the call nobody wanted to get, the call from Bianca Jones requesting the services of a crime scene technician.

They had all heard the rumors about what Bianca really did in the Special Investigation Unit, that the bad guys she hunted down were not necessarily human, that her investigations took her into a darkness greater than any of them could imagine. And while they discounted the stories of vampires, zombies, and werewolves as probably untrue, none of them wanted to chance taking part in a case where the suspects could only be stopped by a wooden stake, silver bullet, or the light of day. They had seen what had happened to Russo -- that drug dealer story was no doubt a cover for something far nastier -- and no one wanted to take his place.

Still, they all knew it was coming. In anticipation, they decided that when Detective Jones did call, the only fair way to decide who had to go was to deal the cards around the table until someone got the black spot -- the ace of spades. A new deck was purchased and kept unopened on the supervisor's desk to be used when the time came.

The day after Bianca returned to work, the phone in the Mobile Crime Lab rang and was answered by Supervisor Eric Scott. He listened briefly, said, "We'll take care of it," and hung up. Then he walked into the common room and threw the now opened deck of cards in the middle of the table.

"Senior man deals," he said.

That was Greg Harris. Harris was nearing thirty years with the crime lab and in six months or so was planning to follow Joe Russo out the door. Harris was a movie fan and knew all too well what happened in cop films to those close to retirement. He took the cards out of their box and slowly began to shuffle them.

"What's the call, boss?"

"Greenmount Cemetery, 0900. Jones has a body to dig up."

"Probably a vampire," said Patty Bailey, breathing a sigh of relief as Harris dealt her the ten of clubs.

"Nah," Harris said, flipping a two of spades towards Mike Stewart, the new guy of the unit with only six months on the street. "I hear she only hunts them at night. More sporting that way. Close one, Mike, and another close one for you, Terry."

"Could be a ghoul or zombie," Teresa Reinhardt offered as she looked at her ace of clubs.

"What's the difference?" Stewart wanted to know.

Movie expert Harris answered again. "Get eaten by a zombie you become one. A ghoul just makes you dead. Seven to you, Marvin."

Marvin Greene was the last at the table. The cards went round again, and a third time without the ace of spades showing. But then on the fourth circuit,

"We have a winner."

Harris flipped the black spot in front of Stewart.

"Four winners you mean," corrected Bailey.

"Tough luck, kid." Greene didn't mean it but someone had to say it.

"Yeah, tough luck," repeated Harris. "But maybe it won't be so bad, Mike. I heard that Detective Jones is part vampire herself, so maybe she'll suck your blood and you'll live forever. Course you'd be stuck on night shift."

"She's a vamp of some kind. From what I heard about Jones and Joe Russo, she's more likely to suck your …"

"That's enough, Patty." Scott interrupted before the conversation got out of hand. "Pack your gear, Mike, and remember that it's just another call."

The still stunned Stewart didn't seem to believe that as he slowly left the office to respond to what he feared might be his last crime scene. The others waited until the "ding" of the elevator told them that he was on his way down to the garage. Then they all broke up laughing.

"Think he'll ever find out that the fix was in?" Reinhardt wondered.

Harris started dealing the cards again, this time announcing what they were before flipping them over. Thirty years of night shift poker had not gone to waste. "If he comes back alive we'll tell him."

There was another round of laughter at the new guy's expense. Then Scott broke the mood by saying, "Laugh now, guys, but remember, when Mike comes back he's had his turn. And the next time Detective Jones needs someone from this shift, like maybe to search a haunted house for something that should be dead but isn't, it's going to be one of you." He gathered the cards from the table and returned them to their box. "These'll be on my desk. When the time comes, don't let Greg deal."

***

Baltimore's Greenmount Cemetery was built on what was once rural land. Now it's in the heart of the city's crime ridden Eastern District where it was once estimated that the number of people gun downed outside its walls was near to equaling the number buried within them. An exaggeration but it says something about the area that people believe it.

Among the cemetery's eternally sleeping residents are mayors and first ladies. A queen and king almost joined them, but the Duke and Duchess of Windsor were permitted a more royal resting place. Napoleon's sister-in-law is there, as are the photographer A. Aubury Bodine and philanthropist Johns Hopkins. Greenmount is also the final resting place of John Wilkes Booth and at least one other of his conspirators, the former being buried in an unmarked grave.

The small party that had gathered was in the newest section in the cemetery, far away from disturbing the rest of anyone famous or notorious. Bianca stood next to the crime lab tech assigned to her, who had nervously introduced himself as Mike Stewart. They had waited quietly as a minister said a brief prayer prior to the opening of the grave and now stood side by side as they watched a backhoe disturb the peace of Devon Maran.

"If he's in there."

"Wha-what was that?"

At the uneasy question from the crime lab tech Bianca realized that she must have spoken aloud, had forgotten that Joe was not at her side.

Bianca looked over at the young man standing next to her. She did not remember seeing him before. He must be the new guy hired when it became clear that Joe not coming back. From the way he was looking at her, then the grave and then the open gates down the cemetery road told her that while she hadn't heard of him he clearly had heard of her. He was probably expecting the corpse to pop out of the coffin like a jack-in-the-box.

And it just might, Bianca thought, the way things happen around here. Ever since she had stopped that creature from another dimension up on Federal Hill, things in the city had been getting weirder and weirder. And there was no sign that the strangeness would ever stop. Or maybe they had always been that way and it was only that she was becoming more aware of it.

Whichever it was, Bianca knew that when the weird and the strange became demonic and evil it was her fate to meet them head on and stop them or die trying. Which she no doubt would some day. She accepted that. In her prayers at night she no longer asked for a long and happy life, just that when the time came and her luck failed, that she fell with her soul intact and that no harm would come to the people and city she loved.

Putting aside such thoughts, Bianca realized that it was time to reassure the new guy.

"Relax, Stewart," she said, "chances are that when the box is opened we're going to find a partly decomposed body in it, either Devon Maran or someone else. We'll know for sure once you take its prints and the Latent Print Unit matches them up."

The backhoe had finished its job and now workers were busy raising the coffin from the ground. Bianca went on. "Or the coffin might be empty. If it is, you're off the hook and my job just got harder."

"If there's nothing to worry about, why is he here?" Stewart pointed to Sergeant Tavon Greggs of the BPD Quick Response Team who was standing close by, shotgun at the ready. Greggs knew more than most of the extent of Bianca's activities and what he knew scared the life out of him. But he also knew his job and that was to blow anything that got past the detective back to the Hell it had crawled out of.

"He's here just in case."

Stewart's voice started to get higher. "In case of what?"

Bianca's reply was cut off by the cry of "Ready!" She looked toward the coffin, now sitting at the edge of the open grave. "Step back," she told the workers, "I'll unlatch and open it."

Slowly she walked toward the box that was supposed to contain the mortal remains of Devon Maran and said a silent prayer that he was still there. Minutes later she lifted the lid and saw that her prayer had been answered.

"Stewart," she cried, "get over here and print this guy."

The crime lab tech walked over, reached into the coffin and gently brought out Maran's right arm, silently hoping that it would remain attached to the rest of the body. He held up the hand for Bianca to see. It was missing the middle finger, the one whose print had been matched to the recovered pistol.

"Well, that explains that." To Stewart Bianca said, "Go ahead and roll the index finger then get it over to Latents just to be sure. After that you're done."

Stewart let out an audible sigh of relief. "Thanks."

Printing Maran took all of two minutes. When Stewart was finished, Bianca signaled to the cemetery staff that they could rebury the body. Then she walked over to thank Greggs for standing by.

"So Maran's not up walking around," the QRT sergeant asked.

"Doesn't look like it. But that leaves me with another problem."

"Which is?"

"Who did the dear departed Devon give the finger to, and when?"

****

"Hello there, little sister."

"Hello yourself, big brother."

Except for the commonality of their last names, Bianca and Dominic Jones had little in common. He was as tall as she was short and as dark as she was pale. They had met when Bianca was still a patrol officer and had accompanied a murder victim to the morgue. Dominic was there to accept the body.

"Bianca *Jones*?" he had said in a beautiful Caribbean accent. He introduced himself then added, "Could it be that I've found my long-lost sister?"

"I doubt it. My father never left this country."

"Ah, but my father did, and he had a way with the ladies."

This got a rare smile out of Bianca. "Just like his son, I suspect."

"You are right about that. Maybe one night I could show you just how much?"

"I'd love to, Dominic, but since we're brother and sister it wouldn't be proper."

At a loss for words for once in his life, Dominic Jones merely smiled his acceptance and the two were "big brother" and "little sister" from then on.

"And what can I do for you today?"

Bianca explained what she needed and soon Dominic had pulled the file on Devon Maran.

"As you can see by our photos, he had all ten digits when he came in." Dominic lowered his voice and looked around to make sure no one was listening. "But maybe not when he went out. There was one who worked here about a year ago, he was with a gang. He was caught removing fingers and taking blood."

"To lay false trails on crime scenes."

"Exactly, little sister. He was let go and things were kept very quiet. Which is why you probably did not hear of it. We take more care now, and so the bad men have to remove the fingers before they leave the body."

"Does that happen very often, Dominic?"

"Not so much, but the other day we did get in a corpse missing his whole left hand."

****

"So what then?"

Her day over, Bianca had gone to meet Joe at Morgan's Rare Books and Collectibles. There she told him about her missing finger case.

"I gave the whole thing over to Gang Crimes and Criminal Intel. Let them worry about the bad guys planting false evidence. I'm just happy not to have the dead roaming the streets of Baltimore again."

Morgan was serving a customer, his last of the day. When the sale was over, the bookseller locked the door and flipped the "open" sign to "closed."

"Miss Jones, tell me more about the body without a hand."

"Not much to tell, Morgan. Dominic said he was brought in from the Pen, another gang murder it looks like. He was part of the Brotherhood so they're looking at maybe the Bloods or M13. The hand thing may be some kind of message."

"Perhaps not, Miss Jones. Mr. Russo, please hand me down *The Haunters and the Haunted* by Rhys. Look for the catalog from the Walsall Museum as well. The manner of the man's death, it was hanging, was it not, Miss Jones?"

It was not quite a chill that went down Bianca's back, just a feeling that her relief that her day's investigation had turned up nothing supernatural had been premature. She had not told either Morgan or Joe how the prisoner had died, yet somehow the bookseller knew.

"Yes, the guards found him hanging in his cell. From the lack of blood it was determined that his hand …"

"His left hand?"

"Yes, his left hand was severed post-mortem. What's this about, Morgan?"

Taking the two volumes from Joe, Morgan flipped through them until he found what he was looking for then turned the books to display their pages to Bianca. The museum catalog showed what looked like a desiccated claw. The book by Rhys had a drawing of a hand with candles for fingertips.

"A Hand of Glory, Miss Jones. The left hand of a murderer who died by hanging. After death the hand is cut off and the fat of the body used to turn it into a candle. Carried by someone who knows how to use it, it can render the bearer invisible or cause those around him to become immobile. It is also said to have the power to open any door, no matter how well it has been locked. It was very popular with burglars in the time before science replaced magic."

"So why would someone go through the trouble … oh hell!"

"Hell indeed, Miss Jones, at least someone very familiar with it. I suggest you call the State Penitentiary to determine if Damon LeVaey is still in custody."

***

In a dark room, close to the hour of midnight, a young girl stood in front of a mirror. Naked except for an inverted cross around her neck, she waited for the clock to strike. When it did she silently counted the strokes.

"One, two, three …"

And as she did every night, Anna Burgess waited until just after the ninth chime to stare into her reflection and chant, "Black Aggie. Black Aggie. Black Aggie."

As she had every night before, Anna stood before the mirror and waited and hoped for the magic to return. And as she had every night before, she went to bed disappointed and laid in the darkness, waiting for the mocking laughter that sometime came. But there was instead a voice that whispered to her, telling her of day, a time, and a place. And for the first time since losing the child she never had, Anna fell asleep with a smile on her face.

***

She knew the address; it was the abandoned garage where Fat Phillip died. The fool had thought to impress her and another girl by trying to raise a demon. It hadn't worked and Phillip paid the price of failure. However just before he died Anna offered what little of his soul there was to Satan. After that her dreams were filled with carnal couplings, each night bringing a new sensation, a different perversion until she started to swell with a dream child fathered by her dark master. The child was stolen by its father, leaving her alone and a virgin once more. That bitch of a detective, the one who had tried to arrest her for Phillip's death, had promised to help but never did.

The garage had not changed much. Yellow pieces of crime scene tape still fluttered from the doorway. Apparently few people had been here since Phillip's botched ritual, a few junkies maybe and some lovers with nowhere else to go. There was little light to see by but along with the used condoms, old needles, and empty vials Anna could make out the chalk marks that Phillip had drawn on the floor.

Why not, Anna thought, and stood in the center of what had been a circled star to await her master and lover. As she did she heard the chimes from a nearby church strike the hour, then the quarter hour, then the half. She had just decided that the message had been a cruel joke, a punishment for daring to bother one who had no further use for her when a dark shape stepped in from the alley.

"Master!" Anna cried in delight.

"I am tonight."

The voice was not one she had heard before and the form approaching her was not a familiar one. The thought that this was not whom she expected came too late. The man grabbed her and forced her to the ground. She fought but he was stronger and soon her clothes were off and he was inside her, brutally ripping away her physical virginity.

The man used her for what seemed like forever. When he finished Anna breathed a sigh of relief, daring to hope that the ordeal was over. That was when she felt the cold steel of a sharp blade at her throat.

In his first night as a newly freed man, Damon LeVaey had dreamt of a girl, a time, and a place. The garage he saw in his dreams was not familiar to him but he knew the hand would guide him.

"Take her," commanded the voice in his dream, "spill her virgin blood then her life's blood and offer both to me."

And so he had. The girl called him "Master" and so he claimed her as his, stripping her bare, holding her down and enjoying her body for as long as he could. And as he finished, as he relaxed his hold just enough to make the girl think that it was over, he took out his knife. He held it against her just long enough so she would know what was coming then slit her throat, sending her from this world into the next.

The girl dead, LeVaey climbed off her body. Touching her throat first and then between her legs he rubbed the blood from both places together then drew a symbol on the corpse's stomach, the same symbol that was burned onto his left palm, one that marked them both as servants of Hell.

Having done all that had been commanded of him LeVaey turned to go, wondering what purpose of his master had been served that night. Then from behind him he heard, "Well done, my faithful servant."

LeVaey turned to see the dead girl rising. He watched as her neck wound closed and her dull eyes came alive again. In the light of those eyes he saw nothing human and he suddenly realized in whose presence he stood. He quickly went down on one knee and bowed his head.

"You may rise," Satan said in the voice of a young girl. LeVaey stood as the devil continued. "And now we watch this city burn."

***

"Hey, Josh, come here. I want to show you something."

"What is it, Ty?"

"It's behind the old shed. Come on."

Ty led his friend to a house at the end of the block. The building had been vacant for a year and showed all the signs of abandonment and neglect. Windows were broken, storm doors flapped in even the slightest breeze and the basement was flooded. Grass and weeds were chest high and who knew what was living among them. No one knew who the owner was and calls to the city went unanswered, as each municipal agency contacted claimed that it was the responsibility of someone else.

Every parent in the neighborhood had given their children strict orders to stay far away from the old house. This of course only caused the kids, the boys especially, to explore what would have otherwise been ignored and a storage shed in the back yard became a sort of meeting place and hangout.

Two other boys, Danny and Andre were at the shed when Ty brought Josh there. The two were looking down at something in the grass. It was an old dog. Matted grass and a trail of blood showed where it had crawled off the road after being hit by a car. That it was still alive was evident by its slow breathing and an occasional twitch of pain.

"My dad says injured animals should be put down."

"It is down, Andre."

Danny hit Josh in the shoulder. "He means killed, you dick." To Andre he said, "Maybe you should get your dad."

"Hell, no. He'd kill me; I'm not supposed to be back here."

"None of us are."

"So what should we do?"

All the boys knew the answer to Josh's question. "We have to do it," Danny said, speaking for the group.

"How?"

"There's a shovel in the shed. Let's smash it." The undisguised glee in Andre's voice bothered no one. They were all beginning to feel the same.

"I got a better idea."

Ty ran into the shed and came out with an old can of lighter fluid and some matches and soon the boys were laughing as the dog's pained whimpers slowly faded along with its life.

That's how things started, with the animals going first. The four boys decided that old Mrs. Groman's nasty little poodle Pierre should be the next to be roasted as elsewhere in the city came target practice with pigeons and .22s, kittens affixed to walls with nail guns, and bizarre mutilations of animals at the Maryland Zoo. Beloved pets were found with limbs cut off and drivers suddenly sped up to hit and run over strays. The owner of a miniature horse farm woke one morning to find all his charges ham-strung and employees at an exotic pet store reported finding peacocks, pot-bellied pigs, and albino ferrets decapitated and the heads switched.

Some arrests were made. Not all of those who had committed these heinous acts were juveniles. No one had any explanation for his action other than "It seemed like a good idea" or "I always wanted to" or "Can't you see, man, it's funny." A few mentioned the devil, but no one took them seriously or thought to make an issue of it.

Drugs were blamed. Some said it was a new kind of gang initiation. Conservative commentators said that it was just another example of what happens in an overly permissive society while liberal pundits claimed it was a reaction to an over oppressive government. Both sides agreed that the media was at fault for publicizing such things and turning sick behavior into popular trends. There were cries for the banning of such on-line videos as frog stomping and hamster hockey.

***

Diane and Steve were the average suburban couple. They worked too hard, played too little and fell asleep every night while pretending to watch The Tonight Show. They had it all -- a nice house fixed up just how they liked, two great kids who went to good schools and played three kinds of sports and a growing IRA that would leave them very comfortable when the time came to retire. They were living the American dream but had forgotten how quickly nightmares could come.

Diane was in the kitchen, fixing dinner while Steve watched the news and complained about the city.

"We have to move out of Baltimore, hon. Did you hear what's going on now? They got drug gangs going after family pets. We should move up to Pennsylvania. It's cheaper up there and we could take I-83 into the city for work. Maybe then we could get a pet, a dog maybe."

Diane only barely listened to her husband. She looked at the clock. Dinner was still a half hour from being finished. That would give her time to start the laundry. What was that he said about pets and Pennsylvania? A dog? Like he'd take care of it. Just one more thing for her to do.

Diane suddenly realized that she was tired, very tired. She stopped moving and sat by the kitchen counter. I can't do this any more, she thought to herself. Kids, a job, a house, a husband -- four full time jobs and only one of me. She'd heard a woman on the bus that day. She was talking to her friend about car troubles, money problems, and conditions in her kids' school.

"Oh, well, what the hell," the woman finally said. "It'll all work out. At least we're happy."

Are we happy? Diane wondered, then changed the question to "Am I happy?" Sitting at her kitchen counter watching a roast thaw she had to admit she wasn't and hadn't been for a long time. She worked so hard she didn't have time to be happy.

A wave of resentment washed over her. She looked into the living room just as Steve said something about the Baltimore Ravens and yelled, "When's dinner?"

Diane's resentment flared into anger. Part of her knew that Steve was not fully to blame for their situation, that they both had played their parts in getting to this point. That did not stop her from studying the carving knife and thinking of her husband's throat.

"Honey! Dinner? When it's going to be? I'm starving!"

Anger grew to rage. Knife in hand, Diane walked quietly into the living room.

Throughout the city, other families were also having problems. Petty squabbles became physical as old arguments were recalled and refought. Husbands and wives turned on each other and then on their kids. Simple family arguments lead to serious injury and sometimes death.

This sudden increase in domestic assaults alarmed no one. No one questioned why reports of this kind of violence were double and sometimes triple what they had been. In a city where the drug problem was out of control and the level of gang activity grew daily, there were few resources left to combat something that most regarded as unpredictable. Everyone agreed that it was a shame when it happened and each and every complaint was handled professionally and responsibly, but the overall sentiment was that as long as people live together these things were bound to happen. That there was another cause, an outside source, occurred to no one.

***

Michael Fitzsimmons, "Mr. Fitz" to most of his students, had been teaching at St. Zita's High School for Girls for over ten years. His manner had always been proper and professional and if he occasionally looked down a blouse or up a skirt when the opportunity arose, no one had ever caught him at it.

But the urge had always been there. Day after day Fitzsimmons taught the girls, all too aware of the fresh young bodies that lay hidden beneath the uniforms. There was always one in each class, the girl with the skirt rolled up to show more thigh than was decent, the one who had one more button undone than the rest. This was the girl that Fitzsimmons dreamed about every night and sometimes imagined when he was with his wife. But fantasy was as far as Fitzsimmons dared go. However much he yearned for tender young flesh, he knew where the line was and the price of crossing it.

It was late afternoon, the last class of the day. The talk in the teachers' lounge had been of a woman who had carved up her husband instead of dinner. Everyone in the lounge knew of someone having major marital problems. One teacher remarked how a few of the students had bruises that could have been from parental abuse and maybe they should be more alert.

But that's not what Fitzsimmons was thinking. He was thinking of Sharon Lester, the redhead in the back row. All through class Sharon had been crossing and recrossing her legs, each time giving her teacher a flash of white. Normally Fitzsimmons would have simply filed the images to memory to be recalled at a more appropriate time, but today there was something, something that caused him to think "What the hell." He knew it was wrong, he knew what would happen. He didn't care. The desire was strong and he didn't want to fight it.

The bell rang. Fitzsimmons shouted a reminder about the homework most of them had no intention of doing, then added "Miss Lester, a minute of your time."

As Fitzsimmons waited for the classroom to empty he imagined Sharon bent over his desk -- her skirt up, her panties down and him inside her. As the last student left he thought about closing the door but remembered that that was against school rules.

The absurdity of that thought suddenly struck him. He started laughing and that banished the urges inside him.

"Did you want something, Mr. Fitz?"

The innocence of the girl's question almost started Fitzsimmons laughing again. Instead he took a deep breath said, "Never mind, Miss Lester" and excused her for the day.

Other teachers in the city lacked Mr. Fitz's appreciation for the absurd. Other students were not as lucky as Sharon Lester. Reports of sexual assaults on school grounds began to increase. Teachers attacked or seduced their students; students assaulted their teachers and each other.

"What's going on this city, Mike," Detective Earl Beasley asked his partner as they left City of Hope's Pediatric ER and headed north up I-83. "That's two sexual child abuses today, added to the three from yesterday, and now there's another teacher who couldn't keep it in his pants."

"Actually, Earl, the complaint we're going to is about the principal, the victim is a teacher."

"Jesus, what's happening to this city? Every freak and pervert seems to be out there. The streets aren't safe for man, woman, or dog and indoors ain't much better. Things are falling apart. It seems like nobody's got any control anymore."

"It's just one of those things. Ups and downs. You wait, Earl, a couple of weeks we'll be wondering where all the crime went."

"Hope you're right, Mike. Because the way things are now, the pressure's building and sooner or later something's gonna blow."

***

The pressure was building. There seemed to be in the city an overall lack of control. Where before people would feel a momentary rush of anger or frustration then shrug it off, some were now acting in the heat of the moment

Traffic accidents increased as did instances of mutual assault following minor collisions. Most of these occurrences were put down as road rage.

Street crime became more vicious. Merchants were not just robbed they were beaten and stabbed. Minor disrespects that would normally have warranted a punitive shot to the arm or leg instead earned the offender one to the gut or head. Drive-bys targeted not just rival drug gangs but the neighborhoods where they lived, with the old and young as especial targets.

It was all too much. With drugs and gangs terrorizing the streets and seemingly normal citizens unable to control their baser impulses, the crime rate doubled, then tripled. The media called for action, politicians demanded answers, no one offered any answers.

The police department responded as best it could. Tours of duty were extended to ten hours, then twelve. Leaves were cancelled and any officers assigned to administrative duties were told to brush off their uniforms and get back on the street. Still there were not enough people on patrol to meet the ever-growing demand for service. Officers worked harder, with little or no breaks between calls, and no back-up available if it was needed.

The city was at its breaking point. Its citizens were scared and angry. Its protectors were tired, overworked and resentful of most of those they were supposed to serve and defend. Emotions everywhere were raw and on knife's edge. Everyone knew something bad was going to happen. The only question was what and how soon.

***

Bianca Jones was back on the street, her search for LeVaey postponed. With real crime running rampant, Major William decided that she could be spared from hunting supernatural monsters to go after the human ones. On being reassigned to the Sex Offense Unit she asked for and was promised two things -- if an occult crisis did arise she could respond and that she partner with Earl Beasley.

The two were driving down to Westport to interview the victim of a gang rape, the fourth one in that area in the past two weeks.

"Glad you're back, Little Girl. Couldn't take much more from Mike. He was starting to get a little too rough with some of the suspects. Damn near beat a child molester to death the other day."

"Time was, Earl, when you would have helped him."

"Never to death, just enough to make the scum think twice about putting his hand down an eight year old's panties. Anyway, I'm a better person now. But even in the old days, Mike would have scared me. It was like he'd lost all control. And that ain't good for a cop."

Beasley looked over at his partner. Bianca's eyes were closed and she was breathing evenly. Thinking she was asleep, he was about to nudge her when she said,

"It's not good for anyone."

Something in Bianca's voice made Earl ask, "Something wrong, Bianca?"

"You said that it was like Mike had lost control. He ever do that before?"

"Not while I worked with him."

"But he did now. Earl, you've read the reports of the crimes going down. Most of them seem to be committed not by gang bangers or drug dealers, but by regular citizens."

"So what? People can't resist temptation all we can do is find them and lock them up."

"Temptation, exactly. It's as if people can no longer control the impulses and feelings we all have but normally ignore or cast aside. That anything bad or evil inside them overcomes the good and has to come out."

Bianca let Beasley think about that for a minute then asked, "When was the last time that happened to you, Earl?"

Beasley thought back. It had not been that long ago that he and Bianca had journeyed to Hell to save an innocent soul from Satan. "When we went down south to save that kid."

"Right, I was so sure that I could storm the gates of Hell myself that I didn't need anyone, especially you. I could have killed you then."

"And I resented you, hated you. I wanted to rape you, then leave you alone in damnation."

Bianca nodded. Neither was proud of what they had felt back then, because the feelings had been real. "Not our finest moment. The worst we had inside us came out that day and between us we used up most of the deadly sins. But we overcame temptation in time to keep those sins from destroying us."

"You think something like that is happening here in Baltimore?"

"I think it's exactly what's happening here. I've told you about Damon LeVaey and who he was working for before I took him down. He escaped just about the same time everything started going crazy. Somehow he's the cause of this."

"You think LeVaey is that powerful?"

"No, Earl, but his boss is and I think that's who we're up against. And this time we won't have to go to Hell to find him. He's come to us and brought Hell with him."

***

The stench was awful, almost unbearable. How could the neighbors not complain? LeVaey knew the answer to his question. In the cul-de-sac where Anna Burgess used to live, there were no neighbors left.

Anna's parents died first. Her father, a weak man to begin with, did not resist when what he thought was his daughter crawled into his lap and began doing very undaughterly things to him. As planned, Anna's mother came home from work and found them together. Before she could protest, LeVaey grabbed her from behind.

Seduction and rape both over, LeVaey slit two throats and dragged the corpses up to the master bedroom, arranging the bodies in a parody of sleeping lovers. Over the few days, he and his master made nightly visits to the other houses in the complex, leaving lifeless bodies behind.

"Summon your followers," Satan had commanded once the initial slayings were complete. "Call them here to worship me."

LeVaey obeyed, calling his former disciples in one by one. The required acts of worship were more twisted and depraved than the magus could ever have imagined, his master drawing out most of a follower's life force before leaving a burnt out husk to die a tortuous death.

It was after one such feeding that Satan called to LeVaey.

"Can you feel it?"

Having been living too close to pure evil to feel anything but despair, LeVaey shook his head. "No, Master, what is it?"

"This city, it's people, they are about to erupt. It takes only a small spark to burn a great forest, and soon that spark will be ignited and Baltimore will burn. Now come and please me."

LeVaey shuddered at the thought of what pleasing his master meant. Had he not known himself to be already damned, he might have prayed for mercy.

***

In the backroom of Morgan' Fells Point bookstore, a council of war was held by four self-appointed soldiers out to save a city from itself.

"It's possible," allowed Joe Russo as Bianca explained what she thought was happening to Baltimore.

"It's more than possible," said Morgan, "it's likely. It explains much. Before time itself began, the Devil was condemned to Hell. Where he goes, Hell is, bringing with it the despair and misery that are its walls and foundation. Weaker souls cannot resist its temptations and in falling, drag others down with them."

"So why haven't we been affected?"

The old bookseller looked at Joe. "Miss Jones and Detective Beasley have faced their demons and conquered them. You, I suspect, have no demons. As for me, I am at the end of what has been a very long life. There is little left to tempt me."

"I think the first step is to find this LeVaey character."

Bianca nodded. "I agree, Earl, we find him and maybe, just maybe the Devil loses his earthly anchor. But how, I've been looking for him since he escaped."

Joe spoke up. "I have an idea." Conscious that all eyes were on him, he went on. "I've been working here since my retirement and Morgan been doing his best to teach me something about magic, or at least the way it works. There's something called the Law of Similarity, how like calls to like. LeVaey escaped using a Hand of Glory, the left hand of a dead man. If like does call to like, why not use the right hand to point the way?"

"That might work," Bianca admitted, "if LeVaey still has the hand. Worth a try."

"Good idea, Russo. I see why Bianca keeps you around. I knew it wasn't for your looks or she'd have dumped you for me."

"Thanks, Earl. I've went ahead and made some calls. The guy we're looking for was released from the Medical Examiners and buried in the old Eastpoint Cemetery. I cashed in some favors with a State's Attorney and got us a court order. He can be exhumed at any time."

Beasley stood. "Well, what are we waiting for? Someone call the backhoe and let's go dig up a dead guy."

They were soon back in the bookstore with a dead man's hand in a mini-cooler. Morgan pulled an ancient tome off a back shelf and opened it to a certain page.

"Clear the table," he ordered, then asked Joe for several items and told him where to find them. Soon a pattern was laid out with the mostly decayed hand on a gold plate in its middle and Morgan was ready to begin.

"This is real magic, isn't it?" Beasley asked.

"Yes," the old man replied, "but not, I should add, black magic. We are simply asking that two parts of a whole be reunited. However, like everything of this nature, what we asking will come at a price. All magic does."

"What's this going to cost us?"

Morgan gave Beasley a gambler's smile. "One enters into these things blindly. The cost, when it comes, may be too high or too low. Either way it must be paid."

Morgan started to read from the book. As he did, the air grew cold and the candles on the table wavered even though there was no wind. The words he spoke were sometimes in Latin, sometimes Greek or Rom and often in a tongue not heard for several centuries. When it was over, he closed the book and spoke a word that some might have translated as "Amen" though most would not.

At first the hand did nothing. Then slowly its fingers contracted into a fist with its forefinger extended. The hand then rocked and turned until it pointed in a specific direction.

"Its mate is that way. Be careful," Morgan warned Bianca and Beasley, "Remember what I said. Magic has its price and it must be paid."

Bianca nodded her understanding. "Whatever the cost as long as we can stop LeVaey and send his boss back home."

The two detectives were almost out the door when Joe called out. "Bianca!"

"I'll wait outside," Beasley told his partner.

"What it is, Joe?"

"Just … come back to me."

"If I can, you know I will. You're the one thing that keeps me going, the only reason I have for making sure I do come back."

"What we talked about last night, when this is over?"

"It will never be over, but later, when I come back, then yes."

Beasley drove. Bianca sat shotgun with the hand on a plate in her lap, giving directions each time it turned. They were led from Fells Point past Canton and into what was once Highlandtown and now called Brewer's Hill.

"Hey," Beasley said in recognition, "isn't this where …"

"Anita Dixon was torn open." And with that Bianca knew where the hand would lead them and what they would find.

The journey ended in an old garage. On the floor not so fresh blood covered old chalk marks while nearby a desiccated left hand lay next to a pair of panties.

"Shit! I should have known she'd be mixed up in this."

"Who's that, Little Girl?"

"Another old friend, Anna Burgess. You remember, she and her demon child are the reason we went to Hell."

Bianca told Beasley of Anna's role in the carbon monoxide death of a young man trying an occult summoning.

Beasley pointed to the hand. "I guess this trail is cold."

Bianca shook her head. "No, Anna's involved in this somehow. After her 'pregnancy' ended abruptly, her parents moved her out to a new development in North Baltimore. Why don't we go see if she's home?"

***

On the bed unable to move, LeVaey watched as the devil dressed.

"Things are happening," his master said without explaining what. "I'm going out. Don't worry, you'll be protected."

Even if he had been able, LeVaey knew better than to ask questions. Earlier on he had questioned his master's actions and the burns he received had still not healed. Instead, lying helpless, he watched Satan leave the house dressed in a plaid skirt and a thin white blouse taken from Anna's closet.

***

While downtown Baltimore had quite a few pubs and nightspots and Fells Point even more than that, the city's Southern District had its share. And it was there, in clubs hiding in the shadow of Raven's Stadium and in taverns along Hanover Street, that things were getting out of control. The crowds at these nightspots, often curious mixtures of rock and country, were usually a bit boisterous and out to have a good time, but that was all. It was always party time with music playing and drinks flowing and everybody was your friend.

That night things were different. Things were tense, emotions were high. Couples who usually enjoyed some light necking while slow dancing found themselves groping and grinding. Some went further and, heedless of the people around them, stripped down and put on a show. Police and private security officers had already broken up several fights and had not been gentle doing so. This only added to the tension. A flashpoint was building and needed only a tiny spark to set things off.

The match came in the form of what appeared to be a teenaged girl. Dressed in a white blouse and plaid skirt she approached a police officer standing in the courtyard of a bar on Waterview Avenue. A live band was playing on the parking lot and the dancing in front of the stage was growing more and more frenzied.

The girl was telling the officer of how she had been separated from her friends and had no way back home. She was asking him if he could call her a cab when the music stopped. That's when she ripped open her blouse and screamed.

The crowd turned became a mob as the girl yelled, "He tried to rape me." Needing no evidence beyond what their eyes told them, they rushed the officer.

With nowhere to escape and no time to call for back-up, the officer drew his gun, hoping that the mere sight of a weapon would stem the tide rushing toward him. One or two heeded it but the rest came on and the frightened cop fired into the oncoming mass of people.

At the sound of gunshots, the bar emptied out to the sight of a now out-of-control policeman firing blindly at whatever targets presented themselves. Drunk on cheap booze and excited by feelings they could no longer control, the partygoers and revelers decided that license and freedom had somehow been granted. "Do what you will" became the rule of the night as what appeared to be a teenaged girl adjusted her clothing and quietly slipped away.

***

A few miles away, unaware of what was happening in Southern District, two uniformed officers sat in their patrol car watching a house on Pimlico Road. The house was belived to be occupied by members of B'more 21, an offshoot of the Crips gang that had recently come to the city. There was no evidence that illegal activity had or was taking place in the house. The marked car was there solely to remind the gang members that their presence was known and that they were being watched.

It was a stupid detail. On that both officers agreed. Bad guys who were being watched, and neither officer doubted that these were bad guys, merely went somewhere else to commit their crimes. But their lieutenant had explained that a police presence eased the community's collective mind and "it sent a message."

The officers were trying to figure out just what message was bring sent by assigning two white cops to openly stake out a house where nothing was happening in the middle of a black neighborhood whose residents, if they didn't hate the police, at least had good reason to be suspicious of them.

That's when they saw the girl.

She was a white girl, about seventeen. If that wasn't odd enough, she was wearing what looked like the remains of a school uniform. Her plaid skirt was ripped and her white blouse was in tatters. She walked from the direction of the house and before they could wonder how they could have missed her coming or going she came up to them and cried, "They raped me!"

"Who raped you?" asked the older of the two police.

The girl pointed to the house. "They did, they all did."

There were procedures for this, ones that the officers knew full well, ones that on that night they chose not to follow. They were tired of the rules, sick of how drug dealers and gang members laughed at the law and the men who enforced it. Looking at the brutalized girl crying in the back of their patrol car, something dark inside them both told them that his was their night to bring a little justice back into their world.

"Got enough ammo?" one asked the other as they approached the house.

"Full clip in my piece, two more on my belt."

"Same here. Should be enough bullets to go around."

The sound of gunfire woke the normally peaceful community. As the neighbors came out, a young girl in a patrol car told them of how two police had brutalized her and then had gone into a house to "teach some niggers a lesson."

Word spread quickly, calls were made, people gathered. The two officers emerged from the house to find themselves surrounded by an angry, righteous mob. Having used the better part of six clips of cartridges in making sure that no one in the house would ever rape a white girl again, the officers had little ammunition left with which to shoot their way clear. Instead they ran back into the house, locked the doors and called for back-up.

It did them little good. Cans of gasoline were found, matches produced and the house set ablaze. And when other police responding the radio call of "Signal 13, officers need assistance" arrived on the scene, the crowd turned its anger and torches on them.

Bad news travels fast, and what was happening in the city was the worst possible. The local television stations broke into network broadcasts with stories of the twin civil disturbances, both of which threatened to spread throughout the city as chaos grew and riot followed.

***

Bianca and Beasley were both familiar with the smell of death and it hit them strong when their car pulled into Underwood Court complex. Twelve houses, all silent as the grave. Without having to look, both detectives knew why.

"We've been here before," was all Beasley said, "at least, someplace very close to it."

"We're standing in an outpost of Hell, Earl. Let's be careful."

"I think it's too late for that."

Beasley pointed out the front windshield into the court where the dead were walking. All those murdered by LeVaey and his master were leaving their houses and slowly shuffling toward the car.

"Seems we were expected," Beasley said dryly.

"You think?"

Bianca watched the undead come out of 9 Underwood Court, Anna Burgess's home. "That's the house we want. Wait for that doorway to empty, then drive straight through the zombies right up to the front door."

The dead came closer. They were almost to the car when the doorway of number 9 emptied.

"Floor it!" Bianca yelled. With a squeal of tires the car raced forward, scattering bodies in its wake.

Beasley hit and went up over the curb, getting almost to the front entrance before getting stuck in the grass.

"Let's go."

"You know, Little Girl, there's probably a few left on the inside."

"I'll take care of them. Can you hold off the ones outside?"

At Beasley's nod, Bianca handed him a shotgun from the back seat.

"Flechette loads. Aim for their head. It's the only way to stop them."

Beasley took the gun. "I got your back. They'll get in over my dead body."

Beasley had named the stakes. This was life or death, and there was every chance that neither of them would leave Underwood Court. The two partners looked at each other in a silent goodbye then left the car.

The undead that Beasley had scattered had turned and were now advancing on the house, most on foot, those who had lost their lower limbs crawling as best they could.

Using his car as a bulwark, Beasley took his position. Behind him, Bianca entered the house. He tried not to listen for the sound of gunfire coming from inside and when he did hear it, did his best to ignore it.

The zombies were coming. Not for the first time was Beasley glad that he had traded in his old service revolver for a .40 caliber Smith and Wesson. Fourteen shots instead of six might make the difference. Saving his shotgun for when the dead came in close, Beasley used his pistol to take them out at a longer range.

As Beasley began to focus on individuals, he realized the hell of his situation. Some of his targets had once been young women, teens, and even children. There were a few preschoolers in the mix and even a crawling infant. All were coming toward him with deadly intent. Knowing what nightmares would be his for the rest of his life, Earl Beasley did what he had to do to protect himself and his partner and opened fire.

Bianca dropped two zombies almost as soon as she entered the house. They came at her from the living room. Having expected such an attack, she put two quick shots into each of their heads, dropping them instantly. Only after they fell did she notice that both were in their early teens.

Cautiously she moved through the house. The place stank of shit and piss and death. Stains Bianca knew to be blood covered the walls and she had to step around puddles of urine on the floor.

As Bianca searched the house, clearing the laundry, kitchen and family room before going upstairs, she was suddenly aware that she'd been hearing gunfire for sometime. Pistol shots, regularly paced. She hoped that Beasley was keeping the dead well back. If they got close enough that he had to use the shotgun they might overwhelm him. As she reached the second floor Bianca recalled what Morgan had told her about the cost of magic and prayed that Beasley wouldn't have to pay the price.

The zombies were shuffling around Beasley, trying to get on both sides of him. So far he'd done well holding them off, using the flechettes only on the ones who dared to get too close. Once Beasley felt something bite his ankle. Without looking he fired downward, hoping that what he blew apart was a family pet and nothing more. The attack had come from under the car, causing him to give up that up as a barrier and retreat to the doorway.

Slowly the dead advanced. There were not as many as there had been but what remained were densely packed. Putting his S&W away, Beasley turned to the shotgun.

As his razor-sharp ammo shredded head after head Beasley thought about going inside and locking the door after him. As he took down one zombie after another, he realized that while right then the creatures were focused entirely on him, closing the entrance he guarded would only force them to seek another. Bianca would not stand a chance if they started coming in through the windows or went around the back.

Keeping his position, Beasley continued to fire into the mass of flesh coming closer. He wondered which he'd run out of first, shells or zombies, and how many walking corpses he could take down using the gun as a club.

Bianca put down two more zombies on the second floor. One came at her from the bathroom. It collapsed when Bianca fired into its eye socket. The other shuffled at her from the master bedroom. Bianca dropped it with a bullet to its knee. As she put two more into its head to make it lie still the detective realized she knew the woman, or at least who the woman had been. It was Anna Burgess's mother.

There came a sudden quiet, a brief lull in the battle. Listening for the sliding steps that would warn her of more undead, Bianca instead heard another sound.

Sighing, weeping, wailing -- it was the cry of a soul in anguish. It came from a back bedroom, one that a feces smeared sign on the door proclaimed to be "Anna's Room." Loading a fresh clip into her pistol, Bianca moved to investigate.

***

In the back room of Morgan's bookshop, Joe Russo looked at his cell phone. "I should call her, warn her what's happening."

"It is likely that Miss Jones is not in a position to answer her phone. Your calling now could be a fatal distraction."

Joe closed the phone and put it away. "We have to do something."

The two had been watching coverage of the riots. What had started as local news had quickly become national as the networks, both broadcast and cable, cut away from their regular programming to cover what some were calling massive civil unrest and others armed insurrection. The major news stations had their top anchors on the job and had tagged the chaos with colorful logos and provocative names.

CBS was the first, using the old Baltimore nickname of "Mobtown."

After the fires started on Pimlico Road began to spread NBC followed with "Baltimore in Flames." ABC continued the theme with "City on Fire," likening what was happening in the city to the Great Fire of 1904. Fox came late and settled on "Baltimore -- the Next New Orleans" predicting devastation greater than that caused by Hurricane Katrina.

"They may be right," Morgan commented, "especially if what we fear is true."

Joe nodded. "As the night goes on, the more raw emotions will be exposed. Fear, hatred, anger -- this situation will bring them all to the surface where they'll be easy prey for Evil's influence."

"You left out Gluttony, Lust, Envy and the rest, but you're right, and we are the only ones who know this. Has it occurred to you that the police are only making things worse?"

"Initially they will, Morgan, as a focus for the rioters' anger and attention. But sooner or later the police will able to control the crowds or at least contain them until the National Guard or State Police can be called in."

"And so you expect these very human officers, who themselves are no doubt feeling everything the mob is, to be somehow immune to the temptations of Hell?"

"Damn," Joe whispered softly as the full implications of Morgan's question. He imagined the police confronting the crowd, each side on edge, each feeding the other and ready to give in to their darkest natures. An endless loop of hatred and violence which, if it didn't burn itself out, could spread past the Beltway and engulf the state.

Again Joe wanted to call Bianca. She was always the one with the answers, who knew the correct action to take to stem damnation's tide. But his love was on the street, possibly already fighting on the front line with Beasley at her side. Joe had faith that those two would resist the call of evil and he briefly prayed that they would be kept safe.

"What can we do?" Joe asked the man whom he knew to have decades of experience in fighting the darkness, possibly more than that. Surely he'd know what must be done.

Morgan shook his head. "It is for you to decide, Joseph, and for you to act."

Joe thought and found the answer deep within. Using his phone he got through to Bianca's commanding officer and, invoking her name, made an appointment with the only man who could break the cycle of violence.

"Very good," Morgan said, smiling to himself with a feeling of satisfaction and completion. He turned to the TV. "It is relatively calm between Fells Point and Police Headquarters. Still, I'd best accompany you."

The two got as far as the Fayette Street post office before having to stop. The traffic was such that there was no room to even pull over. So Joe just dropped his car into park, left it in the middle of the street and continued on foot, their progress slowed by Morgan's age and Joe's need for a cane.

As Joe and Morgan approached police headquarters they saw the reason for the backup. Barricades had been erected at Fayette and President Streets, preventing traffic from coming near the building. Armed tactical officers stood guard so as to make sure no one crossed the line. Joe presumed that the level of security was the same all around the square block that made up the headquarters complex.

Here and there on the other side of the barriers were protesters, camera crews, local and national TV anchors, people seeking solace or those just wanting to help. There were not that many of them, but there number was growing steadily. Joe and Morgan both knew that soon a critical mass would be reached and then with the wrong word, a threatening remark, or a misunderstood gesture another hot spot would erupt and more people would die as the symbol of law itself came under attack.

Already there was a certain tension in the air. Morgan felt it more than Joe and looked around for its source. He found it in the mob of protesters who seemed to be the loudest, the ones most willing to tempt the tactical officers' patience and aim.

Scanning the crowd, Morgan searched for and found the one he had been expecting. His form was not familiar nor was his face, but Morgan recognized him instantly, even if he was in the body of a teenaged girl.

"Joseph," Morgan said, grabbing the young man's arm to halt his progress. "You will have to go on ahead. I have just spotted, well, not exactly an old friend, but someone I knew of old."

Joe looked at Morgan but saw nothing but peace and calm in the old bookseller's face. He looked past the man, but could see no one that could even remotely be considered one of Morgan's contemporaries. Just a young girl coming their way. Still, what Morgan had said and the way he said it worried him.

"I'll stand with you," he offered.

"No." Morgan was firm. "You have the more important job. Go do it. And when you do get back to the bookshop, if I'm not there, you'll find a letter in the top drawer of my desk."

There was no mistaking the finality of Morgan's words. Still Joe said, "You can read it to me when this is all over."

Morgan smiled and said, "Go. Stay safe. For her sake if not yours." Then he turned and walked away.

Joe approached the barricades carefully, not wanting to give any trigger-happy cop a chance to add to his number oaf bullet scars. Standing close enough to be heard but back enough that he could not be considered a threat,

Joe held up the police ID he had so far not turned in and asked to be allowed to enter the compound. But it was not until he mentioned Tavon Greggs's name and the Sergeant was consulted that he was permitted access.

After Joe left, Morgan stood his ground and let the young girl come to him. The one who was wearing the body of Anna Burgess now dressed in black slacks and a white turtleneck sweater. It fit her well, as it had the woman who had been killed for it.

The girl came closer to Morgan. As she did it seemed that nothing else mattered. The noise of the crowd, the shouts of the protesters, the droning of the television reporters, all faded away until there was nothing left for the two but each other.

"Morgan," the devil said with a smile in her face, "it's been a while, old friend."

"We were never friends, Scratch."

"I've always hated that name."

It was Morgan's turn to smile. "I know."

The devil ignored him. "You fought a good fight, I must admit. You and that bitch you recruited held things together for quite some time. But as they say, all good things must come to an end -- fortunately for me."

"It's not over yet."

"For you it is and the girl's time is near."

With unearthly speed the devil reached into Morgan. As the old man felt his soul, his essence, his very self being yanked from his body, he looked toward police headquarters in time to see Joe Russo enter the front door. You fool, he thought, this time it's not about the girl. And he died thanking the One who had made it part of Satan's curse that he would forever underestimate those he warred upon.

***

Bianca had not thought it possible, but the bedroom stank worse than the rest of the house. Every manner of filth spattered the walls, pooled on the floor and dripped from the ceiling. Something that seemed not quite human moved on the bed and as Bianca took aim on it, it moaned the long plaintive wail of one in torment.

Moving closer to investigate, the detective realized that the moans coming from the bed were the only sounds she was hearing. There were no gunshots, no sounds of battle coming from below. For good or ill, whether he stood victorious or lay defeated, Beasley's fight was over.

Bianca resisted the urge to rush down to check on her partner. If he survived, there was no need. If not, then she might be rushing headlong into the surviving undead while leaving potential danger behind her.

Listening for the shuffling and dragging sounds that would tell her that zombies were climbing the stairs, Bianca turned to the creature on the bed.

It had once been a man, she could tell that much. Emaciated and dehydrated, he bore the scars of weeklong ill use. In her years as an officer and detective, Bianca had seen children who had been deliberately starved, the elderly neglected for so long that bedsores had eaten away their flesh, and women who had been tortured beyond the point of human endurance.

The man on the bed looked worse then any of them

Had he not been moving and moaning Bianca would have thought him dead for some time. Still could be, she thought as she moved closer. As she steeled herself to check his vital signs, Bianca noticed something familiar about him. The features that remained on his face were those for which Bianca had been searching since he escaped prison.

"You should have stayed in jail, LeVaey," she said.

Looking down on the man on the bed, Bianca felt a strange mix of anger and sympathy. LeVaey had opened the door to Hell on Earth, and so assuredly deserved his own piece of it. However, no human, regardless of his crimes, should be forced to endure whatever had brought LeVaey to his present condition. This was not justice and Bianca felt no satisfaction in his plight.

As LeVaey looked at her from Anna's bed, Bianca felt that he heard and understood her. Leveling her gun, she pointed it at the spot between his eyes.

"Where's the girl, LeVaey? Where's Anna Burgess? Tell me or I put you out of both our miseries."

Panic filled the eyes of the once proud magus. As weak as he was, he crawled as far as he could from Bianca without leaving the bed.

"No, don't!" he whimpered. "It will be like this forever. No power, no glory, just this and worse. He lied to me! He lied!"

"That's what he does." Bianca kept her weapon steady. "So you're afraid of Hell? That's good, that's a start. But if you don't tell me where the girl is I'm sending you there right now."

Bianca hoped that LeVaey would believe her threat, knowing she would not pull the trigger. However much he deserved it, Bianca was not going to send this pathetic wretch to Hell. She had other plans for him.

Already weak and faced with an eternity of damnation, LeVaey broke. "The girl is dead. My master, Satan, is wearing her."

Bianca heard a noise behind her. She turned suddenly, gun drawn, ready to fire, only to see Beasley standing in the doorway.

The older detective's clothing was torn in several places. Through the tears Bianca could see bruises, lacerations and what seemed to be bite marks. Beasley's left hand was wrapped in a handkerchief while his right held the barrel to what used to be a shotgun.

But all Bianca saw were his eyes. In them she read sadness and horror. Bianca knew what had been outside, what Beasley had had to fight. And in his face and eyes she saw what price he had paid to keep her safe.

"Are you okay, Earl?"

Beasley held up his bandaged hand.

"One of them bit off my finger. He was the last one and I didn't see him coming. He was, had been only ten or eleven and I …"

He looked at the gun barrel in his hand, the metal covered with blood, brain and bone. He dropped it on the floor.

"I can't do it anymore. When this is finished, I'm done."

"It's almost over, Earl."

"No, it's not." Beasley's voice was that of a soldier whose company had just held off an invading force, only to be told that there were ten times as many on the way.

"After I … well, I figured that with all the shots I fired, Northern District had to be on its way. I was trying to come up with a way to explain all the dead bodies when I realized I wasn't hearing any sirens. There should have been sirens. So I got on the radio and called in. And I found out why no units had responded."

Beasley then told Bianca of what had happened in the city, of the riots and the fires.

"And it's spreading. From what the dispatcher told me, it's spreading every minute. You'd think with morning coming they'd tire out, go home. But no, people are fighting each other and the cops. And the cops are fighting back, which only makes thing worse.

"He's out there, Little Girl. He's out there fueling the fire and feeding the flames. Hey, who's that?"

Beasley had finally noticed the figure on the bed.

"All that's left of Damon LeVaey."

"Why ain't he dead? I thought the whole point was to take him out to weaken you know who."

"Change of plans, Earl. I've already stolen two souls from you know who. I'm going for the hat trick and I think his boss knows it.

"Earl, take LeVaey out of here and put him somewhere safe. I'm going to wait here awhile, see what happens."

"Give me a spare clip and I'll stand with you. One more time won't kill me, or if I'm lucky, maybe it will."

Bianca shook her head. "No, Earl. You've paid your price. From here on in, I'm picking up the tab."

***

On the strength of Bianca's name and all she had done to keep Baltimore safe from dark forces, Joe has convinced Major Williams to get him an appointment with the Police Commissioner. With the city's top cop busy with two on-going riots and several more threatening, it had not been easy. It was when Williams assured his boss that what Joe had to say directly involved the situation at hand and might offer a solution that an interview was granted.

Once in the Commissioner's fifth floor office, Joe explained just what that solution was.

"Are you crazy?"

"I really wish I was, Sir."

"You want me to order all the police in the city to stand down? To not take any action against anyone rioting, looting, or committing other civil disturbance?"

"Yes, Sir."

"Because the Devil's has possessed the city."

"Something like that."

"If I may, Commissioner," Williams interposed, "we've had vampires, ghosts, old curses come to life, other worldly rapists, and at least one elf. All well-documented cases. I think the devil was past due for a visit."

"Even if you're right, it leaves me open for a world of trouble. Every bit of damage, every death that occurs after I give the order to secure becomes my responsibility. The press will crucify me and the city council will buy the nails and wood. At best my career is over. I could even be prosecuted and sent to jail."

"Commissioner," Joe said, "isn't a police officer sworn to risk his life, to lose it if need be, to save that of a citizen?"

"You know he is, Mr. Russo."

"Then isn't saving the entire city worth your job and freedom?"

Ten minutes later the order came out over the police bands.

"Attention all police personnel. On orders from Unit 1, all units are to stand down. Repeat, all units are to stand down and secure from any area of civil unrest. Units are to return to their districts for redeployment."

Most officers obeyed. Those that didn't found themselves without back-up and were soon overwhelmed. With police now assigned to guarding public buildings, vital infrastructures and those neighborhoods not yet affected by the rioting, the mob turned its anger on itself and its surroundings. As people died and buildings burned, the Commissioner could only pray that he had done the right thing.

***

Beasley was gone, having taken LeVaey with him. Alone in the house, Bianca waited. Sitting on the sofa in the living room, Bianca dropped the clip from her pistol and replaced it with one she had been saving for an occasion such as this.

Morning ran into afternoon. The radio Beasley had left told her that the Commissioner's plan seemed to be working. In the absence of the police the rioting had at first escalated, but now, although they still continued, the looting, fires, and fighting were, at least, no longer spreading.

It won't last, Bianca realized. All the PC has done is to buy us some time. Bianca knew that there was only one way the nightmare could be ended. She wondered if she shouldn't be out on the street searching for the thing that looked like Anna.

No, she decided, he knows I'm here. His sending the undead after us was proof of that. Let him come to me.

Satan appeared suddenly. Although she had been watching the front door and listening for footsteps, one minute Bianca had been alone and the next something was standing at the door.

Even if she had not been warned by LeVaey, Bianca would have known her enemy. Wherever the soul of Anna Burgess had gone, there was nothing human left in her body. Even worse than the house, the thing before her stank of evil.

"Lucifer."

From Morgan, Bianca knew that names held power, and she hoped the one she used was a true one. The devil bowed, acknowledging and accepting the name as his title. As he did so, Bianca raised her gun and fired several times into his body. Most of the silver-tipped bullets passed through the creature, striking the wall behind him. The rest dropped uselessly to the floor.

Bianca sighed and holstered her weapon. "I had hoped that would work."

The devil smiled. "A waste of good silver, but it was a nice try. You did save one for yourself, I trust."

As the shadows of evening crept through the open door and gathered around her opponent, Bianca made eye contact and held it in challenge. There was nothing in the stare that looked back, only the void.

"While you still can, ask the question."

At first Bianca remained silent, even as the shadows around Lucifer grew longer. But she was first of all a detective, and so she had to know.

"Why?"

The Devil broke eye contact and shrugged. "Because I can. Because I want to. Because humanity is weak and so easily lead into sin. Maybe it's because of a kick in the balls and two stolen souls. Or maybe I just like to see how long it takes before some fool figures out the nature of my game and tries to stop me."

Bianca squared herself up, ready for what she knew was sure to come.

"The game's over."

"Not quite." There was a gloating in the Devils' voice. "You may have beaten me before, Miss Jones, but this round is mine. This time you lose and the game goes on."

The shadows rose up from Lucifer and gathered around Bianca. As they swirled up and caught her in a serpentine embrace, she began to pray. The shadows began contracting, stopping her breath, cutting off her prayer. And in what seemed to be no time at all yet time everlasting, the darkness took Bianca Jones.

Satan looked down at the body lying lifeless before him. "So easy," he muttered, trying to decide to what use he could put the body.

Behind him, someone cleared his throat.

Satan turned to confront that which had once been a man called Morgan.

"You're dead," the Devil said, "I killed you myself."

Morgan smiled. "For once you speak the truth. And from where you sent me I bring a message."

Then as he had been instructed, Morgan spoke a name, a name that could not have been uttered by one alive, a name that was old before the Fall.

And there was Light, Light which began to overwhelm the shadows. Morgan delivered his message.

"It is your nature and your fate that you will never understand those you would seek to destroy, that your evil will always be defeated by the willing sacrifice of good men and women. If you ever do understand that, you will be back on the Path."

The Light grew and filled the room. There was a single scream. When the Light faded, the room was empty.

***

Bianca awoke and found herself on a featureless plane. There was light ahead of her and darkness behind. She was reminded of a journey she had once taken, to save an unborn soul from the one who had just killed her. There had a plane much like this one. But unlike the one on the outskirts of Hell, there was no despair, no feeling of damnation. Where she was, Bianca felt only hope and maybe the beginnings of joy.

In the distance Bianca saw someone between her and the Light. With nothing else to do, she walked toward him and soon was standing next to Morgan.

"Is it over?" she asked.

Morgan nodded. "The Adversary has been returned to Perdition, where he will remain until he comes to know why he is there, or until he's freed yet again by some weak, power-seeking fool. But for now, yes, it is over."

"We're dead, aren't we?" Bianca was sure she already knew the answer.

"One of us is," came the cryptic reply.

"One of us?"

"There's always a price to pay, Miss Jones. The Evil that had to be banished was great and thus, so was the cost."

Morgan pointed to the Light. "That way lies all that is Good and Perfect. It is Happiness and Joy. There you would be forever with those you loved and those you will love. It is the Peace for which we all strive and hope to obtain."

"You said, 'would be.'"

"Yes," Morgan said with a sadness and regret rarely felt in the realm where he stood. "Your sacrifice, however needed, however willing, was merely part of the price. The rest has yet to be paid."

"So I have to go back."

Morgan shook his head. "The road to Paradise is open to you. Should you chose to walk it, no one will stop you."

"Then who will pay … Joe."

"Joe," Morgan affirmed. "Without us, without you, guided only by the teaching I gave him and the knowledge he gains from the books, his road will be dark and treacherous. He may prevail, but there is an equal chance he will not. What you fought for, what you died for, could be lost, Joe could be lost -- forever."

Bianca smiled. "So like I said, I have to go back." She took a long look at the distant Light. "Without Joe, it wouldn't be much of a paradise. Save me a cloud. I'll be back."

Suddenly alone, Morgan took a long look toward the Light. However close it seemed, he knew that his journey would be a long one. He had his own debts to pay.

***

Bianca awoke and found herself in the otherwise empty house. For just a minute she could not remember why she was there. Memory came rushing back. LeVaey, Anna Burgess, their master who had used them both in the most obscene way.

She had stopped him, this she knew. She had offered herself as the means to end the Evil plaguing Baltimore. Her offer had been accepted and …

The rest was gone. She knew that she had had something wonderful, something precious that had been taken from her. But with this sense of loss came a feeling of hope, a belief that one day it would be returned to her.

But for now all she had left was the knowledge that, for now, the fight was over, that her city was safe from the darkness once more.

***

A Northern District car picked her up fifteen minutes after she called in.

"Jesus!" the officer exclaimed, "What the hell happened here?"

"Hell, indeed," was the all reply Bianca offered as she mentally began preparing her report to Major Williams.

Rather than go to headquarters, Bianca had the officer drop her at the Fells Point bookstore. There she found Joe waiting.

The lovers ran to each other's arms. No words were spoken. None were needed as each gave thanks that the other was safe. Finally, after what seemed to be to short a time, they parted.

"Morgan's dead," Joe said simply.

Bianca nodded and realized that she had already known this.

"He left me the store." Joe held up a letter he had found in Morgan's desk, his desk now.

"It couldn't be in better hands."

A few minutes of quiet, then Joe said, "It's over, isn't it?"

Bianca nodded. "Mostly. There are dead to bury and houses to rebuild. There'll be commissions and investigations and everybody will look to place the blame on everyone but themselves but, for now, it's over."

"And for us?"

Bianca smiled, remembering her promise.

***

It was a private ceremony, one held in a small, southeast Baltimore Catholic church. Father Anton Lawrence, just arrived from Italy where he and other members of his order had thwarted a terrorist threat against the pope, waited at the altar. Beside him stood Joe Russo.

At the other end of the church, Bianca Jones fretted.

"I've faced monsters, vampires, ghosts and the Devil himself. Why am I so nervous now?"

Earl Beasley smiled. "I think it's the 'obey' thing, Little Girl. Can't imagine you doing that."

Bianca returned the smile "You might be right. Let's do this."

At the maid of honor's signal, the Wedding March began.

Biography

JOHN L. FRENCH has worked for over thirty-five years as a crime scene investigator and has seen more than his share of murders, shootings, and serious assaults. As a break from the realities of his job, he writes science fiction, pulp, horror, fantasy, and, of course, crime fiction.

In 1992 John began writing stories based on his training and experiences on the streets of Baltimore. His first story "Past Sins" was published in Hardboiled Magazine and was cited as one of the best Hardboiled stories of 1993. More crime fiction followed, appearing in Alfred Hitchcock's Mystery Magazine, the Fading Shadows magazines and in collections by Barnes and Noble. Association with writers like James Chambers and the late, great C.J. Henderson led him to try horror fiction and to a still growing fascination with zombies and other undead things. His first horror story "The Right Solution" appeared in Marietta Publishing's Lin Carter's Anton Zarnak. Other horror stories followed in anthologies such as The Dead Walk and Dark Furies, both published by Die Monster Die books. It was in Dark Furies that Bianca Jones made her literary debut in "21 Doors," a story based on an old Baltimore legend and a creepy game his daughter used to play with her friends.

John's first book was The Devil of Harbor City, a novel done in the old pulp style. Past Sins and Here There Be Monsters soon followed. John was also consulting editor for Chelsea House's Criminal Investigation series. His other books include The Assassins' Ball (Written with Patrick Thomas), Paradise Denied, Blood Is the Life and The Nightmare Strikes. John is the editor of To Hell In A Fast Car, Mermaids 13, C. J. Henderson's Challenge of the Unknown, and (with Greg Schauer) With Great Power…

PAST SINS
Bad Cop...
No Donut
THE GREY MONK
SOULS ON FIRE
JOHN L. FRENCH
THE NIGHT MARE STRIKES
"THE NIGHTMARE IS CO
-Michael A. Black, Autho
OF CHIMES AT MIDNIGHT
AND THE EXECUTIONER SERIE
JOHN L. FRENCH

TALES FROM THE SEA
MERMAIDS 13
Edited by
John L. French

APOCALYPSE 13
THIRTEEN FANTASTICAL
TALES FOR THE END OF DAYS
ANTHOLOGY
DEFCON 1
...WARNING...
MISSILE LAUNCH
EDITED BY
DIANE RAETZ

WHAT WILL THE FUTURE HOLD FOR EARTH?
FANTASTIC
13
FUTURES
ANTHOLOGY
EDITED BY
ROBERT E. WATERS
JAMES R. STRATTON

EDITED BY EDWARD J. MCFADDEN III
LUCKY 13
Thirteen Tales of
Crime & Mayhem
Good or bad, it runs out eventually.
It's all just a matter of luck.
FEATURING
Trent Zelazny
Jessica McHugh
Matt Schiariti
Sarah A. Hoyt
Brady Allen
Danielle Ackley-McPhail
Patrick Thomas
Robert E. Waters
G. Elmer Munson
Diane Raetz
Georgina Morales
John L. French
Michael Laimo

No One Is Above The Lore...
Even In Hell

Hell's Detective

IT'S NOT EASY BEING HELL'S CHIEF OF POLICE
LORE & DYSORDER
THE HELL'S DETECTIVE MYSTERIES
PATRICK THOMAS

MYSTIC INVESTIGATORS
BULLETS & BRIMSTONE
Patrick Thomas & John L. French

GHOSTMAN AND HELL'S DETECTIVE
TERROR
CASE OF THE MOON MAN
PATRICK THOMAS / BLAIR WEBB
FEATURING
GHOSTMAN
HELL'S DETECTIVE
DANTE

MURPHY'S LORE
AFTER HOURS

"Gritty, snappy, very dark
and very funny,"
-J. L. Comeau,
Creature Feature

"Dark... and charming."
- Ellen Datlow,
The Best Horror of the Year Vol. 4